RENDEZVOUS
IN
BLACK

CORNELL WOOLRICH

RENDEZVOUS
IN
BLACK

Introduction by Richard Dooling

THE MODERN LIBRARY

NEW YORK

LIBRARY OF CONGRESS CATALOGING-IN-PUBLICATION DATA
Woolrich, Cornell, 1903–1968.
Rendezvous in black/by Cornell Woolrich.—Modern Library pbk. ed.
p.   cm.
ISBN 0-8129-7145-0
1. Revenge—Fiction.   2. Young women—Crimes against—Fiction.   I. Title.

PS3515.O6455R46 2004
813'.52—dc22
2003066523

Modern Library website address: www.modernlibrary.com

Printed in the United States of America

2   4   6   8   9   7   5   3

CONTENTS

RENDEZVOUS IN BLACK

Introduction

Richard Dooling

Which of these names does not belong with the others: (a) James M. Cain, (b) Raymond Chandler, (c) Dashiell Hammett, (d) Cornell Woolrich? Put the question to the average consumer of mainstream entertainment here at the beginning of the twenty-first century and most would guess (d), and then ask: Who is Cornell Woolrich? The editors of *Benét's Readers Encyclopedia,* 3rd edition (1987), presumably agreed with this assessment, for the popular reference work contained entries for Cain, Chandler, and Hammett, and nothing for Woolrich, Cornell. The volume you hold in your hands, dear reader, should convince you that Woolrich indeed belongs with the others and perhaps even surpasses them, especially if, fresh from a reading of *Rendezvous in Black,* the reader is asked to choose which of the four authors best deserves the overused honorific: master of suspense. (The editors of *Benét's* apparently read *Rendezvous* and came to the same conclusion, because the fourth edition, published in 1996, contains an entry for Cornell Woolrich.)

Revered by mystery fans, students of film noir, and lovers of hard-boiled crime fiction and detective novels, Cornell Woolrich remains almost unknown to the general reading public. His obscurity persists even though his Hollywood pedigree rivals or exceeds that of Cain, Chandler, and Hammett. Try the Internet Movie Database (imdb.com) and compare the filmographies of the four and you'll find more than twice as many films and television dramas based on the writings of Woolrich, with the breakdown as follows: Cornell Woolrich (58 entries), Hammett (25), Cain (24), and Chandler (22). Woolrich also has his fair share of film classics adapted from his works. He was the author of the story "It Had to Be Murder," the source material for the Alfred Hitchcock suspense thriller *Rear Window* (1954), and François Truffaut's *The Bride Wore Black* (1968) and *Waltz into Darkness* (1969) were both based on Woolrich novels. First-rate actors in the forties and fifties played characters in movies made from Woolrich tales—Burgess Meredith in *Street of Chance* (1942), based on Woolrich's *Black Curtain;* Edward G. Robinson in *Night Has a Thousand Eyes* (1948); Dan Duryea in *Black Angel* (1946); and of course, Jimmy Stewart and Grace Kelly in *Rear Window.*

Woolrich's titles alone are pure noir poetry: *The Black Path of Fear, Night Has a Thousand Eyes, The Bride Wore Black, Waltz into Darkness,* and of course, *Rendezvous in Black.* The words *black, night, dark,* and *death* recur with such regularity in Woolrich titles that his oeuvre is credited by some for suggesting the label "film noir."

What Woolrich lacked in literary prestige he made up for in suspense. Nobody was better at it. He achieved financial success and even fame during his lifetime, but enjoyed neither, living alone or with his ailing mother in a series of decrepit New York City hotel rooms for most of his life.

Shortly after losing a leg to gangrene out of sheer self-neglect, he died, miserable and alone, of a stroke on September 25, 1968. Five people attended his funeral. He left his money ($850,000) to Columbia University to fund a writers program.

Most of what we know about Cornell Woolrich is contained in *Cornell Woolrich: First You Dream, Then You Die* (New York: Mysterious Press, 1988), an excellent biography by Francis Nevins, an Edgar Award winner and accomplished mystery writer himself, as well as a meticulous hagiographer of Woolrich and a perceptive literary critic of the Woolrich canon. Nevins's encyclopedic compendium makes for a haunting tale in its own right, because Woolrich was possessed by the same despair and terror that haunts his doomed characters. *First You Dream, Then You Die* also makes discerning use of Woolrich's autobiography, *Blues of a Lifetime* (Popular Press, 1991), written in the early 1960s after the author had put away his typewriter. On the first page of *Blues*, Woolrich wrote in his own handwriting: "I have not written this for it to be well-written, nor read by anyone else; I have written it for myself alone."

Cornell George Hopley-Woolrich was born December 4, 1903, in New York City to parents who were divorced soon after. He spent his boyhood in Mexico with his father, and later moved back to New York City where he lived with his mother and her family. Love and death are twin inescapable terrors in many of Woolrich's tales, so it's worth examining his early experiences of each. In *Blues*, Woolrich recalled his first overpowering intimation of mortality on a starry night while he was still in Mexico with his father:

> I was eleven and, huddling over my own knees, looked up at the low-hanging stars of the Valley of Anahuac, and knew I would surely die finally, or something worse.... I had that trapped feeling, like some sort of a poor insect that you've put inside a downturned glass, and it tries to climb up the sides, and it can't, and it can't, and it can't.

Sisyphus meets Sylvia Plath.

As for love—an implacable, often destructive force in *Rendezvous* and many other Woolrich tales—he wrote in the opening pages of *Blues*: "I never loved women much, I guess. Only three times, that I'm fully aware of.... The first time it was just puppy-love, but it ended disastrously for at least one of us." Woolrich then devoted seventy pages to "the disaster" in chapter two. Lucky for us, Nevins recounts the story of that first love in some detail, weaving in Woolrich's own version of the heartbreak; the reader of *Rendezvous in Black* will recognize the vibrations coming off the prose, and the tragic finale.

At age eighteen, Woolrich met Veronica Gaffney ("Vera") through a pal ("Frank"), and the young Cornell ("Con") was instantly infatuated. Vera was "shanty Irish" and lived in a tenement near the elevated train. Though Woolrich had only just met her in passing on the street, he waited three nights by the El tracks for her to appear (the "love-wait" as he called it, not unlike the vigil Johnny Marr keeps for his Dorothy in *Rendezvous*). Finally, on the third night, young Woolrich and his buddy, Frank, worked up the nerve to go inside the building. They knocked on the door of the flat where Vera's family lived. Her parents were impressed with the skinny, nervous youth because Con was a "college boy," and Vera promptly accepted his invitation to go for a walk.

Later that night, they kissed on a bench by a quaint Catholic church, and Con eventually made a pass at Vera, which she rebuffed, and for which he respected her. Their chaste but intense relationship continued for two or three months, until Con's mother accepted an invitation her son had received to a birthday party on Riverside Drive. Con asked Vera to go with him. Vera vacillated for several days because she was uneasy about attending a party given by rich people, but eventually she accepted his invitation and was thrilled to be going.

On the night of the party, Vera appeared in a new party dress and "a glossy honey-brown full-length fur coat." In Woolrich's words, "She was hugging it tight to her, caressing it, luxuriating in it.... She even tilted her head and stroked one cheek back and forth against it.... She made love to it." Vera explained that she had made a small down payment on the coat and would return it after the party for a refund. On to the party, which was a magnificent success. Vera was so excited to be accepted into that rarefied social swim that when she and Con returned to the tenement flat and found no one home (her family was at an Irish wake), she asked Con in. He suspected that this time his overtures would not be rebuffed, but on this occasion it was young Con who thought better of going too far: "I had this image of her. I wanted to keep it, I didn't want to take anything away from it."

Woolrich left in a state of physical and emotional panic. It was the last time he saw Vera alone. As Nevins (quoting Woolrich) describes it in *First You Dream:*

> She didn't come to their special bench the next day, or the next, or the next. When he knocks fearfully on the door of her flat, her mother glares at him ferociously and begins screaming at him. "Isn't it enough

you've done? Well, isn't it? Stay away from here. There's no Vera here for you."

Devastated, young Woolrich haunted their special bench every night and waited in vain. Several weeks later, Frank told Con what had happened. Vera had been arrested for "borrowing" an expensive fur coat from a rich old lady on West End Avenue for whom she had worked part-time. She served six months in an upstate reformatory. End of story, but for a chance meeting at a block party, which concluded with Con watching Vera and a girlfriend climb into a black sedan full of mysterious, prosperous-looking older men. He never saw her again.

That winter, whenever Woolrich passed Vera's tenement building, he imagined her standing in the doorway, a morbid illusion that reminded him of the suffocating sense of mortality he'd suffered so long ago in Mexico. A "sense of isolation, of pinpointed and transfixed helplessness under the stars, of being left alone, unheard, and unaided to face some final fated darkness and engulfment slowly advancing across the years toward me . . . that has hung over me all my life."

His first novel, *Cover Charge* (1926), garnished reviews comparing him favorably to F. Scott Fitzgerald, and his second, *Children of the Ritz* (1927), earned $10,000 in prize money and a stint in Hollywood as a screenwriter, with all of the usual Faustian temptations and bargains. The Hollywood sojourn also provided the occasion for Woolrich's next experience of "love"—a brief marriage to Gloria Blackton, daughter of studio mogul J. Stuart Blackton. According to Nevins, Woolrich idolized his new wife in a bizarre, platonic way, and was at the same time consumed with self-loathing over his own promiscuous, clandestine homosexual activity. The marriage was never consummated and ended in annulment three months later, after which Woolrich went to live with his mother in New York City.

Several years later, Woolrich returned in print as a writer of hardboiled crime fiction for magazines such as *Black Mask, Detective Fiction Weekly,* and *Dime Detective.* In 1940, he moved on—with many other crime writers—from the pulp detective magazines to hardcover fiction with *The Bride Wore Black,* his first and probably most popular novel of suspense, later made into a film by Truffaut. By this time he was a true professional, so obsessed, reclusive, and devoted to his craft that he dedicated *The Bride Wore Black* to his Remington portable typewriter.

Woolrich's critics would probably say that Chandler, Cain, and Hammett were silver foxes who could do it all—plot, complex characters, lean, precision prose, snappy dialogue—and that Woolrich was a pathetic hedgehog who had an immodest facility for doing one thing altogether too well: fingernail-gnawing suspense. Woolrich, too, judged himself harshly for failing to live up to his youthful literary promise, and in the end he could not bear to have his own work around him. As he wrote to one fan: "I'm glad you liked *Phantom Lady* but I can't help you, you see. I can't accept your praise. The man who wrote that novel died a long, long time ago. He died a long, long time ago."

At the end of his life, Woolrich described himself to his literary agent as follows: "I wasn't that good, you know. What I was was a guy who could write a little, publishing in magazines surrounded by people who couldn't write at all. So I looked pretty good. But I never thought I was that good at all. All that I thought was that I tried to tell the truth."

———

In the fall of 1951, shortly after Woolrich had stopped writing and had begun a long slow descent into alcoholism, loneliness, and illness, he told a fan that, of the novels he'd written, his two personal favorites were *The Black Angel* (1943) and *Rendezvous in Black* (1948).

The life of Woolrich the author, only briefly described above, makes for fascinating reading, but the less said about *Rendezvous in Black* by way of introduction, the better; its hallucinatory clout depends on the reader being as violently dislocated as the doomed lover, Johnny Marr.

> They had a date at eight every night. If it was raining, if it was snowing; if there was a moon, or if there was none. It wasn't new, it hadn't just come up. Last year it had been that way, the year before, the year before that.

Johnny Marr and his girl, Dorothy, aren't characters, they are migratory animals that move with the polar ordination of bees, geese, salmon, or sea turtles. Instead of gravity or geomagnetic forces, Love governs Johnny and Dorothy's every movement, as surely as Fate and Chance will govern Johnny and the other mortals in the tale once Dorothy is violently taken from him.

When a bizarre, improbable accident ends Dorothy's life, Johnny vows insane revenge on five men, only one of whom could have plausibly "caused" the accident that killed his lover. Instead of murdering the five men, Johnny plots a far more diabolical and pathological retribution, and leaves them alive to enjoy it, with a note, asking each of them in turn: "Now you know what it feels like. So how do you like it?"

The reader finds no shelter in a comfortable central character or crime-solving Hollywood "hero" and is instead disgorged onto a doomscape where paranoia, death, and meticulous, unseen vengeance rule with the caprice of wanton boys swatting flies. Instead of the Hollywood archetypes of truth-seeking tough guys, the cops in Woolrich tales are usually sadistic thugs or incompetent bureaucrats. We find both in *Rendezvous*.

Johnny Marr, who is nowhere near ready to face the unbearable truth of his lover's sudden, violent death, still waits for Dorothy every night at their appointed spot, until a helpful cop sets him straight:

> "Your girl's dead. . . . They told me about that. She's buried. She's lying in the ground, in the cemetery up on the hillside, this very minute. I even went up there and seen the plot and the marker with my own eyes. I can even tell you what the headstone says on it. . . . Now move on, and don't let me find you here again."

By contrast, the detective in charge of "solving" the revenge murders orchestrated by an omniscient and nearly omnipotent Johnny Marr is MacLain Cameron, a mere accessory to a story governed by the mighty forces of murder, retribution, and fate:

> He was too thin, and his face wore a chronically haggard look. . . . His manner was a mixture of uncertainty, followed by flurries of hasty action, followed by more uncertainty, as if he already regretted the just preceding action. He always acted new at any given proceedings, as if he were undertaking them for the first time. Even when they were old, and he should have been used to them.

To appreciate the raw power of Woolrich's nightmarish vision, the reader should tear through *Rendezvous in Black,* and then read the portions of *First You Dream, Then You Die* wherein Nevins performs a kind of postmortem of its many plot weaknesses and gross factual errors, not one of which any warm-blooded reader will have noticed on first reading. There are clunkers aplenty; "His heart was frothing hate like an eggbeater" comes to mind, but the reader doesn't care and will suffer any indignity of syntax and strained credibility to find out what happens next. As Anthony Boucher wrote in *The New York Times Book Review,* "Critical sobriety is out of the question so long as this master of terror-in-the-commonplace exerts his spell." Or as the undercover policewoman observes at the end of *Rendezvous,* "Instinct, in the deranged, can be supremely accurate; it has no reason or logic to contend with."

Nevins goes so far as to claim that Woolrich's imperfections are a happy marriage of form and function:

> Without the sentences rushing out of control across the page like his hunted characters across the nightscape, without the manic emotionalism and indifference to grammatical niceties, the form and content of the Woolrich world would be at odds. Between his style and his substance Woolrich achieved the perfect union that he never came within a mile of in his private life.

Sown amid the discord of gushing, purple prose there are gems, often visually splendid ones, which help explain Hollywood's enduring fascination with Woolrich's work. A wealthy, desperate, adulterous husband sneaks out of his mansion after midnight, on his way to murder his blackmailing mistress, offering a camera-ready moment: "He went rapidly down their slowly curving stairs.... A grotesque shadow of himself rippled along beside him over the ivory-pale wall panels ... like a ghostly adviser spurring him on to evil deeds."

At the end of *Rendezvous,* those who know Woolrich's life and work hear his voice speaking through the thoughts of the undercover policewoman who finally lures Johnny to his doom: "How cruel this is. Why does it have to be so cruel? Why couldn't it have been some other way?"

In an afterword to *The Fantastic Stories of Cornell Woolrich* (Southern Illinois University Press, 1981), Barry Malzberg, Woolrich's agent, quotes Woolrich at his darkest: "Life is death. Death is in life. To hold your one true love in your arms and to see the skeleton she will become; to know that your love leads to death, that death is all there is, that is what I know and what I do not want to know and what I cannot bear."

Born fifty years later, Woolrich probably would have graduated from a twelve-step program and gone on a maintenance dose of serotonin reuptake inhibitors. But then we would be the poorer for being deprived of his unremitting nightmares. Handwritten on a scrap found among his papers, Woolrich left perhaps the most honest explanation of his writing: "I was only trying to cheat death. I was only trying to surmount for a little while the darkness that all my life I surely knew was going to come rolling in on me some day and obliterate me. I was only trying to stay alive a little brief while longer, after I was already gone. To stay in the light, to be with the living a little while past my time."

Since his death, some admirers have called him the "Hitchcock of the written word" and even the "Edgar Allan Poe of the twentieth century," but the author of hundreds of short stories and two dozen gripping novels would undoubtedly have none of that, even if, by some miracle, he had lived to hear it. One might as well call him the "Kafka of the suspense novel." Overwrought comparisons aside, the nightmare tales Woolrich wrote are thoroughly modern in one sense: they take place in a godless world where monstrous, irrational, barely comprehensible forces wreak violent havoc on the affairs of doomed innocents, who scatter like cockroaches in the night. Like the author of *Phantom Lady,* God died a long, long time ago, and in His place we have "the authorities," cruel, corrupt, or merely and tragically incompetent.

Woolrich never found a shred of comfort or happiness in such a universe, nor does he see any reason to spare his readers the full brunt of his misery and terror in his frantic, deranged recreations. Instead he traps us under the glass of his airless prose and, with the studied care of Johnny Marr plotting his insane revenge on five passengers who once flew in a plane together, he introduces us to his world. When we finish *Rendezvous,* it's easy to feel like just another one of Johnny's victims. We half expect to find a note, this one left by Woolrich the author: "Now you know what it feels like. So how do you like it?"

———

RICHARD DOOLING's novel *White Man's Grave* was a finalist for the 1994 National Book Award. His writings have appeared in *The New York Times, The Wall Street Journal,* and *The New Yorker.* His most recent novel is *Bet Your Life,* a modern take on noir detective fiction. He also writes for the ABC series *Stephen King's Kingdom Hospital.*

. . . for now mine end doth haste.
I run to death, and death meets me as fast.
—JOHN DONNE

Rendezvous
in
Black

1.

Parting

They had a date at eight every night. If it was raining, if it was snowing; if there was a moon, or if there was none. It wasn't new, it hadn't just come up. Last year it had been that way, the year before, the year before that. But it wasn't going to keep on that way much longer: just hello at eight, good-bye at twelve. In a little while, in just a week or two, their date was going to be a permanent one; twenty-four hours a day. In just a little while from now, in June. And boy, they both agreed, June sure was slow in coming around this year. It never seemed to get here.

Sometimes it seemed they'd been waiting all their lives. Well, they had. Literally, no figure of speech. Because they'd first met, you see, when she was seven and he was eight. And they'd first fallen in love when he was eight and she was seven. Sometimes it does happen that way.

They would have been married long ago; last June, the June before, the very first June that he was a man and she was a grown-up girl. Why hadn't they? What's the one thing that always interferes, more than any other? Money. First no job at all. Then a job so small it wasn't even big enough for one, let alone for two.

Then his father died. In October, after one of those wasted Junes had gone by. His father had been a brakeman on the railroad that went by there. A switch had been defective and cost his father his life; and though he hadn't asked for anything, the railroad must have been afraid that he would, and so in order to save themselves money, they hurriedly, almost eagerly, paid him a smaller amount than what they were afraid he was going to ask for later, as soon as it had occurred to him to do so. And thus they came out ahead.

It was still a vast amount—to him, to her. Eight thousand odd, after the lawyer turned it over to him. It had originally been fifteen. But most lawyers, the lawyer told him, would have taken a straight fifty per cent out of it, and he hadn't, so he was quite a considerate lawyer. Anyway, now they could get married the succeeding June, and that was all they cared about. It had to be June, she wanted it June; it wouldn't have been like a marriage at all if it had been May or July. And anything she wanted, he wanted too. And figures above five hundred lost their reality, they weren't used to them. One thousand was as much as eight, and eight was as much as fifteen. It became just theoretical at those heights, even when you were holding the check in your hand.

And it was all his, all theirs. His mother had died when he was a kid, and there was no one else to share in it. Gee, June took its time about getting here! It seemed to purposely hang back and let all the other months get in ahead of it, before their turns.

His name was Johnny Marr, and he looked like—Johnny Marr. Like his given name sounded. Like any Johnny, anywhere, any time. Even people who had seen him hundreds of times couldn't have described him very clearly, he looked so much like the average, he ran so true to form. She could have, but that was because she had special eyes for him. He was a thousand other young fellows his own age, all over, everywhere. You see them everywhere. You look at them and you don't see them. That is, not to describe afterward. "Sort of sandy hair," they might have said. "Brown eyes." And then they would have given up, slipped unnoticeably over the line away from strictly physical description. "Nice, clean-cut young fellow; never has much to say; can't tell much about him." And then they would have run out of material on that plane too. He would perhaps take his coloring from her, starting in slowly from this June on. He was waiting to be completed, he wasn't meant to stop the way he was.

Her name was Dorothy, and she was lovely. You couldn't describe her either, but not for the same reason. You can't describe light very easily. You can tell *where* it is, but not what it is. Light was where she was. There may have been prettier girls, but there have never been lovelier ones. It came from inside and out both; it was a blend. She was everyone's first love, as he looks back later once she is gone and tells himself she must have been. She was the promise made to everyone at the start, that can never quite be carried out afterward, and never is.

Cynics, seeing her go by, might have said, "Why, she's just another pretty girl; they're all about like that." Cynics don't know about these things. The way she walked, the way she talked, the little slow smile she had for him as they drew toward one another upon meeting, or the same smile in reverse, going backward as they parted—those things were only for Johnny Marr to see. He had special eyes for her, just as she had for him.

They had their date always at the same place, outside the drugstore down by the square. There was a little corner of the lighted showcase there that belonged to them—that part where, if you stood before it, the powders and the toilet waters were at your back. Not the part where the boxes of chocolates were, tied up in crimson and silver ribbons. Nor yet the part where the scented soaps were, displayed in honeycombed boxes and looking like colored easter eggs. No, only that far end where the powders and the toilet waters were, where there was a shallow little niche, an indentation, formed by a projection of the brick trim between the drugstore and the next shop on. That was their place, right there. The reflectors at the back of the window, striking through the flasks and bottles, made little sunbursts of amber, gold and chartreuse green; acting on the same principle, though quite unintentionally, as the glass jars of colored water it was once customary to display in apothecary windows for just this purpose and no other. That was theirs, that little segment of the window, that little angle of the wall, that little square of the paving in front of the drugstore. How often he had stood there, when it wasn't quite eight yet, eyes oblivious of everything else around him, whistling a snatch of tune upward at the stars. Tapping his foot lightly, not in impatience, but because his foot was singing love songs to the ground.

That was their meeting place, there by Geety's Drugstore, their starting-off place. No reason; it had just come to be so. Whatever they were going to do—a soda, a movie, a dance, or just a walk—they did it from there.

So you have them, now.

One night, *this* night, the last night of the month, he was a little late getting there. A minute or two maybe, not more. He came hurrying along, because he didn't want her to stand there waiting for him. He was always there before her, as it was fitting he should be. But she'd be there ahead of him tonight, he was almost certain, and that was why he was hurrying so.

It was a spring-like night, one of the first this year, calendar to the contrary. The sky had hives, it was rashy with stars. And, he remembered afterward, a plane had just finished going by somewhere up there, just about then. He could hear its steady drone lingering on for a minute or two after it was gone, and then that had stilled into silence too. But he didn't look up, he had no eyes for it; he was saving them for her, for when he'd get down there to the square and find her standing there outside the drugstore.

And then when he'd finally turned the last corner and was in the square, the people were so thick, he couldn't see her for a minute anyway. They were like bees. It was as though the drugstore had been robbed, or there had been a fire, or something like that. They stood there in clusters, with scarcely a lane of clearance left in their midst. A strange hush hung over all of them. They weren't talking, they were standing there utterly quiet, not saying a word. It wasn't natural for that many people to stand there in such dreadful silence. It was as if they were frozen, stunned by something they had just seen, and unable to recover from it.

Whatever it was, it was over already. This was the aftereffect.

He threaded his way through them. He went first to the place where she should have been standing, *their* place, right up against the lighted window, with the powders and the toilet waters at her back. She wasn't there. There were others standing there, ranged along there, but she wasn't one of them.

She might have simply strayed off a little way, into the crowd, in the excitement of whatever this was while waiting for him to come. He rose up on his toes and tried to look over the heads of those in front of him. He couldn't see her anywhere. So then he went out into the crowd himself, once more, to try to find her, elbowing them aside, looking this way, looking that.

Suddenly he came to the curb line, hidden until now by the almost solid phalanx of people standing between him and it. They ended there. The roadway was clear, they were being kept back on all sides from it, in the form of a big hollow square. There was a policeman there to do it, and another man who wasn't a policeman, but who had deputized himself to help him do it.

There was something lying there in the big hollow square. A rag doll or something equally limp, lying there in the road. A life-sized doll. You could just see the legs and the twisted little body. They had newspapers spread over its head and face, but the newspapers had gotten soaked through with something. Something viscous and dark, like gasoline or . . .

There were jagged pieces of broken glass lying about here and there, dark bottle glass. The entire neck of the bottle, intact, was resting a few feet away.

Some of the people were craning their necks to look up at the windows of the houses overlooking the scene. Some were even looking higher, along the cornices of the roofs. Some higher still, toward where the sound of that plane engine had come from before.

Johnny Marr moved at last. He took a peculiar tottering step down from the banked curb and went out alone into the open space—and what it held.

Instantly the guardian policeman was standing beside him. His hand came down on Johnny Marr's shoulder, to halt him and turn him back.

Johnny Marr whispered, "Turn the newspaper over a little at the top. I—I just want to see if I know who it is—"

The policeman stooped, briefly curled one of the sodden newspapers back by its outermost corner, then let it straighten out again.

"Well, do you?" he asked in an undertone. "Do you?"

"No," Johnny said sickly. "No, I don't." He was telling the truth.

That wasn't what he had been going to marry. He hadn't been going to marry *that*. The girl he'd been going to marry—she hadn't looked like that. Nobody'd ever looked like that.

His hat had fallen off. They picked it up and gave it back to him. He didn't seem to know what to do with it, so finally someone put it on his head for him.

He turned and went away as though he hadn't known her. The crowd gave way, as he bored his way through it, and then reclosed its ranks after he had passed, and he was swallowed up in its midst.

He regained that meeting place of theirs, by the drugstore window, by the powders and the lotions shining amber and chartreuse, that one little place of theirs, and leaned up against it with a palsied lurch.

No one looked at him any more, everyone kept looking the other way, out at the roadway.

Something with red headlights, a chariot from hell, was jockeying around out there, backing into position. Something was being shoved into it. Something that no one had any use for, something that no one loved, something to be thrown away. The rear doors of the chariot from hell slapped shut. The red glare swung around, glancing across the crowd for a minute, staining its lurid crimson, like a misfired rocket on the Fourth of July that fizzles around on the ground instead of going up; then it streaked off into the distance with a dolorous whine.

He was still there. He didn't know where to go. He didn't have any place to go. In the whole world there was no place to go but this.

The shock wasn't so bad at first. It was more a numbness than anything else. You couldn't tell. He just stood there quietly, swaying a little at times like a highly volatile weathervane in a breeze that couldn't be felt by others. The showcase behind him and the little projection at the side kept him upright between them. But the harm went in deep. Deep, into places where it could never be gotten out again. Into places that, once they're sick, can never be made sound again. Deep into the mind—into the reason.

Then presently his eyes struck upward, as if the memory of a drone, the winging-away of death, overhead in the sky, had briefly recurred to his foundering senses.

He clenched his fist, and shot it up toward there, aimed it toward there. And holding it like that, shook it, and shook it again, and again and again, in terrible promise of implacable accounting to come.

And on that note of dedication, the darkness came down over him.

———

Twelve struck from the steeple of the church just off the square. The crowd had gone long ago, the square was empty. Empty but for him. There was nothing in the roadway now. Just a few leaves of newspapers, stained and darkened, like the kind butchers use to wrap fresh meat in.

She was a few minutes late tonight, but she'd come. You know how girls are; maybe a last-minute run in her stocking, or something that had to be done to her hair. You had to give them a few minutes overtime, on any date. Any minute now, he'd see her running from the opposite side of the square toward him, the side she always came down on, and waving to him as she crossed, the way she always did. They didn't have enough lights on tonight, maybe something had gone wrong with the transmission, it was pretty dim for eight o'clock. But light or dark, any minute now.

That steeple clock was a liar; it was completely out of kilter; it should be fixed. Four strokes too many. He looked at his watch. That had gone back on him too; that was haywire too. Running ahead, *killing* her, lacerating him. He tore it off his wrist savagely, swung up his heel, and stunned the watch against it with a vicious impact. Then he put the hands back to where they belonged, just a minute or two before eight.

Then he held it to his ear and listened. It was silent, it was still. She was safe now. She was still coming to meet him, somewhere just around the last corner out of sight. And no harm could happen to her now, no harm such as had befallen that other poor unknown girl before; he'd taken care of that. As long as it wasn't quite eight, she was still on her way. She'd stay alive all night now. She'd stay alive forever.

It would always be eight o'clock now, on his watch, in his heart, in his brain.

A good samaritan had accosted him. "Where do you live, Mac? I'll take you home. You don't want to stand here like this any more."

Johnny Marr looked around and it was daylight. The early-morning sun was peering into the square.

"I guess I'm too early," he faltered. "It's not until tonight. Funny how I—how I got all mixed up."

He let the other fellow take him by the arm, lead him away from there. He was talking softly, in an indistinct mumble. He was even smiling a little.

"... the last day of May, the thirty-first of the month ..."

"Yeah," said the good samaritan, who thought maybe he'd had a glass of beer too many, "that was yesterday."

"Once a year," Johnny Marr murmured softly, "once a year it will come around again—for somebody else."

The man beside him didn't hear him or if he did, didn't know what he meant.

"... into each of their lives, some day, sooner or later, will come a girl. A girl always has to come into the life of each man. *They* won't die, their girls will. When you die, you don't feel anything more. They'll live, they'll feel what it's like...."

"What's the matter with you, Mac?" the man assisting him along asked with gruff kindness. "Whadderya keep looking up like that for? Did you lose something up there?"

He only said one thing more, Johnny Marr.

"Everybody else still has *his* girl," he grimaced protestingly. "Why haven't I got mine?"

———

Every night now, all alone, a motionless figure stands waiting in the niche by the drugstore window where the lotions and the toilet waters are. A figure with patient, ever-seeking, haunted, lonely eyes. Waiting through the hours for eight o'clock, an eight o'clock that never comes. A lifelong stand-up, a stand-up for all eternity. Waiting in the mellowness of June, the sizzling violence of a July electrical storm, the star clearness of August and September nights—waiting in the leaf-strewn wind of October, coat-collar upended about his throat, shifting and scuffing patiently in the bite of November.

Watching, waiting, for someone who never comes. Looking now and then at a watch that doesn't run, taking his consolation from that—a watch that's always short of eight. The eight of eternal hopefulness. The eight of a love turned macabre and cancerous.

Until the lights go out in the window behind him. Until the drugstore man locks up and goes by. Until the eight that never moves has become the midnight, the one, of reality.

Then the pathetic drugstore cowboy shuffles away, loses himself in the darkness. "Tomorrow night she'll come. Tomorrow night at eight. Maybe she stayed away on purpose; you know how girls are, trying to tease me, keep me on my toes." The wan footfalls die away, the figure loses itself in the gloom.

No one knows where he comes from. No one knows where he goes. No one cares, much. It's just another life, and the world's so full of lives. He doesn't live where he used to live; they wouldn't have him there any more. They touch their heads and nod to show what they mean. He doesn't work where he used to work; they wouldn't have him there any more, either.

But you can always find him, down by the drugstore, down by the square. On a date that never comes true.

Lots of people get so they know him by sight, even the ones that didn't know him before. But the ones that did, they pass him by with the rest. What can they do for him? "Don't look. There's poor Johnny Marr waiting for his dead girl again."

A few of them try to be kind to him in odd, haphazard ways. Human beings are funny. One of the young fellows he used to know goes by one night, silently puts a package of cigarettes into his hand, goes on without a word. To keep him from being quite so lonely while he waits.

One particularly raw night the drugstore man suddenly comes out to the door, thrusts a mug of steaming coffee into his hands. Again without a word. Takes the mug in again when he's emptied it. Just that once—never before then, never again.

Human beings are funny. They are so cruel, they are so kind; they are so calloused, they are so tender.

He becomes a landmark, a fixture, a cigar-store Indian. Only, a cigar-store Indian with warm blood coursing through it beneath its stoic rigidity.

Another night, a well-meaning middle-aged lady, who didn't know, hadn't heard the story, who had just come out of the movie-house a few doors down, stepped over and accosted him.

"Pardon me, young man, but can you tell me what time it is? I'm afraid I stayed in there longer than I intended to."

He looks at his watch solemnly. "Three to eight."

"Why no. You must be mistaken!" she protests volubly. "It can't be. It was that when I went into the show, and I've been in there all of two and a half hours. Is it too much trouble for you to give me a civil ans—"

Suddenly she shuts up. Her jaw hangs slack. Something about the look he gives her strikes terror into her heart. She backs away, a step by a step, until she has increased the distance between them sufficiently. Then she turns suddenly and waddles away as fast as she can carry herself, looking back repeatedly to make sure he hasn't started after her.

She has just seen imminent death peer forth at her from a living face.

She is one of the wise ones, one of the forewarned ones; she ran away in time.

And then one night they changed the cop down there by the square. The old one got too old, or was shifted, or went away. The new one was officious, overconscientious, as new cops are so often apt to be.

He made his tour of the square, and Johnny was there. He made his return tour, and Johnny was still there. He came back again the third time, on his last tour of duty, and he stopped and went over to him.

"Now, what is it?" he said. "You're getting on my nerves. You've been here three solid hours. You don't dress up the square. I don't care what Simmons put up with, but I'm in charge now." And he nudged him in the hip with his stick to get him to move his leg.

"I'm waiting for my girl," Johnny said.

"Your girl's dead," the cop said brutally. "They told me about that. She's buried. She's lying in the ground, in the cemetery up on the hillside, this very minute. I even went up there and seen the plot and the marker with my own eyes. I can even tell you what the headstone says on it—"

Johnny Marr suddenly flung up his hands and covered both ears, with desperate intensity.

"She's never coming here again," the cop said. "Get that through your head. Don't do that when I'm talking to you, understand? Now move on, and don't let me find you here again."

Johnny Marr swayed a little, like someone coming out of a trance. The cop's stick nudged him, and he moved one foot. The cop's stick nudged him again, and he moved the other foot. The cop's stick kept it up until finally he was moving his feet of his own accord. Then the cop stood there and watched him, until he was out of sight.

And from that night on, suddenly he wasn't standing there in that same place any more. No one saw him any more.

A few of them wondered about him, where he'd gone, what had become of him. Then they forgot to wonder about him. Then they forgot about him.

One or two people claimed they'd seen him standing, the next day, with a packed grip beside him, waiting on the station platform for the train to take him away. But nobody knew if that was true or not.

Maybe the cop should have let him stand there, should have let him alone. He hadn't been hurting anybody, until then.

———

Tri-State Airlines were well satisfied with the services of the employee down on their rolls as Joseph Murray. He'd been with them about three months. His job was filing clerk. That gave him access to flight schedules, lists of reservations, and all the multitudinous archives accumulated by such a large organization. He seemed to take a great interest in his work. He was constantly at the files, burrowing through them, looking up former bookings, scanning old-time passenger lists. He even stayed after hours, did it on his own time. He went back, back, back—years back in the records. Then suddenly he lost interest.

He would even have been in line for a small raise. It was the policy of the company, at the end of the first six months. Only, all at once he wasn't there any more to get it. He didn't resign, he didn't even give notice of quitting. He just walked out the door and never walked back in again. One day, in the morning, he was working there. But that same day, in the afternoon, he wasn't.

They waited for him to come back. He didn't. They checked. He'd left the address he'd given. Nobody knew where he had gone.

They couldn't understand, but they couldn't stop and worry about it either. They took on somebody else in his place, they had to. But his successor wasn't nearly as diligent or conscientious about his work as he had been. He only went near the files when he had to.

Liberty Airways Inc. were well satisfied with the services of the employee down on *their* pay roll as Jerome Michaels. He, too, was constantly at the files, winnowing through them, noting dates, frowning over hours of departure and hours of arrival, plotting courses of flight on the reference maps. Then suddenly he just stopped being around. One day he was there, the next he wasn't.

Continental Transport had the same experience. So did Great Eastern. So did Mercury. It happened once to each of them. To each of their ground staffs.

And then the smaller companies started running into this oddity. One by one, all down the line. Down to small concerns, with about six planes to their name, operating nonscheduled flights. That is, flights without any definite timetable—flights to order, so to speak, chartered by private individuals or small private groups just for the one occasion itself. However, they too kept records and accounts, they were required to by law, for the sake of the licenses permitting them to operate, for tax purposes, and so on.

Such as the little shoestring organization calling itself, with a grandiloquence that fooled no one but that sounded good, Comet Trips. It had a very small headquarters of not more than two subdivided rooms, an office staff of exactly two, some very patchy planes that passed inspection by the skin of their teeth, and two very worried and harassed partners to run it. But it had files of a sort.

One day one of the two employees, Jess Miller by name, made a funny sound at those files. The other, the girl who worked in the dusty, decrepit office with him, looked around, said, "What's the matter, Jess? You sick or something?"

He didn't answer. He never said a word.

He just ripped one of the yellowed file cards bodily out of its fastening.

"Hey, don't, the bosses'll have a fit!" she exclaimed.

The file drawer stayed open, the office door stayed open, he wasn't in there with her any more.

He never even took his hat with him. It stayed there on the rack. It stayed there for days until they finally threw it out. He had six-twenty-five coming to him too, for a half week's work. And believe it or not, it was a boon to Comet Trips, just then, not to have to pay it.

She told one of the bosses what he'd done, and the boss took a look, tried to find out for himself just which card it was that had been torn out. He couldn't. The whole file was so out-of-date, so jumbled up, he couldn't even tell.

However, in addition to getting a lot of dust all over his cuffs, he did get one good idea out of it. He extracted and dumped out the whole file then and there, into a trash basket.

"That should have been done years ago," he said. "I didn't even know it was still in there. Glad he reminded me."

The card said in faded typing:

Number (and then a set of numerals that meant nothing any more).
Chartered by: Rod and Reel Club, Amateur Sporting Organization.
Destination: Lake Star-of-the-Woods.
Rate: $500.
Time of Departure: Six P.M., May 31st, 19—
Pilot: Tierney, J. L.

And then these names, as passengers, each with an accompanying address as of that time:

> Garrison, Graham.
> Strickland, Hugh.
> Paige, Bucky.
> Drew, Richard R.
> Ward, Allen.

On a map, by secret lamplight, card at hand for quick reference, a ruler and a pencil plot a careful straight line between the large city, where the flight had its origin, and the small star-shaped lake, where it had its terminus. The shortest line between the two. As the crow flies. Trains don't run that way on tracks, nor cars on the roads. They can't. But a plane can, in the unobstructed air.

And between the city and the lake, this pencilled guide line passes directly over a little place called—

The pencil-point snapped off. The body of the pencil struck the map and bounced off again. A fist clawed at the map, and as it vengefully closed and squeezed and choked it, the map rippled into furrows, was sucked up into a crushed mass between its remorseless fingers.

"He's dead," the weary-looking woman in the doorway said without emotion. "Been dead two years now. He was my older sister's eldest boy. Better off, too. Ah, it was no life for any man, risking his neck in them rotten old crates held together by wires and spit. All for a few measly dollars. Carrying drunks to conventions and lodge meetings and fishing trips and what not. No, he didn't drink himself. But the passengers all brought bottles on board, he told us so often enough. They were not supposed to, but he had to shut one eye. What could he do? It was his living. They'd hide the bottles from him, and then when they were empty they'd throw them over the side. He never actually caught them at it, but they must have. They'd all be roaring, singing drunk when they got there, and not a sign of a bottle in the plane."

"How'd he die?"

"Like his kind do," she said simply. "Deep down under the ground, and only three blocks from his home. He was jostled off the edge of a subway platform, and a train cut him in two."

———

The list now read:

    Passengers: Garrison, Graham.
              Strickland, Hugh.
              Paige, Bucky.
              Drew, Richard R.
              Ward, Allen.

2.

THE FIRST RENDEZVOUS

GARRISON, Jeanette (nee Wright). On May 31st. Beloved wife of Graham S. Funeral services private. Kindly omit flowers.
—OBITUARY COLUMNS, DAILY NEWSPAPERS, JUNE 2ND.

The blinds were down over all the windows. There was a wreath on the door. It was raining softly, and the red-brick, white-trimmed Georgian house looked cold and lonely. The drops falling from the trees that stood around it, more clearly visible than in the open for they were held back and thickened by the screen of leaves they had to filter through, made the trees all seem to be weeping in unison.

The blinds were down on the limousine too as it turned into the rain-polished driveway and slowed to a stop before the entrance steps. The driver alighted, opened, and held the rear door.

A man got down, his face solemn, turned to face the inside of the car, and extended his arm helpfully to someone else, who was yet to appear.

A second man emerged. His face was more than solemn, it was ravaged with grief. He accepted the supporting arm, and painfully made his way up the steps. The door had already been opened to admit them by the time they reached it. A butler stood behind it, his eyes decently cast down.

Inside, there was that hushed, brooding melancholy of a house in which a death has just taken place. The two men went into a library just off the main hall. The butler tactfully closed the door after them, left them in privacy.

The one helped the other into a chair. The sitter turned his head and looked up at him presently in a sort of pathetic appeal.

"She looked natural, didn't she?"

"She looked beautiful, Gray," his friend reassured him. He clutched him hard by the shoulder for a moment, turned his head away as he did so, let his hand trail away finally in helpless inability to do more than just that.

"Don't you want to go upstairs and lie down for a while?" he asked him.

"No, I'm all right. I'll—I'll make it." He tried, rather bravely, to smile. "It comes to everyone, and whining or whimpering doesn't make it any easier to bear. She wouldn't have wanted me to take it that way, anyhow. I want to be like she wanted me to be."

"Do you want some brandy?" his friend said softly. "It was damp out there."

"No thanks."

"How about some coffee? You haven't eaten a mouthful all day today and most of yesterday."

"Thanks, no. Not right now. There'll be time enough for all that. I'll have all the rest of my life for food and drink."

"Do you want me to stay here with you tonight? Morgan can put me up in the guest room."

Garrison raised a protesting palm. "You don't have to do that, Ed. I'm really all right. It's pretty far out here for you, and you've got an office waiting for you tomorrow. You go home and get some sleep. You've earned it. You've been swell. Don't know what I would have done. Thanks for everything."

His friend gripped his hand. "I'll call you in the morning, see how you're making out."

"I'll go up to bed in a little while," Garrison promised. "I'll sit here first and look over some of these condolence messages Morgan's stacked up here. It'll take my mind off . . ."

"Good night, Gray," his friend said quietly.

"Good night, Ed."

The door closed.

He waited until he'd heard him leave the house. Then he waited a little longer, for Morgan's inquiring good-night tap that he'd known was coming, to sound upon the door.

He told him the same thing he had his friend when he opened the door and put his head in. "You can go up now, Morgan. Don't wait for me. I'm just going to sit here awhile and look over these messages. No thanks, I don't want anything. Good night."

He was alone now. The way he wanted to be. Even in grief, it's better to be alone than with someone else.

He cried a little, first. In the way of a man who is not used to crying, who has seldom if ever cried before. In a subdued, stifled way, head within his arms. Then that was over. He raised his head, and presently his eyes had dried of themselves. He sat there thinking of her for a while. Her laughter out there in the hall; her voice, when she came home and asked Morgan, "Is Mr. Garrison here yet?"—the sight of her in the open door, all bustle and animation. "Oh, there you are! Hello there! Did you think I was lost?"

So sudden. So sharp. So swift.

It hurt much worse, even, than the crying had. It would never stop, either. It would always go on hurting, because he would always go on thinking of her.

He tried to dispel it, assuage it, presently, by turning his attention to the messages of condolence. He began to go through them one by one. "Our deepest sympathy," "our most heartfelt sympathy," "in your loss." There was something monotonous about them. But then, he realized, what could they say? What *should* they say?

He went ahead. The fourth one from the top said—

He jolted a little and his eyes opened wider.

He sat staring at it for some time. Then he sat staring off into space, but still holding it tight in his hand. Then he returned to staring at it again.

He rose and stood there now, but still staring at it. He'd placed it on the table with his hands flattened, one on either side of it, and his head inclined, acutely, tautly, staring down at it from directly above.

Then, in some kind of swift decision, he strode for the door, flung it open, and went out into the hall. He went back to where the telephone was and taking it up, dialed with nervous haste. Then he stood there waiting.

When he spoke at last, his voice dropped to a bated urgency.

"Is this the police department? This is Graham Garrison. Sixteen Penrose Drive. Could you send someone over here? An investigator? Yes, right now. As soon as possible. Of a homicidal nature. I'll discuss that with the person you send. I'd rather not over the phone."

He hung up. He went back to the library, back to the table where he'd left it. He looked at it some more.

It was unsigned. It said simply:

Now you know what it feels like.

They sent Cameron over. It was his baby from then on.

Cameron was nothing too confidence-inspiring. Perhaps because there hadn't been anyone else there at that hour, or perhaps because, in their book, that kind of a call only rated that kind of a man. Or perhaps because the draft law was already beginning to be felt and standards were going down.

Cameron's first name was MacLain, through some odd ancestral switch from front to back. It was of no consequence to anyone but himself, anyway. He was too thin, and his face wore a chronically haggard look, probably due to this fact. His cheekbones stood out and his cheeks stood in. His manner was a mixture of uncertainty, followed by flurries of hasty action, followed by more uncertainty, as if he already regretted the just preceding action. He always acted new at any given proceedings, as if he were undertaking them for the first time. Even when they were old, and he should have been used to them.

There must have been times when his clothing had been at least passable, if nothing more than that. But he must have been entirely alone when that happened, because no one else could ever remember having seen him at such a time.

On the present occasion his shirt hadn't been changed in far too many days, and it wasn't only your eyes that told you that.

"Mr. Garrison?" Cameron asked. And then he told him who he was.

Garrison said deprecatingly, "I'm sorry I did that. I guess I lost my head for a minute."

Cameron just looked a question mark at him.

"As a matter of fact, immediately after I'd called the first time," Garrison admitted, "I thought better of it, and was going to call back and tell your office not to bother. But I was afraid of making even more of a fool of myself than I had already. I'm sorry you had your trip for nothing. . . ."

"Well, what was it that you *thought* it was, Mr. Garrison? Would you care to tell me?"

"It isn't anything. It's just that it hit me at the wrong time, tonight of all times. I'm jumpy, you know. Overwrought. And for a moment, when I first picked this up, I had a horrible impression. . . ."

Cameron waited, but he didn't finish it.

"You see, I buried my wife today," he explained.

Cameron nodded sympathetically. "I saw the wreath on the door as I came in. What is it you say you picked up?"

"This. It came among the condolences."

Cameron took it from him, studied it.

Then he raised his eyes, looked at him rather steadily.

"It's nothing, of course," Garrison said finally. "Rather cruel; bad taste; perhaps from somebody who's brooded over a loss of their own too long; but outside of that—"

Cameron had sat down suddenly, without being invited to. As though he intended staying for some time.

"Let me ask you to finish something you started to say a while back," he said. "What was the 'horrible impression' you say you had for a moment, when you first picked this up?"

Garrison seemed reluctant to answer that. "Why, er—my wife's death was from natural causes, of course. But for a moment, when I first read this, I thought maybe it—it hadn't been after all. Without my realizing it. It almost sounded as if—as if someone had had a hand in it, had had something to do with it. It was just a horrible, mistaken idea that flashed through my mind." He ended with an apologetic smile.

Cameron didn't return the smile. "It's an idea," he concurred sombrely. "And it's horrible. But whether it's mistaken or not—that's what we're going to try to find out, starting in right now."

He picked up the note once more and balanced it, unfettered, across the tips of his upturned fingers, as though he were testing it for weight. It wasn't its physical weight that he was interested in.

"I think you did the right thing, in calling us in on this," he said.

——

"I'm not a patient," Cameron told Dr. Lorenz Muller's receptionist. "I don't mind waiting until the doctor can give me his full and undivided attention. In fact I'll even come back later if I have to."

"There's a gentleman here from the police department to see you about Mrs. Garrison—" And she repeated the rest of the message.

The doctor seemed to possess his full share of normal human curiosity. "You can go right in now," she relayed. A barrage of black looks from a number of stylishly gowned women who had preceded him in the waiting room followed him as far as the inner door.

The doctor seemed to like the idea of chatting with a non-patient for a change. He even seemed to like the idea of chatting with a member of the police force, as a novelty. He lit up a cigar, offered Cameron one, and leaned back comfortably at his desk.

"At least I don't have to hold your hand, Inspector, and inhale a lot of sachet," he told him. "I wish I'd been a detective. You get out among healthy people more."

"Healthy criminals," Cameron remarked drily. "And you end up poor."

"But think of all the excitement you've had."

Following which amenities, they got down to business, Cameron already with a considerable liking for the doctor and a fairly strong impression of his honesty.

"You treated Mrs. Garrison, doctor?"

"I've been their family physician for years. He's a former classmate of mine. I was called in on—" he looked it up—"May the thirty-first, in the small hours of the night. I didn't like what I saw, but I couldn't diagnose right away. I made a second visit later that same day. I rushed her immediately to the hospital." His voice dropped. "I didn't waste any more time, but it didn't do any good. By evening she was dead."

"What was the cause of her death?"

The doctor's face clouded. He glanced away for a moment, as if averse to speaking. "Tetanus," he said quietly. Cameron noticed he put his cigar aside for a moment, as if it didn't taste so good right then. "I wouldn't wish that on my worst enemy."

"You say you didn't recognize it right away, the first time you were called?"

"A physician is seldom that fortunate. It wouldn't have mattered much if I had. I suspected it on the second visit, and I didn't wait to make sure, I took her out of there fast. The tests at the hospital confirmed it." He took a deep breath. "It was already too late for vaccine to be effective. The deadline had already expired. There's a time limit on the injections, you know. If you go past that, no power in heaven or on earth can save you."

Cameron was beginning to feel chilly down his back.

"How did she happen to get it?"

"She grazed her leg on a nail as she was going in the doorway. The main thing was she had it, not how she got it."

Cameron nodded understandingly. "That's the chief difference between us, I suppose. The detective works backwards, the physician works forwards."

"But this wasn't a crime, so your comparison isn't valid."

Cameron just dropped his eyes for a moment as if to say, "Are you sure?"

"Can you tell me something about the disease, Doctor? In the simplest language, please. I'm not a medical expert. Frankly, I don't think I have ever heard of it before."

"Yes you have. It's what you fellows call lockjaw. It's transmitted through a break in the skin. Even a scratch or pinprick will do the trick—always providing the virus is present. Which fortunately isn't usually the case, or most of us would be dead. Even a torn hangnail, for instance. Or if the wound was already there previous to going near the source of infection."

"Any other way? Contact with a person?"

"No. It's not contagious in that sense. It can't be transmitted from person to person."

It can, thought Cameron as he got up to go, but I don't mean it in the way you do.

———

Garrison came down the stairs in bathrobe, pajama trousers showing under it.

"Sorry to get you up, Mr. Garrison," Cameron said from the foot of the stairs. "I know it's three in the morning, but I've been chasing around all night and didn't have a chance to get out here any earlier."

"It doesn't matter," Garrison said dully. "I don't know what it is to sleep any more, anyway."

"I want to ask you some questions," Cameron said, "about that nail that was the cause of your wife's death."

Garrison looked surprised, as though wondering what there was to ask about such a thing. "It was just a nail," he said.

"Can you show it to me?"

"It's gone. I yanked it out and threw it away."

"Can you show me where it was?"

"Yes, I can do that." He led him out to the front door. "Right down there," and pointed. "Can you see that little pit there in the woodwork? That's where it was, sticking out of the frame. We came home late that night, and as I opened the door for her and she went in, the darn thing grazed her leg as she went by. We couldn't understand what it was doing all the way down there. It served no purpose. There's no split in the wood to be held tight. It seemed to have been driven in at random."

"Random?" Cameron said dryly, querying with his eyebrows. "Any idea how long it had been in there?"

"It might have been there for years. If it was, we'd never noticed it before."

"Had it ever grazed her leg until that night, or yours?"

"No, never. Neither one of us."

"Then it was never in there until that night. If it scratched her leg that night, it would have scratched her leg before, if it had been in there before that night. That takes care of that." But he sounded sombre about it, not pleased.

They both straightened up, being unable to hold the acutely bent positions of their backs any longer.

"Had anyone heard any sounds of tapping or hammering?"

"There wasn't anyone here *to have* heard. We'd been away for the weekend. This was a Sunday night and we'd been away since the Friday before. The house had been closed for those two days. The servants only came back *after* we did, the following morning, Monday."

Cameron tried the door. Brought it around to full closure, swung it inward to full opening once more.

"The nail stayed on the outside, even with the door tightly locked. The door swings in, so the nail didn't block it. Now let's see. You as the man would take out your key and unlock it. Then you'd step aside to let her go in first. But she'd be a little crowded. Your hand would still be on the knob, pushing the door open for her. Your whole body'd be on this side of her. So she'd have to veer over to that side where the nail was. That's how it would reach her. Otherwise, if she'd gone in dead center, she would have avoided it. Going in a door is a habit," he explained. "You never think of it, but you never vary it either." And to himself he added, "I wonder who else thought of that, besides myself?"

"You drew it right out," he said, "and threw it away?"

"Should you keep a thing like that?" Garrison countered. "I drew it right out then and there, so it wouldn't happen again. She got sore, so I got sore in sympathy. Morgan wasn't here, so I brought a pair of pliers out here and did it myself. And you want to know something funny about it?"

Cameron said with deadly earnestness, "I want to know something funny about it, yes."

"It was driven in the wrong way around. The head was the part imbedded in the wood, the point was the part sticking out."

"Then it wasn't hammered in. A nail *can't* be hammered in in that position. It would simply bend over and fold up. The entering wedge has to be sharp, not flat."

"But it *was* all the way in, deep. It was a long devil, almost as long as my hand."

"A hole could have been bored with an awl first, and then the nail simply slipped in backward, filling it. If it was as long as you say, the very depth it took would have held it fast. Did it come out easy?"

"One good wrench."

"Notice anything about it?" Cameron asked him. "Was it bright, was it rusty?"

"I didn't hang on to it long enough to really take a good look at it. I was sore, as I've said. And with one and the same gesture, I drew it out of the wood and swung the pliers up over my shoulder and let it fly off into the dark. But it did pass before my eyes for a moment, on its way up, and it seems to me there was a dirty little strip of gray rag caught around it, or tied around it under its head. Just a wisp. Such as you often find clinging to stray nails. But I can't say for sure, it traveled past my eyes too fast."

"Stray nails," repeated Cameron, in that same dry way he'd used before.

Garrison waited for him to say something more, but he didn't.

"Is all this any good to you?" he asked finally.

"Not now any more. The nail is gone beyond recall," answered Cameron cryptically. "Your wife is dead."

"I don't get what you were driving at," Garrison told him blankly.

"That's the answer right there. You've just given it yourself," Cameron assured him dourly. "As much of a one as there'll ever be."

———

Cameron's chief handed him a thin sheaf of clipped-together papers. "I'm assigning you to this," he said tersely.

Cameron looked them over. Then his mouth became an open oval. "But this is another matter," he said. "This isn't the Jeanette Garrison—"

"Drop the case," his chief interrupted. "Or rather, since there never was a case in the first place, drop the informal investigation you've been engaged upon. Oh, yes, I know all about that. I don't like these personal sidelines. You're on homicide, and you stick to homicide. I can give you enough to keep you busy."

"But sir, this woman—"

His chief pasted his hands flat down upon the desk, in such a way that his elbows went up on each side of him. As if he were about to hoist himself to his feet, though he wasn't.

"The woman died of lockjaw. Her personal physician attests to that. The specialists he called in, who have nationwide reputations, attest to it. The death certificate of our own medical examiner attests to it. As if that weren't enough, you obtained an exhumation order and I allowed you to carry it out. The findings of the autopsy only corroborated what was already known before. If there is any mystery there, and I grant you that there is, it's a biological mystery, for the department of health to worry about, and not ourselves. Even there, you only covered ground that they had already been over. I think, by this time, it's entirely incapable of solution. You could spend the rest of your natural life, Cameron, and never find out how that germ got into her bloodstream. And your business isn't germs, it's two-legged killers. If you wanted to go after germs, why didn't you enter a medical school?"

Cameron tried to say something. This time he didn't even get a "but" out. His chief seemed to read his mind. He swung his arm impatiently.

"Oh, don't give me any more about that note! Every time we have a homicide on our hands, about eighty-five people write in claiming that they did it, you ought to know that yourself. The people that really do these things are the ones that *don't* write in and claim the credit. I told you she died of lockjaw. What more is there? Now report to—"

"Yes sir. But she could have been *murdered* by lockjaw. There can be two kinds of lockjaw, the accidentally contracted and the purposely contracted. Lockjaw could have been the weapon, just as a gun or a knife or an axe is the weapon."

His chief's voice became very subdued. He pronounced each word very slowly, very distinctly. There were red flags out all over them.

"I—told—you, drop—the—investigation. That's an order."

There was only one answer Cameron could make to that. And stay on the force. "Yes sir," he said quietly.

———

Garrison came heavily down the stairs, all the spring gone from him. He sat down at the breakfast table. Morgan brought in a half grapefruit bedded in ice, set it down before him. He placed the morning's mail to one side of him.

After a while Garrison turned to it, began listlessly going through it piece by piece.

It was the third one he came to. It said, "Now how do you like it, Mr. Garrison?"

It had no signature.

For a moment, a moment only, he roused slightly from his lethargy. He turned his head and looked toward the door, and beyond it, where the telephone was. He even seemed to be on the point of leaving his chair, getting up and going out there.

Then a look of wearied wisdom crept into his eyes. He stayed where he was. He pursed his lips. He shook his head slightly, to himself. As if to say, "I let myself be fooled once, by one of these. I won't let myself be fooled a second time."

He crumpled it, threw it under the table, away from sight. He went back to his grapefruit.

3.

THE SECOND RENDEZVOUS

The telephone call came at a fiendishly inopportune moment.

They were both together in the room there.

Florence was dressed before him; the hostess usually is dressed sooner than the host. She should have been downstairs seeing to the last-minute arrangements. She would have been, in all probability, by then. Something about a bracelet had kept her in the room. The catch balked, it took her several moments to get it to work right.

They had an extension there in their mutual bedroom. His blood froze, afterward, to think how narrowly the call had escaped being intercepted by her. She was even standing closer to the instrument than he was at the moment, within arm's reach. If it hadn't been for that bracelet-catch, occupying both her hands . . .

"Hugh," she said, indicating it with a nod of her head. "I hope it's no one calling up with a last-minute refusal, after my arrangements have all been made."

He was preoccupied with his bow tie. "Let them get it from downstairs," he said.

It rang again. "You'll only make one of them come all the way up here, when they're needed down there every moment of the time tonight." If she had released the bracelet, it would have slipped from her arm to the floor; she hadn't been able to succeed in joining it yet.

It had stopped.

A maid knocked on the door. "Telephone for Mr. Strickland."

The bracelet was bringing out all the latent stubbornness in Florence's nature now. She sat down at her vanity table with it. She took a hairpin to the catch and worked on it, like an expert repairing a watch.

"Party or no party, I'm going to sit here until I can get this to work. I planned on wearing it and I won't go down without it. You really should take it back and have them fix it for me, Hugh; I had this same trouble last time."

He was already at the telephone.

"Hello?" he said incautiously.

"Hello," a mocking soprano echoed.

The shock was like a pailful of icy water dashed full into his face.

Luckily she wasn't looking at him just then, only had eyes for the catch. He turned sharply the other way, phone and all, so that his back was to her.

"Hello, Grainger," he said.

"Grainger?" the soprano jeered. "Since when? All right, you talk your way and I'll talk mine. And I'll be at the punch line afore you."

If he hung up, that would be worse; Florence would wonder about his curtness.

"I'm a little busy right now," he said.

"This comes under the head of business. Haven't you forgotten something this month? You're a little overdue, aren't you? It's already past the fifteenth. I've waited as long as I can, but my expenses go on just the same, you know."

"I told you about that," he said curtly. "You'll have to handle that yourself from now on, the best you can."

"I'm not taking what you told me. You can't walk out of it that easy."

"Look, call me at the office tomorrow."

"Oh, no you don't. I tried that all this week. And all last. And all the week before. I don't get through down there. You've got it fixed. That's why I called you tonight, where you are now. Now I've got you where I want you, haven't I? I should have thought of it before."

Florence had finally fixed the bracelet. She had risen, was leaving the room. At the door she turned, flung her arm out toward him with impatient disgust. "Oh, for heaven's sake, get rid of him, whoever he is, Hugh! I need you downstairs with me, they'll be arriving any minute now."

The door closed. But it would be even worse now. She might pick up the main telephone below and accidentally cut in on the two of them.

He hurried the conversation to a ruthless close.

"Listen, you bitch," he said savagely, "I'm through with you. I've carried you long enough."

"Oh, she left the room, hunh? You owe me fifteen hundred dollars for this month and another fifteen hundred you didn't give me last month. Are you coming down here with it?"

"Go out and shake your tail on the streets."

"Either you come here or I'll come up there. I'll walk right in, in front of your wife and all her guests, and let the whole world know about us. I'll give you until nine o'clock."

"I'll kill you!" he vowed maniacally. "You show your face anywhere near here and I'll kill you with my own hands!"

She cut short her own peal of derisive, silvery laughter by hanging up.

—

The dancing began at about nine, after what had turned out to be one of Florence's more memorable and brilliant dinner parties. The second-string guests, invited only for the dancing, easily tripled or even quadrupled the number of people present. It was by any standard a full-fledged ball, complete even to hired name band and interspersed cabaret acts. When Florence entertained, she pulled out all the stops.

He was doing his duty by one of Florence's more mature and less appealing women friends, the kind the good host deliberately singles out to be attentive to simply because they are in that category; not for their sake, but for the sake of his own party, to keep it from developing dead spots. And as she moved backward before him, overrouged, over-jeweled and oversimpering, in a skippy little hop that was probably the last actively surviving example of the 1905 two-step, the wide entry-way to the ballroom slowly turntabled around into frontal perspective and came before him.

Suddenly he saw her out there. Tall and lithe and coruscating in spangled white; knew her unmistakably, even at that distance. She was giving the butler her stone-marten wrap. The stone-marten wrap *he* had given her, once long ago when they were in love. He knew her way of posing, he'd seen her prepare to enter so many rooms. Turning gracefully half sideways, and drawing one knee slightly in toward the other. He knew her way of smiling complacently, eyelids half down, in a way that infuriated women, but wasn't meant for them anyway. She was doing it now. He knew that trick she had of upturning one forearm and gently stroking whatever bracelets she happened to be wearing *down* toward the elbow. She was doing that now too.

She'd changed her way of doing her hair, in the weeks since he'd been avoiding her. There was a time she wouldn't have had time to change her way of doing her hair, without his almost watching her in the act of doing it; now she'd had plenty of time.

It wasn't good. Nothing about her could have pleased him; no change and no remaining as before. He didn't like her any more.

It even overcame his fear, his rage and hate, and somehow held him steady, where otherwise he would have crumbled in dismay.

He looked around, and Florence was at the upper end of the over-sized room. (They really had an enormous room, for dancing, and for the first time he was glad of it.) She wouldn't see her yet until the slow progress of the dance brought her around in turn to where he was now. But once she did— Even though they'd never met, she was an anonymous guest, an arrival at her door, and Florence was punctilious about such things. He had to get out there first.

He made a sudden, a crazy swing to the side, simply to get his encumbering partner off the floor and spare her the humiliation of being left standing alone in the middle of it. Then released her without a word, paused for a moment just within the room opening, then strode forward down the entrance gallery. His face was a little gray, but stonily composed. His heart was frothing hate like an eggbeater.

"Good evening, Mr. Strickland," she said sociably. "So nice of you to ask me."

"Did I?" he said in a deadly undertone, his lips scarcely stirring.

She gave that famous vacant smile of hers, eyes half-shuttered. "What a lovely party. And one of my favorite tunes. Shall we go in?"

Again his lips scarcely moved. "I told you what I'd do." There was a butler hovering in the background. "Just a minute. Don't put that away yet."

She'd always had great presence of mind. And tonight she was relying on it entirely, anyway; it was what had carried her here. She motioned negligently, backhand over one shoulder. "Very well, then leave it out. It's insured. You can't very well expect me to keep it on on the dance floor." Her hand sidled through under his arm. "And you *are* dancing with me, aren't you, Mr. Strickland?"

He motioned the butler back now, out of earshot. "You won't get away with this," he breathed apoplectically.

She wasn't listening. Her eyes had strayed over his shoulder, into the distance. "She *is* lovely," she murmured almost raptly. "Why, you've never done her justice. You must be blind or something. How could you ever have preferred—?" She didn't finish it. For a moment she had seemed to be completely, obliviously sincere.

He glanced around briefly, and Florence was slowly coursing past the ballroom opening in the arms of a partner. At that instant she wasn't looking out at them. She might have been just a second before; she might be just a second from now. He didn't keep looking to find out.

Sweat peered out on his forehead.

"Will the money handle it?" he said swiftly.

She gave her answer in the strangest way. She raised her wispy, gauzy, scented handkerchief and gently patted his brow with it.

"Stand over here on the side a minute," he said. "Don't talk to anyone."

"I never do at parties of this kind, without an introduction," she promised him. "Well, give me someone's name, just in case. . . ."

"You're a friend of Bob Mallory's. He's in there half-stewed. He wouldn't know the difference even if he came out here to you."

He left her swiftly and plunged into the library. He'd already started to lock the door, when he became aware of a spooning couple nestled in the lamplight. They reared their heads from a semiprostrate position and looked at him.

"Would you two excuse me?" he said harriedly.

"Oh, that's all right," the youth assured him. "We don't mind who comes in here." And they both prepared to settle back again.

"I mean, could I have this room for a minute."

The girl nudged her companion in the ribs, whispered audibly, "Must be our host," and they went out hand in hand, snickering together.

"We didn't know it was out of bounds," the boy said impudently over his shoulder. "Should have told us."

Strickland locked the door. He opened up the wall safe, took out the cash box. There was an even thousand in it. He took that, tremblingly scratched out a check for the additional five hundred, made out to bearer. She wouldn't have accepted it any other way, he knew. He was so unstable and in such haste, he spoiled the first check, had to write a second.

Then he unlocked the door and went out to her.

She was there where he'd left her, sitting now; she'd remained undiscovered.

"Let me have your evening bag a second," he said out of the corner of his mouth.

He put it in, handed it back to her.

"Now . . ." He looked meaningly at the door.

She rose, graciously unhurried. She motioned slightly, with merely the tips of her curled fingers, and the butler came over, put the stone-marten cape around her.

"It *would* have been a lovely party," she said with pleasant ruefulness to Strickland. "And I dressed so carefully too."

"Harris," he said, "will you get the lady a taxi."

For a moment they were alone in the open doorway.

"You'll never live to do this to me again," he promised her grimly.

———

Then the Rogers left, and there were only two couples left, the Whitings and the Devraux. And when they were on the point of following suit, it was Florence who coaxed them into remaining a few moments more. She who was always so anxious to be rid of the rearguard, after a tiring event like tonight's.

"The last part of every party, you know. How did the old song go? 'Is the real part, the best of all.' Let's go into the study and have a nightcap all around. I'm sick of this railroad station."

They went in and had their nightcap, just the six of them.

"Look, I'll show you what I mean." She sprawled back on a sofa, deliberately unstrapped her sandals, let her bare feet play upon the floor.

"Why do we give parties, anyway?" she asked. "It feels so good when they're over."

"That's why we give them," somebody answered. "It's like hitting yourself on the head with a hammer."

"Strick looks tired," one of the other women said commiseratingly.

She didn't even turn to look at him. "Hugh always looks tired," she said somewhat waspishly.

Were they never going? He wanted to bend down over the table and pound his fist on it, again and again, until it was splintered. See them start to their feet, see their stunned expressions, see them hurriedly make for the door.

He didn't. You never do the things you really want to do, he reflected.

He just looked down at the polished tabletop. And then put his glass down on it rather heavily, so that it thumped out.

Unintentionally, it worked nearly as well as the more explosive alternative that had passed through his mind.

One of the women stood up at once. The other within seconds after. Women were quicker at getting nuances that way.

"Well, now we really must, Flo—"

"Yes, before we're thrown out."

Nobody looked at him, but he knew the whole five people in the room were acutely aware of him as being the cause of the exodus.

The amenities be damned.

He was already up in their bedroom, before she had even finished seeing them off at the door.

He stripped off his coat, put on a business jacket in its place, the first thing his hands fell on.

Then he went over to the bureau, opened a drawer, and took out the revolver they'd kept there ever since that time they'd been held up and robbed right here in their home six years ago. Everything had been recovered later, but they'd had a bad few moments facing a gun.

He put the gun away inside his coat.

She came into the room, cool and charming. As cool and charming as though it were eight instead of three. As though there had been no party. As though there had been no extra, uninvited guest. (Well, maybe for her there hadn't been.)

She closed the bedroom door. She was smiling benignly.

"Well, dear—" she said sweetly. She put her hands to the back of her neck and started to undo the diamond necklace. She crossed the room while she was doing so. "—what'd you think of it? I think it was one of our more successful ones, don't you?"

"What was?" he said, coming back to her with an effort.

She laughed indulgently. "The party, dear." Nothing could seem to ruffle her tonight.

Oh, God, that party! He shuddered inwardly.

"You weren't very cordial at the end."

"My head," he said. "It's ready to burst."

"An aspirin wouldn't—" he started to say.

"Why don't you take an aspirin?" she said.

She finished it for him before he could. "No, an aspirin wouldn't help, would it?"

He looked at her askance. What did she mean by that? What did she know?

Apparently she didn't mean anything by it, she didn't know anything; it was just his own self-consciousness. She was out of her party gown now and into a silk negligee, placid, untroubled.

Suddenly, he became aware she'd been at the bureau a moment ago, at that same drawer; she'd already quitted it, was coming away, by the time the fact registered on him.

"What'd you want there just now?" he asked her sharply.

"Why, I was putting away something," she said vaguely. She chuckled, as you would at a cross child.

"Can't I even go to my own bureau drawer?"

She couldn't have seen the gun was gone. She would have said something about it, and she didn't, not a word.

She didn't even notice the contrasting stripe on his evening trousers, beneath the business jacket. She was all taken up in herself, in a world of her own; probably reliving and resavoring the party. Women had a habit of doing that, he knew.

He put his hand out to the bedroom doorknob. "I have to get some air," he said. "That's the only thing'll cool off my head."

She didn't oppose him.

"Be sure you take your key, dear," was all she said. "The servants are all dead to the world, poor souls."

"I won't disturb you," he promised sombrely.

She came over to him, quite innocuously. "I'll say good night to you now," she said, and gave him one of their perfunctory cheek-kisses.

He stiffened, too late.

Her fingertips had just lightly strayed past the place where the gun was. So deft were they, he only realized it once it was done and they had gone on by. No pressure, just a surface stroke.

She gave no sign. She must have mistaken it for that bulky cigar case he carried in there sometimes. He looked slyly past her, and saw it lying there as big as life across the room. But she didn't glance over that way.

She went over to her bed and lightly whisked the covers aside. She was smiling, she was charming, she was cool to the last. You would have thought their guests were still present.

She airily touched two fingertips to her own lips, then fluttered them toward him, sending him a final little good-night salutation.

His last glimpse of her, as he closed the door, showed her to him sitting propped against the pillows, about to take up a book and read herself to sleep; a rosy halo from the bedside lamp pinking her face and shoulders; her snowy hair, soft as a young girl's, falling in thick curls below her shoulders.

She looked like an eighteenth-century marquise ready to hold court at a levee in her bedroom.

He went rapidly down their slowly curving stairs (he'd always hated those stairs; they took so long getting you down). A grotesque shadow of himself rippled along beside him over the ivory-pale wall panels, cast from the night lamp left burning in the broad hall below. Like a ghostly adviser spurring him on to evil deeds.

In the hall as he passed, he noted a strange thing, a trifling yet somehow bizarre memento, overlooked from that party, that now seemed to have taken place a thousand years ago. A goblet of flat champagne left standing forgotten on the edge of a table beside the wall, an empty chair drawn up alongside it. It must have been hers, it now occurred to him. That was where she'd been sitting waiting those few moments, in that very chair. And though he could no longer remember seeing her hold or sip a glass of champagne, she must have asked for one or the butler must have offered her one unasked.

Suddenly, in a flash of anger, he went over to it, pitched it shoulder-high in venomous oblation, and downed it, flat as it was. He had just toasted her death with her own drink.

A flicker of chill night air needled the hall, the door clumped shut, and he'd left the house.

———

He didn't ring, he didn't knock. He didn't have to. He took the key she'd given him, once long ago, and unlocked the door with very little sound.

He took the key out, went in, and closed the door. With not much more sound than its opening had made.

He knew right where the switch was, knew where to put his hand without even having to look. He snapped it, and the garish peach ceiling lights she affected went on in a little ringed cluster.

He knew the place so well. Knew everything about it. It had once been like a second home to him. No, once it had been his first home, and the place he had just come from, that had been his second. Funny how you changed.

Every piece of furniture, every object, every chair, had some part in his history. There—that one over there—he'd sat there that night when he'd been a little drunk, back in their early days, and vowed he was never going home to Florence again; he was going to break off clean with her, that very night, that very hour. She'd had to sit beside him on the chair arm, and cajole and talk him out of it, and finally gently disengage the telephone from him, which he'd been holding in his hand then. She'd smoothed his ruffled fur, and winked at him knowingly, and said, "We're doing all right; why go out of our way looking for trouble? Here, have another drink and pretend you're single; it works just as good."

And on election night they'd both put their money there, on top of the radio console. He'd bet the Democrats were coming in, and she'd had to take the Republicans, by default; there wasn't anyone else. But maybe she hadn't been so dumb after all. He'd tried her out, just to see how she'd take it, and she'd been a good sport; hadn't sulked or whimpered, insisted he pocket the whole bet, forced it on him. And the next day she'd gotten the stone-marten cape, and her whole original stake back along with it. How could she have known it would work out that way? It was like lending someone five hundred dollars (which was originally his, anyway) just overnight, and then the next day being paid a fur coat for interest. Good business.

And on the piano rack, as he passed it, there was a sheet of music open. He glanced at it, and his lip curled as he read the lyric. "Sooner or later you're gonna be coming around—"

Wrong this time; not any more. He clawed at it with one hand, bunched it up into a crumpled ball, and gave it a venomous fling across the room.

The mirrored bedroom door stood half open. He drew it back the rest of the way, and stood there looking in at her. Enough light came through from the blazing living room to reveal everything with utter distinctness, just a tracing of azure shadow to tone it down here and there.

She was asleep there in the bed, resting on her side, her back toward him. The sight of her, so oblivious, so unconcerned by what she'd done, began to pump up his rancor again.

The stone-marten cape had been dumped over a chair; it made a tent over it, with the chair back for a tentpole. The white dress had been put onto a hanger, but then instead of being restored to the inside of the closet, the hanger had simply been hooked over the top of the door, and the dress hung there, slipshod, against it.

Her perfume was heavy in the air. She'd once told him the name of it. Styx. (And he'd added an "n" to it, and they'd both laughed.) She hadn't had to tell him the price, he'd seen it on too many a charge account. Those charge accounts that had all been stopped some time ago, before the real pressure and the real blackmail had begun.

He stood looking at her for a while, nursing his rage.

Then with quiet, cold deliberation he unbuttoned his double-breasted jacket, heavy with gun. He took the jacket off completely, and folded it over lengthwise from the collar down, and placed it that way over a chair back.

Then he went over and latched down the windows tight, so little or no sound—sound to come—should escape from them. Then he came back again to where he'd been, rearward of her undulant back, and unfastened his belt buckle. He drew the belt out in its entirety, and took hold of it by the buckle end, using that for a grip.

He reached down and flipped the lightweight covers off her, with a single billowing wave. Rustling taffeta spread and hissing silk sheets. She lay there now in all her sculptured shapeliness, filmy black open to the waist shadowing her.

He grimaced vengefully and flung the belt up overhead, like a writhing snake caught by the head. *This* was the way you treated women like her! *This* was what they deserved! *This* was what they got! *This* was the only treatment they understood!

The sound it made coming down was like slow, spaced handclapping. Again, and again, and again; faster, and faster, and faster. Now across her rippling shoulder blades and now across her hips and now across the undersides of her thighs. White rents appeared in the black shadowing, as though it were no more than dust that was being removed here and there with the blows. It billowed out, and rippled, and settled again, with each impact.

But that was the only movement. . . .

Suddenly the steaming hate that had misted his eyes cleared enough to let him see that she hadn't screamed, she hadn't jumped, she hadn't rolled away in an attempt to escape. And she should have, long moments ago.

He dropped the belt in a looping little puddle. He reached down over the bed and pulled her head around his way, by the hair. It came around too easily, it came around too loose. It came around, and nothing else did. Her neck had been broken.

He had, for the past several moments, been whipping a corpse.

———

All the way up those deliberately curving stairs now, that shadow pursued him along the wall panels, and he fled away from it. But as the stairs curved, it relentlessly overtook him, then swept around before him, to confront him accusingly as he reached their top. He creased his eyes protectively and warded it off with the flat of one hand; plunged through its blue impalpability and gained the bedroom door and the bedroom beyond. It didn't come in there after him. But it was waiting outside.

He drew a shuddering bowel-deep breath, and turned the key in the bedroom door.

She was, or seemed to be, asleep. The aureole of rosy light was out. Her head though, was little, if any, lower on the pillows than when he'd left her. Her eyes were indisputably closed. The daylight came through the spaces of the Venetian blinds like bars of lead bullion.

He put the gun away, giving careful back-shoulder glances at her. Her eyelids never stirred.

He went into the bathroom, and shook a little, even wept a little, with sheer reflex nervousness. Then he wiped his eyes on a towel, and sat on the edge of the tub for some moments, in a dismayed apathy. At last, still sitting there, he partially undressed; took off his coat, his tie, opened his shirt as far as his belt, but went no further.

Sleep, sleep, he had to get sleep; that was the only way to get away from this, to elude it: sleep. He struck his own head a few times with the heel of his hand, pounded it lightly, as if to settle it for sleep. But sleep couldn't be injected into it in that way. Within was a turmoil of nightmare-wakefulness.

He opened the cabinet and took out the bottle of sleeping pills. He poured two into his hand, then three. Raised his hand halfway, scoop-shaped. Then suddenly flung them from him with a whimpering grimace. That would only lock it up inside his own head, that kind of sleep.

He couldn't go through it alone. Couldn't keep it to himself. He had to talk to someone. He had to talk to *her*.

They'd come here anyway. And she had to help him.

He went into the bedroom again. The bars of lead bullion had become bars of silver bullion now. Before long they would become gold, but not yet.

Then, before he got to the bed, he saw that she was awake after all. Must have awakened just now.

"Florence—" he said breathlessly. "Florence—"

"There is something you want to tell me?" The intonation of a question mark was so faint it was almost nonexistent. It wasn't a question, it was a declarative statement, but he had no time for nuances of speech.

"I do, I do. Listen carefully."

He sat down beside her on the bed. He got up again. He moved around to its other side. He sat down there. That was the side her heart was on.

"Are you awake enough to understand?"

"Quite enough." There was something clipped about it.

"That woman—" He stopped again, and wondered how to go on. "There was a woman here tonight. I don't know if you noticed her or not—"

She smiled with the faintest shadow of irony. "Let me see. A Hattie Carnegie dress, white, in the hundred-and-fifty-dollar bracket. But I think it was bought at a discount, after the season was over, and then charged at full price—to someone. Perugia originals on her feet. Probably 5-A's. No more than that. Everything in very good taste, excellent taste, but—" she shook her head and crinkled her nose. "The foundation is cheap, she can't do anything about that, it shows through. Thirty-five in actuality, but could pass for twenty-eight."

"She *is* twenty-eight," he wanted to blurt out protestingly, but checked himself. Maybe she had been thirty-five at that, without his knowing it.

"Her perfume would be something like Styx, sticky and syrupy."

His eyes were round and he was speechless.

"Yes, Hugh. Yes, I believe I know whom you mean."

She lit a cigarette, as if giving him time to recover. She even offered him one. He refused.

"I—er, I don't know how to say this, Florence. There was an involvement that you never knew of—"

Again the ironical smile. "Shall I help you out there too, Hugh?"

She flicked first-ash from her cigarette into the little cloisonné platter on the stand, savored the smoke, rolled her eyes thoughtfully ceilingward, as if marshaling her facts in order to be of the greatest possible assistance to him.

"Her name is Esther Holliday. She lives at Sixteen-o-four Farragut Drive, Apartment D-seven. She pays a hundred and five a month for it. Telephone, Warfield seven one seven six. She's been in your life—or shall I say in your hair—oh, roughly, about four years now, a little bit over. I'm not a clairvoyant, Hugh. I can't give you the exact day you met her, nor the exact month. These things come on slowly. I *can* give you the exact season and year, spring, 1943. 'In the spring an older man's fancy—' I shouldn't have gotten so involved in my war work." She said this quite parenthetically, with a charming and not very fierce admonishing upthrust of her index finger. "You loved her for three years. For the past year and a half, you've no longer loved her, but you've been too lacking in backbone to do anything about it."

He seemed ready to come apart, as if he was strung on loose wires; like a puppet with the puppetmaster's fingers off the strings. "You know. You know about it."

"I've known for years," she said offhandedly. She decided she'd had enough of her cigarette, put it out; it had only been used as an aid to the conversation, anyway. For his sake.

"And now, what is it? What brings you to—unburden yourself at this particular time? Not that I don't appreciate it. Small favors, you know, are better than none at all."

"Florence, I went there to—to—"

This time she let him flounder his own way out.

"To kill her."

"I know you did."

"Oh, Florence," he said at last, and slumped back, as if wearied of trying to tell her anything she didn't know already. She left him no virtue in his confession.

"It was so obvious," she said disclaimingly. "A business jacket over your dinner trousers. A lump under your coat. The revolver gone from the drawer. You weren't very subtle about it, you know." Then she added, quite neutrally, "And did you?"

He stared his horror at her.

"I'm only going by the indications you gave. You showed every intention, and yet you look at me so appalled when I—"

"But do you have to be so brittle about it?" he pleaded almost poignantly.

"Forgive me," she said. "I'm sorry." And she sounded quite penitent about it. "I'm not used to living with violence, you know. I'll have to learn to drop my drawing-room glaze."

His head was drooping far downward, showing her the part in his hair. He was holding his hands cupped to his face, and speaking between them. His voice was stifled.

"She was already dead. I found her lying there already dead. Someone—I don't know who—I only know I didn't."

She reached for his hand and held it. She patted the back of it, almost maternally.

"Of course you didn't. Of course."

He raised his head, became a little more alert, as a sudden recollection struck him. "I can prove it. I can show I didn't. Wait a minute, where is that—!" He grew frightened for a moment, at finding he no longer had his coat on. He jumped up, went into the bathroom, came back with the coat. "Here. Here it is. I found this lying there in the room." He handed her the note.

She read it aloud. " 'Now how do you like it, Mr. Strickland?' "

Her thinking was always so much quicker than his. "You should have left it there," she said instantly. "There's where it should have stayed, where he put it. Not here, where they can't see it."

"But I didn't want to be linked—"

She changed her mind, abruptly. "Maybe it's better. Yes, maybe you were right. But keep it, whatever you do. Make sure you hang on to it. If you have to, you can show it to them. But you see, you've already destroyed the greater part of its value. You can't prove you found it there in the room, now that you've removed it. You can prove, or they can, that it wasn't written by you; but you could have found it anywhere. It could have come from anywhere else. It's too late now." Then seeing the dismay this had brought into his eyes, she added: "But even without the note, you're safe enough. They can't saddle it on you, when you really didn't do it. There would have to be a complete miscarriage of justice. Those things don't happen."

"But they'll come here. They're bound to. They'll ask questions. . . ."

She nodded regretfully. "They'll go back into her past. And the association was—a rather long one."

"Florence, you've got to help me! No matter what they find out about the past, that won't count so much; at least, if we can keep them from finding out about tonight. Don't you see? This big party you gave tonight. What a marvelous thing. Dozens of people; they all saw me here all evening, to the very end. Florence, I *didn't* go out of the house after our guests left tonight! I never left it, do you understand? Florence, you won't go back on me, will you? You'll stick by me? You're my only hope."

"I'm your wife, Hugh," was all she said. "Are you forgetting? I'm your wife." There was only tender devotion in her eyes as they met his.

His head fell forward against her breast, with a deep choking gasp of relief that was almost a sob.

Softly, reassuringly, her hand stroked his hair. Forgivingly, understandingly, with all the wifely solicitude there was in the whole world.

———

She'd died the night of Tuesday to Wednesday. Nothing happened Wednesday. Nothing happened Thursday. It was just flat, impersonal; it was just cold print, black on white. He held his breath. Then on Friday it finally leaped out of the papers, came to life, and took the form of a man standing on his threshold.

"Show him in," he said to Harris.

Then he checked the order. "No, wait a minute." He tried a pose at the desk, scanning some papers. No, that didn't look right, this wasn't an office. He tried a large leather-covered chair, sank back in it, crossed his legs. He got up again, selected a book from the shelf and a cigar from his humidor, returned to the chair.

"All right. Now show him in."

The man wasn't very impressive. He was a tall, scrawny fellow, hollow-cheeked. He acted uncertain, a tyro. He hadn't changed his shirt in days; there was a regular ruff of frayed threads peering out at his wrist.

He said, "Sorry to bother you, Mr. Strickland. I'm from the police. Mind if I ask you a few questions?"

Strickland said, "Sit down. No, I don't mind."

The man sat down, inclined too far forward; there was too much wrist left over. He looked around at the room in awe. He looked at Strickland in awe. As if he hadn't known people lived in places like this.

"Have a cigarette," Strickland said, to put him at his ease. "That's your light, there."

He took up the inkwell first, by mistake.

"No, right there beside you."

Even after he had it, he couldn't get it to work.

"You just push down. Prod a little."

But by that time he'd given up, and used a match of his own.

Then he didn't know what to do with the match; had to keep it pinched between his fingers.

Good Lord, what have I been afraid of? thought Strickland.

"What are the questions?" he prompted.

The man gave a start, as though he'd forgotten what he'd just said, himself. "Oh—ah. Yes. Er—did you know a woman—a lady—named Esther Holliday?"

"Yes I did," Strickland said immediately.

"Well?"

"About as well as a man can." He let him get that first. Then he said, "I'm frank about these things, you see." Then he said, "But that was at one time. That ended a year and a half ago."

The man fidgeted with his cigarette. It was painful to watch him. He was the questioned and Strickland the questioner, you would have thought.

"You know, she's dead."

"Murdered," Strickland corrected. "I read about it in the paper. All about it."

"You haven't seen her lately, have you, Mr. Strickland?"

"No."

"When was the last time?"

"I should say over six months ago."

"Oh." Then he said, "Well—" It was about as flat as last week's ginger ale. "In that case—" Then he didn't seem to know what more to say. He got up.

Strickland rose too. He happened to put his book down on the table beside them.

The man fidgeted with it, in that way typical of an awkward person who doesn't know how to conclude an interview gracefully, extricate himself properly from someone's presence, and so fiddles around with this and that.

"New?"

"On the contrary," said Strickland patronizingly, "it's quite old."

"Oh. I only thought, because some of the pages haven't been cut yet . . ."

"I hadn't got that far yet." The thing to do in cases of this kind was to shoot the answers at them fast, not take time enough to draw breath between question and answer.

Cameron abstractedly ran his thumbnail down the edge of one. It was the opening page. The following three or four adhered to it.

Then he closed the book and forgot about it and went away.

—

They were preparing for bed, that same night. He was sitting on the edge of his bed, already in his pajamas, but unwilling, or unable, to lie down and rest. Back arched, shoulders slumped, hands loosely clasped, staring disconsolately down at the floor.

She, on the contrary, was sitting before her dressing table. Head also lowered somewhat, but intent on what occupied her at the moment, and not lost in abstraction as in his case. She was shaping her nails with a file, tapering them.

She spoke at last.

"How were her hands? *Hers,* you know."

He knew. He grimaced, and wiped the edge of his hand across his mouth, as though to remove a bad taste.

"Does it disturb you if I remind you?" she asked tactfully.

"No," he said with a sigh. "I was thinking of it anyway. I have been, the whole time. They were—oh, I suppose like any woman's: soft and whiter than a man's—"

"No, I mean where were they? How were they? You said, you said, it was the neck."

"Oh." He understood her this time. "They were up like this." He showed her. "Trying to protect her neck, trying to free it. Frozen into claws, you know. Anyone's would be."

She mimicked the gesture, with her own. Studied it in the mirror.

"Then she must have clawed and scratched at his. Left marks on them."

"I suppose so. That was the only thing she could do."

Presently, since she said nothing further, he raised his head and said, "What made you ask me that?"

"Association of ideas, I suppose. I was looking at my own hands just now, and I thought of hers. I'm sorry if it—"

"It's all right," he said. His head went down again.

She tweaked the two silk-shaded lamps on her dressing table, and they both went out. She got up and came over to the second bed. The silk of her dressing gown whispered soothingly as she agitated it in removal. Then she stopped, held it arrested at elbow height. She turned and glanced at him concernedly.

"Will you be able to sleep?"

"I'll try."

"Yes, but will you succeed? That's the important thing."

"Don't worry about me. You can put the light out."

"Yes, but you can't just sit there on the edge of your bed all night."

"I'm afraid if I go on my back, it will come back again. I had it all last night. Every time I'd come out of a doze, I was covered with perspiration. After all, it was a terrible thing to see. It's the first time I've ever seen anything like that. And then to stumble in on it like that, unexpectedly..." But the crux of the matter he still hadn't told her: the way he'd used his belt.

She scratched slightly, ever so slightly, at the extreme corner of her mouth, with the nail of her index finger.

"You can't have that happen again tonight," she said. "You'll need a doctor if you keep up like that. I think I know what we'll do."

She readjusted her wrapper, went into the bathroom for a moment. She came out with the bottle of sleeping pills in her hand.

"Try these," she said. "Until the shock wears off. Hold out your hand."

He extended it docilely, like a child.

She tapped the bottle slightly, until two of them had rolled onto his palm. Then she righted it, read the label. "Two is the ordinary dose, it says. I think you could stand three, in your condition." She tapped out a third one. Then she held the bottle poised, asked him, "Would you be afraid to try four?"

"No," he said. "Anything's better than—"

She tapped out the fourth one, stoppered the bottle. "I'll bring you some water," she said.

He swallowed it and flushed them down his throat, when she returned. He'd already had them in his mouth.

"Now lie back," she said. "And don't fight against them. Would you like me to hold my hand on your head?"

He smiled sheepishly. "No, thanks," he said. Then he shot her a quick, shamefaced look. "You're being very kind to me, Florence."

"What did you expect me to do?" she asked with an affectionate twinkle.

"After all, she *was*—"

"That's all over and done with," she said. "I'm sorry it had to end in such a grim way. But that's all water under the bridge, as far as you and I are concerned."

She arranged his pillows for him. She even drew the sheet up over his shoulder. She put out the remaining light.

"Thank you, Florence," he said with a half sob.

"Shhh," she answered softly in the dark. "Sleep. Just sleep."

It took a while to work.

Several times he was on the point of succumbing, and his hypertensile nerves, like springs, would ricochet him back again through the surface of consciousness. Then at last he sank down into the murky waters of oblivion and didn't come up any more.

Once a dream, like a patch of light oil on the surface, floated over him, illumined him with its hazy half light for a while, then floated on past.

———

In the morning his sudden cry of astonishment brought her to the bathroom door in inquiry.

He was holding his hands perpendicular, backs toward his eyes.

"Look. All over me. What did I do to myself? Where did I get these? I only saw them this minute, as I was reaching for the water faucet."

She hurried to his side, took one of his now-trembling hands in hers, examined it. Red tracks across its back, in serried lines; some short, some long; some pale-pink with surface shallowness, some red-black with depth.

"Don't be frightened," she urged. "You must have done it to yourself, in your sleep." She took the other one, and looked at that in turn. She clicked her tongue, in mild commiseration. "Maybe you're allergic to that barbiturate you took. It may have irritated your blood or skin in some way, made you itch uncontrollably. Is it anywhere else?"

He drew back his sleeve. "No, not past the wrist bone. There are some on there, but that's as high as they go." He looked at her almost with superstitious dread. "I remember now, I had a dream. *She* was in it. The thing came back to me after all, but in a different way. Oh, it was horrible—" He shuddered violently, and planted one hand against the cabinet mirror, to support himself. "She wanted me to—she kept trying to get me to do what was really done to her. (*You* know.) She had both my hands in hers, and kept trying to lead them to her own neck. And the more she tried, the harder I kept trying to pull them away. In the dream it was I who was screaming, not she. She had a grip of steel, she dug her nails into my hands, and I couldn't free them. Finally I tore them away, and her face sort of faded out, like an electric bulb that dies down slowly." He mopped at his newly perspired forehead. "And she—she had on your dressing gown! It was she, but she had on your dressing—"

"Shh," she said. She put her finger briefly to his lips to silence them. "Don't bring it back. Look what it's doing to you. Wait a moment, let me fix you up."

She took a tuft of cotton, moistened it with witch hazel, and dabbed gently at the coagulated lacerations.

"It still smarts," he marveled. "This long after."

"They'll go away," she promised. "Within a week you won't be able to find them."

———

After he'd been summoned, as he was coming down the stairs, he met Florence. They exchanged a look—hers of concern, his of foreboding.

They didn't speak, but he silently raised two fingers to her, to show her this was the second time.

She nodded, gnawed her lip, as though she didn't like that any too well herself.

At last, she gripped his upper arm, in unspoken encouragement. Then, as she did so, suddenly her eyes went to his hand, with those mysterious nocturnal scratches still perceptible upon its back, even though now they had turned brown and encrusted with healing.

She motioned him agitatedly to wait where he was, not to go down any further. Hastily she ran down the few remaining steps herself, ran back along the hall to where his street garments were habitually kept. He could see her fumbling within the pockets of his topcoat.

Then she came back and in her hand she held a pair of his gloves.

"Put these on you," she breathed.

"But won't they think it strange? In the house?"

"But those marks . . . They may believe they came from . . . It's better if they don't see them."

He drew in his breath sharply, in excruciation. "I never thought of that, until this very minute!" he gasped, appalled. "My God, they may think—"

"They won't think anything, if they don't see them. Try to keep them from seeing them."

"But indoors! How can I?"

"Well, then you've just come in. Here, like this." She ran down again. This time she brought him hat and topcoat. Put the hat into his hand, draped the topcoat over his arm as though he'd just doffed it.

"But they know I was in when they got here. He told them."

"Then you're just going out, you're on your way out. Whatever you do, *see that those gloves stay on your hands.*"

The library door suddenly opened, and Cameron's face appeared, looking out inquiringly to see what was detaining him.

Their stricken, conspiratorial tableau dissolved into motion. But there was a guilty aftereffect to it. They separated; he resumed his descent, she resumed her ascent. But they had been caught motionless; they were just a few seconds too late. It wasn't very well done. Particularly on her part; she'd given a noticeable start back from him.

He went down, reopened the door, which Cameron had closed again after that one brief glimpse, went inside and closed it after him.

"Gentlemen?" he said suavely.

There were three of them in there, two newcomers and the one from the other day. He didn't like that.

They took in the hat and topcoat.

"Were you on your way out, Mr. Strickland?"

"I just was going, yes."

"I'm sorry. This will have to take priority." It might have been veiled, but it was a distinct order.

"Very well," he said tractably. "Just as you say." And threw the topcoat down on a chair, and the hat on top of it.

"Sit down, make yourself comfortable." This was Cameron. Still veiled, and still an order.

He sat down. And now he suddenly found that she—her advice, rather—had somehow emphasized the gloves, and the hands they covered, instead of detracting from them. Thrown a veritable spotlight on them. He was caught with them; he couldn't take them off without attracting attention to his hands, and he couldn't leave them on without doing the same thing.

"Just a few questions." Cameron again. Easy, almost engaging, you might say. Little of his usual gaucheness today.

He was sitting now. He'd had to. He tried to move his gloved hands subtly, get them as much out of the way as possible. He tried to sandwich one down inside, between his thigh and the chair arm. Then perhaps if he could slip the other one partly inside his jacket, between the two buttons . . .

Cameron's eyes hadn't once seemed to go to his hands. They didn't even now, as the hands began to slide. He could tell, because his own eyes were watching Cameron's. He was going to get away with—

Suddenly a little glossed-over white package appeared, came toward him. "Have a cigarette, Mr. Strickland."

His hand made a false start, then recoiled again. "No, thanks. Not— not right now."

"Oh, come on, join us. We'll all have one all around. Be sociable."

"Not just now. I don't care for one."

The little white package retreated, disappeared. It had failed; or yet, maybe it had succeeded.

"Is there any reason you should keep your gloves on in the house, Mr. Strickland?"

The blood in his face did a turnabout; backed from flow to ebb. "I— I was going out."

"But you took off your hat and coat."

He sighed curtly. He summoned arrogance. "Does it annoy you if I choose to keep my gloves on?"

"No," said Cameron courteously, "but I should think it would annoy you. You're wearing them inside-out."

The seam that encircled each finger was thick and thready. She must have held them the wrong way when he shoved his hands in.

He ran out of arrogance. Also, facial coloring.

They were waiting. He had hands, now, four feet long and two feet wide. They were in close-up.

"Don't you think you'd like to take them off, Mr. Strickland?" If Cameron could ever have been called urbane, he was urbane then.

"You can't compel me to take off my gloves in my own house, if I don't want to," was the best he could get off.

"No. But then you must have some very strong reason for not wanting to."

"I haven't! None whatever!" He was perspiring liberally now.

"Then why don't you? You seem warm. Far warmer than the rest of us."

His hand went to his opposite fingers, tugged; the glove fell to the floor.

His breathing was audible in the silence. It sounded like footsteps going through sand.

"Is that what you didn't want us to see? Where did you get them?"

"I—I don't know. I woke up one morning, and they were there. In—in my sleep I must have ... I'd had a dream. ..."

They didn't say a word. Their scorn was louder for that, louder than any derisive playback could have made it. Their very eyelids seemed to curl up scornfully at him.

He'd got them in a dream.

—

Their questions, as a matter of fact, turned out to be only two.

"Do you deny that she was here? That she came here to your house, earlier that very evening, seeking admission to the party your wife was giving?"

"Yes, I do!" he said fiercely.

"Call in the butler," Cameron said dispassionately. "And get out that picture of her that we brought from her place. The one he's already identified for us. We'll have him do it over again, in front of you."

He just held up his hand, in a warding-off gesture; then let it drop down again, all bent and broken.

"She may have come to the door. I—I didn't see her."

"We can't prove that you did. Your eyesight is your own affair. We *can* prove that you said to somebody, at your door, 'You'll never live to do this to me again.' And we *can* prove that that somebody was she. Which gets us, indirectly, around to the same result."

They gave that time to get in its corrosive action. He was crumbling away now like sandcastles at high tide.

Then the second question came. The second and last.

"Now, how about this? Do you deny that *you* went over to *her* place, later that very same evening, sort of—you might say, returning her visit to you? Returning it with interest."

"I do! I was in full view of dozens of people, here at the party. I went upstairs and went directly to bed!"

"We can't handle dozens of people. Just one will do. How about—" Cameron seemed to be improvising. He turned his head toward one of his cohorts. "—that taxi-driver, who's already identified him from his photograph; who took him right up to her door. Bring *him* in and we'll have him repeat the identification from real life."

Again Strickland's hand climbed falteringly to an arresting height, dropped back again exhausted. He'd paid him a thousand dollars to keep quiet! What was more than a thousand dollars? His mind answered it numbly, without taking in the real meaning. Why, fifteen hundred, or even two thousand dollars, paid him afterward *not* to keep quiet. By someone else.

"Where'd you get a photograph of mine?" he asked them vacantly.

They didn't answer that. They had, he thought, a curious look on their faces. Elusive. He couldn't put his finger on what it was.

—

Suddenly, they brought Florence into the room. Two of them came in with her between them. A reluctant, wincing, sympathetic-eyed Florence. So shrinking, so helpless, between these rough men.

He half started to his feet. "Gentlemen, I protest—you can't do this—I demand you leave my wife out of this!"

They turned a deaf ear. They sat her down, with great show of courtesy and consideration. She was no random witness, to be shunted about in their midst, to be baited, tricked and trapped. She was a great lady, stepping down from her pedestal for a moment, of her own gracious complaisance, to mire her feet in the muddy affairs of a man's world.

"You have said, Mrs. Strickland, that your husband did not leave the house, in the early morning hours of the thirty-first of May, following the party that you gave here that night."

"Not precisely," she said. "I said that my husband did not leave this house to my knowledge, during the early morning hours et cetera."

"Why do you persist in qualifying it that way?" Cameron asked her.

"Why do you persist in amending it as I first gave it?" she countered quite charmingly.

"We are going to ask you now if you care to correct or alter that statement."

"I do not," she said simply.

"You're fencing with us," Cameron told her politely. "I'm afraid your intellect is far superior to ours. I see what you just did there. Because I used the words 'do you care to,' you were answering me literally. 'No, you do not care to.'"

"I can only answer what you ask me," she said winningly. "If I am not literal, then how shall I be?"

"This is a serious matter, Mrs. Strickland."

She looked up into his eyes ruefully. "Extremely serious."

"We are not on the same basis we were when I first asked you the question. That is why I have brought you in to repeat it to you once more. A taxi-driver, Julius Glazer, has identified your husband as being in his cab that night." He took out an envelope. "I have here one thousand dollars that he turned over to me, which he accuses your husband of having given to him as a bribe, in order not to make just such an identification. Your loyalty is understandable, Mrs. Strickland, but it can serve no further purpose. Now, once more: did or did not your husband leave this house during the early morning hours following that party?"

"Can I be compelled to give evidence against my husband?"

"No, you cannot."

She sighed deeply. She lowered her head. She made no further answer.

But she had given it, nonetheless!

He saw them all glance at one another triumphantly. Panic seized him suddenly. It was time to play his trump card. Nothing else could now save him.

"Florence, show them the note!" he burst out. "The note, Florence! The one I turned over to you!"

She looked at him, as if baffled.

"Florence, the note!" He was almost screaming it by now.

She shook her head bewilderedly. She gave him the poignant look of one who longs to help someone, who will do anything within her power toward that end, but who doesn't quite grasp what it is that is expected of her.

"What note, Hugh?" she pleaded gently.

"Florence—Florence—" They had to hold him down in his chair.

She was touching her handkerchief to her eyes now, weeping in sheer frustration at being unable to understand what it was he wanted of her. "The only thing you gave me—"

"Yes? Yes?" they all said in one voice.

She glanced inadvertently at her handbag, betraying the item's location in the very act of attempting not to do so.

Cameron held out his hand for it. She didn't offer to give it to him, but she didn't struggle to keep it from him either. She was too much the great lady to offer physical resistance. He took it from her lap, and opened it, and examined its contents.

In a moment he had produced a strip of paper.

"A check for five hundred dollars," he read from it. "Made out to bearer. Dated one day previous to the murder . . ."

She'd burned the wrong thing. She'd made some ghastly mistake. She'd burned the note that could have saved him, instead of the check as he had told her to. But the damage wasn't irremediable; the check was made out to "Bearer," at least. It could have originated anywhere, not just at the scene of the murder. There was nothing about it to link it to—

Cameron had turned it over, was reading it laterally.

"Endorsed," he said, "by Esther Holliday."

There was a knell-like silence. Then Strickland's berserk voice shattered it.

"No! No! It wasn't endorsed when I brought it ba— That's not her signature! It couldn't be! She was already dead when I picked it— That's a forgery! Somebody else must have—"

Suddenly he met Florence's eye. There was something about it. . . .

Cool, tearless. There was a smile deep in it somewhere, that others could not see. He stopped speaking; his voice went off as at the throw of a switch. Not another word issued from him.

Cameron tilted his hand in exposition, let it fall again. " 'When I brought it back,' you just said. 'She was already dead when I picked it up.' Sure she was. You had to kill her first, to get at the check."

He looked around at the others. "There's our case, gentlemen. Sealed, signed, and delivered." He pointed to Strickland's hands. "Signed by the lady's nails, right here. We'll take a photograph or two, because that kind of handwriting soon fades."

He opened the door to the hall, called out to someone, "Bring Mr. Strickland's car around. He's got someplace to go with us."

They stood Strickland up on his feet. He was incapable, for that moment at any rate, of standing unaided. She had remained sitting as she was, however. He saw, or thought he saw, a horrible thing, that must have escaped the others, who hadn't eyes that knew her so well.

For she was sitting as if her head were bowed with grief; as if crushed by an affliction that did not cry out or make a scene. Her elbow was upon the table beside her, and her hand was to her face, concealing her eyes, in fact sheltering from view all the upper part of her face. But he could see the corner of her mouth, from where he stood; it peered out. And though the constricting furrow that pulled the edge of her mouth ever so slightly awry, might have seemed to them a grimace of grief, he knew better than that what it was, for he'd seen it before this. It was a fixed, unholy smirk of ultimate vindication. The stencil of a triumph that is bitter, but is savory just the same. The ghost smile of an exquisite revenge.

More horrible than the death grimace on Esther Holliday, and yet fully as cold.

He turned and looked pleadingly into Cameron's compassionate (by comparison), humane face. "Let me speak to my wife a minute. Alone a minute. Just for a minute, before I go."

"We can't allow you out of our sight, Mr. Strickland. You're in custody from this moment on."

"Right here in the same room with you, just over to one side a little—"

"Your handbag, madam." They took that away from her first, as a precaution, lest she slip him some self-destructive agency. They needn't have worried, it occurred to him dismally. She *was* that agency in herself, in her entirety.

She rose and stood there, a little apart from them, over toward the wall, and waited acquiescently for him to come to her. She was so cool, so smiling, so charming. In all her, what she had once spoken to him of as her, drawing-room glaze.

"Why have you done this to me, Florence? I didn't kill that woman."

She modulated her voice carefully, so that it could not possibly have reached anyone but him. Her lips barely stirred, yet he could distinguish every word with a terribly clarity. (She had always had such beautiful diction.)

"I know you didn't, Hugh. And that perhaps was your greatest mistake. For if you had, that would have paid your debt to me. I would have stood by you then, through thick and thin, and fought for you and with you to the bitter end. But *you* didn't, it wasn't *your* hand that rid me of her. So that leaves your debt to me still outstanding. And I don't leave my accounts unclaimed. You'll have to pay the bill yourself, Hugh. And those three years of misery and humiliation come high, come very high."

In the background there was a metallic clash, as someone readied a pair of handcuffs.

She stood there smiling at him; so cool, so charming, so unmoved.

4.

The Third Rendezvous

It was still night, the tailings of night, and she was lying there very quiet, but very wide awake, praying desperately for it to last a little longer. She'd never thought she'd ever be praying for night to last a little longer. She'd always liked the day, not the night; she'd always liked the light, not the dark.

"Let it stay dark just a little overtime. Keep the day away just a little longer. You can do it. I know it has to come sooner or later. But Lord, make it come *slow*."

Praying there flat on her back, eyes looking up at the dim ceiling, just beyond which Mars, the god of war, presumably was hovering low above her, about to tear her in two.

And while she prayed, she was holding a hand tightly in both of hers. The most valuable hand in the world. A hand she didn't want to let go of, ever.

Not a pretty hand. Shapeless and lumpy, sinewy and strong, rough-skinned on the inside and . . . But, oh, that hand!

She turned her head and touched her lips to it again, for about the fifteenth time.

The cleverly constructed alarm, which had two tones, loud and soft, went *brrrr*, softly; and her prayer had been turned down. The mechanism vibrated more than it actually rang. When it was soft that way, it was for one. When it was loud, it was for two. She quickly clapped her hand to it and it stopped.

She transferred the hand back to its owner's breast, and reluctantly left it lying there. Like something you've borrowed and have to give back. She got out of the bed, picked up her dress and undergarments and stockings, and closed herself off in the tiny bathroom, to dress in there without disturbing him. The light was like a flash of calcium to her unaccustomed eyes, but she quickly closed the door to keep it in there with her, and out of the bedroom.

Then she started to cry. She cried good, because she knew this was the last chance she'd have, until after it was all over. The government said you had to be cheerful. The forty-eight states said you had to be sunny, even willing. The forty-eight states were just flat things on a map; they didn't have a heart and arteries.

She was busy for fifteen minutes, all over the little flat, in and out, without once waking him.

And now everything had been done and there was nothing left to do. Now the tough part came. Now the showdown. She took a good deep breath to see her through. Now the curtain was up. Now she was on the air.

She went over to the bed, and put her hand down softly.

"Darling," she said. "The whole war's waiting."

He opened his eyes and grinned, lazily.

"Oh," he recollected, "today's the day I go." And jumped fast.

"Your razor's ready on the edge of the washstand," she said. "I even got the blade in without cutting myself." She licked her thumb. "Well, without cutting myself *much*. And the cap's off that tube thing you use. A little of it popped out; I must have pinched it without noticing. That was about all I knew how to do in that department. No, not those. There's a clean set waiting for you on the chair over there."

"I'll be taking them right off again, anyway," he said.

"Oh, do you even have to do that?" She was slightly disapproving of them. After all, they didn't have to get *that* personal, did they?

"They give them to you," he said.

He shaved and dressed.

"Did I take very long?"

"Not long en—" she started to say. Then changed it to, "Not long at all."

"I never shaved so fast before. My skin's on fire."

"Why didn't you use your lotion?"

He laughed. "I don't think I better today. It smells kind of sweet."

They went in to breakfast.

"Are you frightened?" he said.

"No," she lied with a dazzling smile. "Are you?"

He shrugged. He was more truthful about it. "Not frightened exactly. A little scary though. And a whole lot excited. Like I used to feel in school, the day the finals were going to be announced, when I didn't know if I'd flunked or passed. And like I felt the day of our marriage. Before, I mean. Not after."

"I'm not going to sit on my own chair today. It's—it's so far away. Would I crowd you if I— Could we both sit on yours?"

"I'll hold my arm around you to keep you from falling off. I only need one arm to feed with, anyway."

"Hold it tighter," she whispered.

"Do you want the radio?" she faltered presently.

He looked at it dubiously. "What's on this early? We never heard it at this hour before." Then, "Let's just be by ourselves."

She sighed. That was what she'd wanted too.

He put back his napkin. "Guess I'd better . . ."

"Just one more cup of coffee," she interposed quickly.

"How about you?"

"Let me drink it from your cup." She pushed her own away.

She prayed again. She prayed over a cup of coffee. He couldn't hear her. "Make it last. Don't let it get down to the bottom. Keep filling it up in some way, from below. By magic, by miracle. You can do it."

She got turned down again.

"Bottoms up," he said with finality. And tilted the cup, and set it back on its saucer with a click of conclusion.

He wiped his mouth with his napkin. Then he wiped hers with it too.

He took his arm away from her, and she had to stand up, or she would have fallen off her half of the chair. He stood up after her.

Breakfast was over. Forever. Never again, never an— She quickly shut her mind against that image.

He was all packed, from the night before. The little he was to take.

"Now, we went over everything last night," he reminded her, "so we don't have to go into it again. You have our two bank books. Don't lose them. The one with the green cover, they pay two per cent. The one with the blue cover, they only pay one and a half per cent. So whatever you have left out of what I send you, you put into the one with the green cover."

"Green. Blue. I'll try to remember." But inside, she was all water-logged, and the two colors were running together, in a mess.

"On those checks you've seen me use, you have to pay ten cents each time you write one. So just save them for important things like the rent and the gas. It's safer than cash."

His voice trailed off disconsolately. "What do I care about checks and interest—"

"What do I care either—"

Suddenly they were crushed together like two people in a subway.

"Now don't cry," he warned between kisses. "You promised."

"I'm not. I won't."

She helped him on with his hat and coat, handed him the little pre-packed bundle he was taking.

"I want to go to the train with you," she said. She'd been saving this to the last, afraid of being turned down if she came out with it too soon.

"I don't go there direct. I have to stop off at the draft board first. They assemble us. Then we all go from there." He added, as though this were very generous, "They pay our carfare."

"Well, then let me go just *up* to the draft board with you." She had a peculiar and recurrent image, whenever the word was mentioned, of a huge planed-down pine board, on which men lay down one at a time to have their outlines traced in pencil; although from the first she'd known better, of course.

"The other fellows may think . . ."

"I'm not ashamed to have anyone know I love you."

That did it. "All right. But only up to the corner, not right up to the draft board door."

She closed the door without looking behind her. She didn't want to look at the place.

They rode the bus, and there was just one vacant seat, even that early. She pushed him down into it. "Today," she whispered, "I want you to take it, and I'll do the standing."

"Aw but everybody's looking at us—" he demurred.

"What do we care?" she said firmly.

A man stood up and tipped his hat and offered his seat. She looked and then she shook her head. "Too far away," she whispered to him. It was all the way across the aisle.

They got out. "It's up this way," he said.

She took his arm. It was like walking to your execution. Of your own accord, without guards around you.

They came to the corner. "There it is, that one down there," he said.

It was just a big gray apartment house. People went right ahead living in all the other apartments, she discovered with surprise, while the draft board was busy disemboweling people on the ground floor. She even glimpsed a woman shaking a mop out of the window two stories above it.

"I wish it would blow up," she prayed. "I wish the whole building would collapse, right while we're standing here looking." She got turned down again. And it would only have moved to another building anyway, she supposed.

They were standing turned toward one another, face to face, now. They didn't seem to know what to say. There was too much to say, that was it, not too little. It stuck in your throat.

"Look," she said, pointing to a couple halted nearby. "They did it too. She came this far with him too."

He took advantage of it to give her an object lesson. "See? She's not crying, notice that?"

She may have you fooled, she hasn't me, she thought; I'm a woman.

A man by himself darted around the corner, went running by them. He recognized Bucky, evidently from some of the processings they'd been through together. He even seemed to know him by name.

"You better not stand there, Paige," he called back warningly. "I've got two to six."

"You're not late," Bucky called after him jocularly. "Make 'em wait for you."

"Hasn't he got anyone to see him off?" she asked curiously.

"Naw, he's a lone wolf, poor fellow."

Some girl's awfully lucky, and doesn't know it, she thought.

"Well, I'm going—" They kissed, and then they kissed again. And then again, again, again. Then he put a stop to it by stepping back out of reach.

"Now go right back home. Don't hang around."

"I will. I won't."

The last thing she said to him, already walking backward along the sidewalk, and spreading her hands out at her sides in a gesture of virtuous self-esteem, was, "Look, Bucky. I'm not even crying. Didn't I say I wouldn't? And look. I'm not."

"I bet you will later though," he said grudgingly.

"No I won't. You'll see—"

And then suddenly the meaning of her own words struck her, and her face twisted ungovernably for a moment. She turned and went away, so he wouldn't see it. She went faster and faster. First she was trotting. Then she was running. Then she was fleeing up the street. There was a drugstore on the corner, and it was already open, luckily. She plunged inside. She made for the telephone booths, all the way at the back. They were all empty. She sealed herself up in one. She dropped down to her knees inside it, all the way down out of sight.

She cried like she'd never cried before. She cried for all the years ahead. She cried a whole war's worth, at one time.

Once a man tried to get in, pulled the door open before he saw her huddled there. Then he said matter of factly, "Oh, excuse me!" and closed it again. But she didn't care, she went right ahead crying.

She was standing in the drugstore entry, waiting and watching for him, fifteen minutes later when he and his mates went by. She'd known they were bound to pass there sooner or later; the bus stop was right around the corner.

The drugstore had a double set of glass doors, and she lurked between the two, and didn't let him see her. It was a good vantage point. But she saw him.

They were in a double column, walking along with their packs and bags, and he was on the inside line, third from the very last man.

He was talking to the man next to him. He'd already made a friend. He was turned, saying something to him.

She only saw the side of his face. But oh, it was a lovely side of a face!

She put her hand up against the glass trying to hold him still, where he was, but he slipped right by because he wasn't really there: Only the glass was.

"Good-bye, Bucky," she breathed. "Good-bye, my heart."

The side of his face went away, and only the glass stayed behind. And she didn't want the glass; it wasn't Bucky.

———

He carried it off by himself, like something precious, to be guarded against the whole world, to be kept for himself and to himself alone. He went into the barracks where there was no one at this hour. He curled up in his bunk with it. And that was the right word, curled; he lay on his side and brought his knees up until they almost touched his chin, made a protective half circle around it. Something of his own. A little luminous square in a dark dreary world. A letter from her.

My beloved, my own husband:

I've written you eleven letters before this one But you won't get them. I never sent them. They keep telling us on all sides, "Lift up their morale, write only cheerful things, keep them smiling." I know. I know all that. I tried. But it wouldn't work. Why should I lie to you now? I never lied before.

And this is the twelfth. The true one. Let some censor frown and shake his head and scissor it all out. I don't care.

I can't go on. I see you everywhere, you're every way I turn, you're everywhere I go. God didn't mean this to happen to anyone, so much of it all at one time. God didn't mean eyes to cry so much. He didn't mean insides to ache so much. He couldn't have, or He would have built them stronger.

If I sit down to eat, you're there across the way from me, but you won't talk, you won't say anything. I beg you and I plead but you won't say anything. If I walk down the street, it feels so empty and so lonely there by my left arm. The cold wind comes nipping around the corner and I feel all open on that side. If I go shopping to the A. & P., I turn around and hand you the parcels to carry for me, and suddenly you're not there, I'm holding them out above the empty floor.

And when I take the Sunday papers in from the door, the comics are always on top. . . . Why do they always *have* to be on top? But there's no one to snatch at them, like there used to be, and rumple up all the other sections of the paper in the process of extracting them. No one's hand to slap down, like I used to every Sunday. "*Wait*, can't you? *Wait.* How old are you, twelve years old?" They stay so smooth all the way into the flat. No one wants the funnies, I sit holding them all morning, waiting, and no one takes them from me, no one giggles like a little boy over in the corner, all hidden behind them. I have to cram them down the incinerator at last, because funnies shouldn't do that to you, they're supposed to make you happy. Then I repent ("He still may come out of that bedroom, he only overslept this morning.") but I can't get them back. I run all the way downstairs to the basement, but it's too late, I can't get them out of the furnace.

You're everywhere. You're nowhere. I can't go on. I *can't* go on. I wasn't meant to be a hero's wife. I was just meant to be Bucky's wife. And they won't let me any more. What can I do, how shall I last? Tell me, oh tell me, my darling, tell me quickly, for I can't hold out much longer.

Sharon.

———

. . . I've taken your advice. I've applied for a war job. They asked me what I could do; I told them "Nothing." They asked me what I wanted to do; I told them "Anything." I told them I wanted to work where there was the most noise, the most glare, the greatest number of machines and people. They didn't ask me why. They just looked at me and they seemed to understand. . . .

. . . It's like a strange new world, but it keeps me from thinking of you. There's such a clatter, I can't hear your name. There's such a glare, I can't see your face. It's what I wanted. We'll wait out this war that way, you and I. We'll fool them yet. . . .

———

. . . I'm a machine now. I don't feel or think. I don't *hurt*. All day long I'm numb from the noise, too numb to hurt. All night long I'm numb from exhaustion, too numb to hurt. I look like a machine too. Dark goggles, you can't see my face. An aluminum hood, you can't see my hair. Heavy gauntlets, you can't see my hands. Overalls, you can't tell I'm a woman. They all laughed at me because I wore a dress the first day I reported to work. I was the only one in the whole plant in a dress. The men asked each other, "Where have I seen one of them before?" And then they'd say, "That's a girl; you remember. One of them soft things they used to have around before the war." And then they'd say, "What was they for? I forget."

At least I don't *hurt*.

And time is on my side. On our side. Every day is a day longer the war has lasted; but it's also a day shorter it still has to go. Don't you think the halfway mark has already slipped by without anyone knowing it? Say you do, say it has! Maybe it was yesterday, maybe even the day before.

There once *was* a thing called Peace. Remember it? Remember? Long ago and far away . . .

———

. . . My bench mate looks as much like a machine as I do, but she's still a girl underneath, very much so. (She doesn't have to be afraid of hurting, I guess.) She loves without getting hurt. I don't know how it's done, but she has some kind of a system. "It's just like crossing the street," she says. "Go fast, and dodge a lot, and you don't get hit." She has dark red hair, I've seen it on the street, going home, and so they call her Rusty. If you call her by her right name, she doesn't recognize it any more, she doesn't know it's her. "I wondered who that was," she says. I have clocked her. They usually last about a week apiece. "Stores give you a week on returns," she says. "Why should I take any longer? Otherwise they're liable to show wear." Wednesdays seem to be her days for "taking 'em back and shopping for a new one." Don't ask me why. Every Wednesday regularly she has a new one out "on approval." I have to hear all about them, over our sandwiches.

She has a new one now. He came up to her just outside the gates, as she was leaving the plant with the rest of the crowd. . . .

When she saw that he was corralled, cut out from the rest of the herd, and practically pleading to be branded, she gave him an armful of rope. She practically gave him a whole lariat. Let him step into it and then tugged the knot closed.

"What do you know?" he said. A question that wasn't to be taken literally. He didn't care about her mind.

"What do you know yourself?" she replied. She didn't care about his mind either.

He tipped his hat, that outdated, forgotten prewar custom in these circles, and that pleased her. It was almost like having your hand kissed.

She just kept going, and he trotted along beside her, fast to her saddle now.

Demureness was even more outdated than hat-tipping. It would have been about like throwing a curtsey.

Nobody kidded anybody else. There was no time. You came to the point.

"You taking me anywhere?" she wanted to know.

"You name it."

She did. "All right. Harry's, down by the Square." And then, just so there wouldn't be any financial obstacle, she added, "Don't let it throw you. I'll go Dutch if it worries you; I'm making ninety a week, and the damn stuff's getting in my way. I gotta kick it under the mattress at nights."

"Who said it worries me?" he said. "It's just on account of looking like I do. . . ."

"Everybody goes in there looking like us. What're we supposed to do, *change clothes?* There's a war on."

On the way he said, "Where's your friend tonight?"

She said, "Oh, her." Then she said, "Oh, you noticed her, hunh?"

He quickly said, "Only because she was with you."

"You can't get her to go out," she said. "She's one of these war widows. Just sticks around the room all night. Y'ought to see her. She even changes to skirts when she gets back home."

They went into Harry's dine and dance joint, and they fought their way to a table. They had to share it with another couple, but though their elbows grazed and their smoke drifted into one another's faces, the two parties were as isolated from one another, as exclusively self-contained, as though they were a thousand miles apart. Neither one existed in the other's awareness.

They had a warm-up drink. They gave each other their names. His, he told her, was Joe Morris.

"Have another," he said, when that stage was past.

"Do you want me drunk, or do you want me to know what I'm doing? It don't have to make any difference, because I can be just as easy to get along with when I know what I'm doing."

They had another. Then she said, "Let's limber up. It'll help make the drinks go down."

They got up and went out where the dance floor was. You could see flashes of it at times under people's feet, but only very briefly.

The eighteenth century had the minuet. The nineteenth had the waltz. The nineteen forties had arrived at a state of delirium tremens, which could be turned on and off, however, without the intervention of straitjackets and attendants.

He spread his legs and shot her through to the other side, like a mail sack going down a chute; then braked her and jerked her back again, and she—miraculously—found her feet once more and stood upright before him. Then he bent down and rolled her across his back, from the left side to the right, and dropped her down to the floor.

Nobody collided with anybody else. Or if they did, it was just like another dance step anyway, you couldn't tell which was the mistake and which the intent. Except that the accidents looked a little better, maybe.

They got through and they complimented one another.

"You're good," she said.

"You're all right," he said.

They had two more drinks. Then they each had a sandwich, to soak up some of the liquor. Then, with the room this gave them, they had a final round. Then they got up and went out. They'd had a quiet, pleasant, completely average wartime evening together. A little on the slow side, maybe. No fights or anything.

He walked her home to the door of her rooming house.

There he took his arm away, and left hers hooked around an empty space. "I'll be seeing you," he said.

She gave him a blank look. Not a resentful one so much as a completely puzzled, uncomprehending one.

"Then what the hell was the whole evening's build-up for? Just nice sisterly companionship?"

He took a moment to answer, looking at her steadily the while as though wondering ahead of time how she would take a projected answer he intended giving her. He smiled at her with an odd mixture of candor and sheepishness.

"I wanted to get to meet your friend," he said.

Her slam of the door was like the explosion of a cartridge shell.

He withdrew one foot from the doorsill, but that was the only move he made. As though he had read her deep and unerringly, in that look of a moment ago.

The door reopened. He was still standing there. Her bray of laughter split the night. She thrust her hand out in proferred partnership.

"I never could stay sore at anything in pants longer than thirty seconds. Come around tomorrow night. I'll fix it for you."

———

She said to Sharon the next night, about a quarter to eight. "Come on downstairs to the company-room, I want you t'do something for me." She seized her arm, tried to propel her forward with windmill energy.

Sharon said, "What?"

"I want you t'meet a friend of mine."

"Can't she come up here? What's the matter with that?"

"It's a fellow, it's a guy."

Sharon drew back, dug her heels in. She couldn't budge her after that.

"Look," Rusty pleaded, "I want you t'do something for me, I want you t'do me a favor." She spread out her hands in excited expostulation. Then she dragged a chair out into the middle of the room and sat Sharon down on it, by pressing against her shoulders; as if there were a better chance that way of getting her to listen to reason. Then she dragged another chair over, set it face to face with the first, and sat down on that one herself.

She leaned forward in intensity of inquiry, palms to knees and her elbows cocked out akimbo.

"Look, you like me, don't you?"

"Yes, sure, you're all right," Sharon said, a little uncertainly, as if realizing that if she committed herself on this point she was probably also committing herself to more than just this.

"Well, wouldn't you do something for me if I asked you to, wouldn't you get me out of a fix?" And then to influence the answer, she added craftily, "I would, if it was you asking me."

"What kind of a fix?"

Rusty dropped her voice to a hoarse whisper, though there was no more danger of their being overheard now than there had been a minute before. It made for better dramatic effect, however.

"I been going with this guy for some time now," she rasped. She semaphored her hands violently. "He's a nice guy, nothing wrong with the guy himself. Only tonight I—well, I made other arrangements. He's down there now waiting for me; I don't want to just turn him down flat." She took hold of one of Sharon's hands, patted the back of it coaxingly. "Take him off my hands just for tonight. I've got a date with somebody else, and I *can't* break it. I would if I could, but I just *can't.*"

"Can't you tell him that yourself?"

"I don't want to do it that way. I don't want to hurt his feelings. You go out with him in my place. Will you do that for me?"

Sharon rose from the chair and stepped around to the rear of it. "I'm married. I don't—"

Rusty squinted, in an effect intended to convey chaste abhorrence. "This has nothing to do with that. It's not that kind of a date. I wouldn't ask you. Poor fellow's all alone, it's just *friendship.* You don't have to *care* for him. Can't you just keep'm comp'ny for me? In half an hour you ditch him and you're home." She threw up her arms overhead, in dramatic termination.

"I don't like the idea," Sharon said, narrowing her eyes in remote speculation. "In all the time Buck's been away, I never did that yet. I'm not going to begin it now. I don't see why I should let you talk me into—"

"What's the matter, don't you trust yourself?" Rusty couldn't resist flinging at her cattily. "All right," she said, without giving her time to answer that, "all right." She did some more hectic hand passing, this time before her own forehead, as if warding something off. "We won't talk about it any more. Subjick's closed. We won't say another word about it. Forget I asked you."

She slung the two persuader chairs back where she'd gotten them. Her mien was that of a thoroughly disillusioned but patiently forebearing person. "Just goes to show you," she said. "Human nature's a funny thing. You pick a girl to be your friend. You break her in at the plant. You speak up for her when the foreman bawls her out. You share a room with her. You do everything you know how. And then the first little thing you ask—" And then, quickly warding off any prospective appeasement, though none had been offered up to this point, she concluded, "All right, skip it. Let's forget I mentioned it."

Sharon shook her head hopelessly. She gave a deep sigh. She looked at her whimsically. Finally she stepped up behind the martyr and took her briefly by the shoulders.

"Oh, for heaven's sake, if you're going to take it that big— All right. I'll go. You and your social complications."

Rusty suddenly launched into a flurry of grateful preparation and assistance without wasting time on any intermediate stage. "All right, here, this all right? Or how about this one, you want to wear this one?" She danced around her in circles, she tried to become so helpful so fast. "Want a little of my lipstick, the new shade?" She tried to apply it herself, on the hoof, but Sharon deftly averted her face.

"All right, now come on, I'll take you down and introduce you." She hustled Sharon out the door before her, as if afraid she'd change her mind if given the chance.

He'd been sitting there in the downstairs room listening to the radio, carefully ignoring another man waiting for some other girl in the same house at the same time.

He stood up. He didn't look as bad as she'd feared.

Rusty gave them a whirlwind introduction, above the radio.

"Joe Morris, this is Sharon Paige."

"*Mrs.* Sharon Paige," Sharon said quietly but firmly.

He gave her an odd look that she couldn't quite fathom. Certainly, whatever it was, it wasn't disappointment. Almost, you might have said, there was a grim satisfaction in it.

Rusty gave each of them, impartially, a clap on the back. "All right, you two run along," she said. "Don't wait for me."

"Would you like to take a walk?" he asked Sharon deferentially.

Her acceptance was almost driven out of her by Rusty's vigorous nudge in the kidneys, unseen by him behind her back. She didn't answer directly, but turned and led the way out into the hall, to show him she agreed.

He followed. Rusty brought up in the rear.

After he had already gone through the front doorway, however, she brought him back to her momentarily with a surreptitious but sharp hiss. He returned to where she was waiting, and they stood there with her forehead almost meeting his chin, they were so close.

"How's that for fixing?" she breathed.

Without a word he took something out of his pocket, in such a way that Sharon couldn't see him do it from where she was, peeled off the top layer, and crushed it into Rusty's unprotesting hand.

She didn't look down. But she wasn't surprised either. Her hand closed up like a small, voracious pink octopus feeding on something.

She gave him a portentous wink.

He winked back at her.

Somehow, there was something a little cold-blooded about each wink. They weren't the lighthearted glancing things winks are supposed to be.

She thumped him familiarly on the chest with the back of her hand.

"Don't keep her out later than all night," she snickered.

———

They walked down to where the pleasure lights were. Then when they got there, the orange tide sucked them up, drew them slowly along, almost without any further effort of their own. The thickly peopled sidewalk seemed to carry them along as if they were on a moving belt.

She didn't know what to say to him, so she said nothing. He, whether for the same reason or not, didn't say anything to her either. She decided to wait and let him do the talking.

"Would you like something to drink?"

"I don't drink," she said without looking at him.

"No, I meant a soda or orangeade. I wasn't offering you anything else."

"No thanks. I just had supper."

They kept on walking in the crowd, like two people who don't know what to do with themselves.

A marquee, studded all over its underside with lighted bulbs like nailheads, came drifting toward them overhead.

"Would you like to go to a picture?"

"No!" she said, this time almost vehemently. "No—they're all about the war."

"I understand," was all he said.

She repented a little. A very little. "Don't let me spoil your evening. Why don't you go and do something, if you feel like it?"

"I'm doing exactly what I want to do," he assured her.

She couldn't think of anything to say to that. It seemed to stand by itself.

They kept on walking.

"He's in the war, isn't he?"

"My husband. Yes." She thought, Why aren't you?

He said, "I know what you were thinking just then. 'Why aren't you?' "

She admitted it tacitly by not answering.

"I've tried three times. What more can I do?"

She didn't say anything.

"And I know what you were thinking that time too. 'That's what they all say.' "

This time, inadvertently, she turned her head sharply toward him for a moment. Which again was a tacit admission.

He reached for his back pocket. "Look, I'll show you my classification card."

She waved him not to. Again he read her thoughts. "I know, you're not interested." He took it out anyway and offered it to her. She wouldn't look at it. He put it back again at last.

"I have arrested tuberculosis," he said.

Then he smiled and asked her. "Are you afraid to walk with me, now?"

"No," she said. "No. Of course not." And meant it. But suddenly she became aware that, somehow, without quite realizing how it had come about herself, she had been maneuvered into a false position. If she quitted him now and turned around and went back, it would be a reflection on her, and not on him any longer. A large part of her freedom of action had been subtly stripped away from her in the course of just those few harmless remarks.

Nevertheless, she'd begun to feel a little sorry for him. She wasn't conscious of it herself as yet, but it had already started. And pity is so inevitably a precursor to . . .

"Anyway," he said, "now you know you don't have to be afraid of me in any other way."

"What other way?"

"Oh, you know what I mean. A fellow in my position, he counts himself lucky just to be walking around at all, he doesn't try to—" And then he looked at her quite frankly, even cheerfully, and he smiled.

So she smiled back. That wasn't much to give anyone, a smile. You couldn't be *that* hard-hearted. Even Buck would think less of you for it if you were.

They came to where the park was, opposite.

"There's a bench over there," he said. "Shall we cross over and sit down?"

"I'm not going *inside* that park," she warned him.

"No, just let's sit on the outside, under the light over there. Rest ourselves a minute."

He's sick, she reminded herself. The walk probably tired him. What harm could there be?

They went over and sat down, under a bleaching needle-like shower of violet-white arc rays.

"I have to be going back soon," she let him know.

I'll get up in about three minutes time, she promised herself, and start back.

"Tell me about him," he said.

"What do you want to know?"

"Oh, everything. What he does, and what he says, and what he's like. . . ."

———

She put the picture away. "What time is it now?" she sighed blissfully. "It must be nearly ten o'clock." She hadn't been so happy; she hadn't known such peace of mind since the war had begun.

He looked. "It's five after twelve," he said quietly.

They'd been sitting there for three and a half hours.

———

He was waiting there for her by their bench—they called it that, "their" bench, now—under the dazzling orchid-tinted arclight. She came hurrying along, crossed the street at a little run to get to him even quicker.

He stood up. His hand was out, waiting, and hers went to it, and they shook.

"Hello, Joe."

"Hello, Sharon."

They settled down together, side by side, like the old friends they were. He spread out his arms along the top of the bench, but he didn't encircle her shoulders with the one that extended behind her, he just left it there inert on the top of the bench.

"I got another letter from him today," she confided happily. "I couldn't wait until I got here and showed it to you."

"Read it to me," he said comfortably, "while I light our cigarettes for us."

She only left out one or two short passages, that were too personal. And the number of passages she left out was growing smaller with each succeeding letter.

"I'm getting to know him so well," he said when she'd finished. "I'm almost beginning to feel like a brother to him."

"I wonder what he'd say if he knew I read them to you?"

"Don't tell him," he said again, as he already had before. "It might spoil things. You and I know there's no harm being done, but— His letters might become self-conscious, lose their wonderful . . ." He didn't finish it.

"You don't think it's wrong, do you?"

"Do you?"

"No," she said with fervor. "No. Oh, Joe, you've been a godsend to

me. You don't know what you've done for me. You make the hours pass so—I'm so happy whenever I'm with you. Just by being able to talk to you like I do, read you his letters, brings him so much closer to me. Sometimes I even get a little mixed up, and I mistake you for him and—him for you." She laughed a little in a shy manner.

"And I'm happy when I'm with you too. It does something for me. It's hard to explain but, through him, vicariously, I'm allowed to share in—in things I've never had in my own right, and never will have. A wife, a happy marriage, someone of my own to care . . ."

"We're two funny people, aren't we?" she mused.

———

"Read it to me," he said, "while I light the cigarettes."

She stripped the envelope away, unfolded it, held it slanted favorably to the light. Then nothing came.

"What's the matter?" he said presently. "Why don't you read?"

"I don't know," she said helplessly. But still nothing came.

"Is there something you can't? Does he say something about me?"

"No," she said. "I've never told him I know you."

The letter fell to the ground, disintegrated into its two or three separate sheets at her feet. Even from there, in the clarity of the arc-light, its salutation could be made out. "My own darling little wife."

"What is it?" he said. "Why are you crying?"

A stricken sob burst from her. "Because—all of a sudden—I don't care about his letters. I don't know what's happened! I'm not interested in reading them any more—or even getting them. It's coming here to the park, to sit with you, that—that—"

"Yes?" he prompted her. "Yes?"

She pressed her hands to her forehead despairingly. "I don't love him any more. It's you I love. Oh, Joe, what's happened to me? I saw you once too often, and I *didn't* see him once too many times. The two of you have changed places. Something went wrong. I didn't mean it, but—you're him now, and he's you." She was shuddering hysterically. "I'm sitting with my love on a park bench, but I keep getting letters from a stranger, in a uniform, in a faraway encampment."

He put his arms around her quivering form, he tried to console her. "What'll we do? Shall I get up and leave you? Shall I walk away, and stay away, and never come near you again? If you say so, I will."

She cried out in alarm. She clung to him with both hands.

"No! No! Joe, don't leave me. I couldn't bear it without you. You're all I have now. That'll leave me without *anything,* because I haven't got him any more."

"I can't lick it," he said in a smothered voice, "if you don't help."

"Don't fight it. Don't. I don't want you to. I can't help myself—Oh, here I go—"

Their lips met in their first kiss. They clung together as if they had vertigo. The whole night somersaulted around them, stars and arclight and all. .

On the ground her foot, unnoticed, shifting with her eagerness for his caresses, was now planted full and firmly on the fallen letter, grinding it into the dirt.

"My own . . . wife:" peered out, crushed, from under her heel.

Bucky, dear:

I'm sorry I missed writing you last week, but what with one thing and another . . .

There's really not much new to tell you. Things have been going along about as usual, no change. . . .

The weather has been lovely lately, we seem to be getting a real break. . . .

I have to run now, the pooled car just stopped by for Rusty and me. More next time, dear.

My love, Sharon.

He looked at the second one curiously. It had come right with hers. "Soldier," it began. And then:

Somebody should tell you. So I guess I will. And just in case you think I'm making a mistake, have the wrong party, she's got brown hair and hazel eyes. She's five feet four, weight one hundred and five, stocking size eight and a half, and she wears a little locket, a four-leaf clover in gold. Now does that mean you or doesn't it?

Every night she meets him on a bench in City Park. You know where City Park is, don't you? Sure you do. Every night she comes

running full tilt to meet him, as fast as her little legs will carry her. Did she ever run that fast to meet you, soldier? They kiss. Then I see them sit there, for the whole town to see. But they don't even know it, they only have eyes for each other.

Poor soldier, I feel sorry for you. Soldier, you're losing your wife.

(Unsigned)

He cried out so sharply that heads popped up all over the barracks, and voices asked, "What was that? Who did that? Somebody must have got a pin stuck in him just then."

And his buddy in the bunks nearest to him, said, "What is it, Paige? Paige, what is it? What're you covering yourself up like that for?"

And the blanket, shaking all over, said with a strangled cough, "Nothing."

—

Always in twos now they came, always in twos.

. . . People do change sometimes, Bucky; you must look at it that way. Love isn't like concrete that's poured just once, and then for-ever after stays hard and fast. Love is fluid, and once in a while it leaks out before you can stop it and runs away.

When two people find they've made a mistake, don't you think the most sensible thing for them to do is not to try to hang on to one another for dear life (that doesn't help any, that just prolongs the mistake), but to admit it to one another and try to find some way out? I wouldn't have mentioned this to you, now of all times, but you're the one who has pleaded so in your last letters, asking if anything's wrong. . . .

—

. . . They don't sit on the bench any longer, soldier. Where do they go? What do they do? I tried to find out for you, but I couldn't. They disappear from the time she meets him at 8. Then he brings her back, sometimes at 12, sometimes at 1. Where have they been all that time?

She's going, soldier, going fast. Going, going, gone. Any day now. Kiss your wife good-bye.

(Unsigned)

His C.O. had had kippers for breakfast. Kippers never agreed with him. His C.O. had a corn on his left foot. It was speaking up today, rain coming. His C.O. didn't like something about his face. It was too woebegone. He hated soldiers with woebegone faces. In fact he hated soldiers with faces. In fact he hated soldiers. In fact he hated.

His C.O. had been deserted by his own wife ten years before. Ever since, he'd wanted every other man in the world to be deserted by his wife. He was jealous of all happily married men.

He was very gracious about it. "Of course," he said soothingly. "Glad you came to me about it. That's what we're here for, you know. To listen to your personal problems. We want you men to be happy. We're only too glad to stop the whole war for you—well, hold it up a short while—while you're getting your private affairs in order. I'm sure Washington won't mind. I'll send them a telegram at once. 'Private Paige has a little matter at home to attend to; suspend all operations.' Would two weeks be enough? Or do you require a thirty-day pass?"

The punchline came like the crack of a whip. It stung like one too. "Get the hell out of here. Request refused. Dismiss."

"Yes sir." Private Paige saluted, wheeled, and went out. Then he lurched a little, on the other side of the door; put his hand briefly to the wall to steady himself.

———

The barracks washroom was deserted in the early-morning darkness, icy-cold; it reeked of ammonia fumes.

He came in just in his trousers and undershirt, holding a concealed bulge against his side. He looked around first, to make sure there was no one in there. Then he raised his shirt and took the gun out, and rested it on the edge of the washstand.

His breath formed vapor in front of his face. Well, that was easy to stop, very easy; that was the first thing that would stop.

He dragged a forlorn cigarette out of his pocket, lit it. The one he'd been saving for this. Then he kept walking back and forth, making quick turns each time, like something caged.

Finally he'd had enough. He threw down the cigarette and stepped on it out of old habit (otherwise it would have lasted longer than him, most likely). Then he swept the gun up, to cut out the fooling and get it over with fast.

The swing-door, which had fluctuated subtly once or twice before now, unseen by him, suddenly swept wide open and his buddy, Rubin, jumped in and dove at him. He caught Paige's upraised arm and brought it down, and twisted it around rearward so that the gun fell out of it. Then he held him pinned there against the washstand, kicked the gun out of the way, across the floor.

They wrestled a little, briefly. The plume of steam kept issuing faster than ever from Paige's nostrils. It had fooled him after all; it was still coming from him.

"I *thought* there was something up," Rubin heaved aggressively. "I been watching you."

"Get the hell out of here. Who asked you to butt in?"

"Sitting on the edge of your bunk—holding your head—it was written all over you this was coming."

"Take your mitts off me. You don't have to keep pawing me."

"Now, steady. Now, take it easy. Turn around and douse some cold water in your face."

He held Paige's face down by main force and did it for him. Then let him raise it and get his breath back.

"How's that?" he wanted to know.

"Wet," was the sullen retort. "How'd you think it would be?"

"I know," said Rubin with a chuckle, "but it snapped you out of it." He packed a fist and pretended to swing it at the point of Paige's jaw, but just let it glance off easy. "What the hell. I don't want to have to start breaking in somebody new for a buddy, after all the trouble I've gone to with you. Who'll I borrow money offa, and forget to pay it back? Who'll I bum my smokes offa?"

"I can't take it, Rube. I can't stand it. I can't sleep any more."

"So all right. Be a man. Go there. Find out. Have a showdown. But don't lie down on it." He shrugged mountainously. "How do you know, anyway? It may not be true."

Paige took out a crumpled letter from his pocket, handed it to him.

… They disappear from the time she meets him at 8. Then he brings her back. …

"It is true," he said bitterly.

"Then go there anyway. What you got on the end of your arms here, lily pads?" He hoisted one of Paige's wrists, let it drop again. "They were put there to use, weren't they? Fight for her. You have to fight to hold them. The way I look at it, if nobody else wants 'em, then you ain't much of a picker, they're prob'ly not much good in the first place. I had the same thing. I hadda bust a guy in the jawr on the Coney Island boardwalk over my Sadie, back in the beginning. Since then—" he gave his hand an edgewise cut—"I ain't had a bit of trouble. All she does is stay home and have kids."

"I can't get a pass."

"What's a pass? You got feet, ain't you? There's a road out there, ain't there?" He stiff-armed him inquiringly, against the shoulder. "Just ask yourself one thing, that's all you gotta do. All right, I'll save you the trouble, I'll ask it for you instead. Do you want her?"

"Do I want to live?" Paige echoed.

———

Just before he reached the confines of the hamlet, he stepped aside into a clump of roadside trees, hurriedly changed over into the civvies Rubin had managed to obtain for him and which he'd carried until now packed into a tight roll under his arm. Or rather superimposed them, for the most part, on what he was already wearing, for it wasn't a complete outfit by any means. He discarded only his army jacket. This he folded neatly and buried under a large stone. He slid a pair of tight-skinned oiler's pants over his own trousers, buttoned a greasy mackinaw concealingly over his Government Issue shirt, and pulled a battered felt down over his head. The unaccustomedly generous brim felt as wide and overshadowing as a down-turned umbrella at first.

It wasn't a good job; he was a walking risk. The shoes, the haircut, the very way he moved his limbs, had "army" written all over them. He was a pushover for the first stray M.P. that took a second look, and he knew it. And besides, the very impersonation in itself was a liability. The war was in its five-alarm stage and you didn't see them his age out of the army and on the hoof any more.

The war. The war. He hated the war, he cursed its guts. The war had taken her from him. The war should have picked somebody its own size. Why did it have to bust him up? He'd never done anything to it.

It was beginning to get light when he showed up in the hamlet, just a roadside stray. The light didn't do the place any good; it only made its mangy clapboards look twice as dilapidated as before. Even the trees all around it acted like they were ashamed of it, the way they tried to cover it up. A rooster crowed; a dog barked at him as he went by. A kerosene lamp lit up with a slow glow behind one of the upstairs fronts. Not on account of him, but because it was time to get up.

If he'd had any feelings left over from his own misery, he would have felt sorry for anyone that had to live in a godforsaken dump like this. Better they should stay in bed all day and not have to come out and see it.

At least a train ran through it and there was a station shack where it was supposed to stop.

He had to wait around a half-hour for the agent to open it up and go in there, and that didn't look too good.

He had money on him. They'd all chipped in, they were all in on it. They'd pooled whatever they had. All to keep a man from losing his wife. All to ease a fellow-sufferer's pain.

He went up to the window.

"Young feller?" the grizzled old man said brusquely.

"What time's the train go by?"

"The train where?"

"The train the hell out of here."

"Six."

"It's nearly that now—"

"Six t'night."

He went back onto the highway that ran through the place.

Everything was going in the other way, to camp, and he was on borrowed time. But after a while an outbound truck came by, and he got it to stop by throwing his hat in front of its wheels. The driver instinctively braked before he'd had time to tell that it was just a hat, with nobody in it.

"What're you, a wise guy?"

"How's chances for a heist?"

"All right, latch on," the driver said weariedly, "as long as you got me to a dead stop."

The truck moved on. The road started to come at them like a roller-coaster chute, spreading open as it got near.

The truck driver was wise. He glanced at him covertly once or twice. Then he said, "Where you from, the camp back there?"

"No," Paige said resolutely. He pared a bill off his scanty stake, handed it to him.

The truck driver looked at it, jammed it into his pocket. "I guess you ain't, if you say so," he said. He winked at him.

After a while he said, "Where d'you want to go? And that question's all paid up; you don't have to worry."

"East," Paige said grimly. "Just east. Straight east, all the way."

———

The day-coach went hurtling through the dusk like a ploughshare cleaving its sepia murkiness apart. And the fill it turned up on either side was speckled with the reflection of rows of lighted windows, so that it seemed to ripple and swim, like sod actually disturbed, as the car went slicing by.

It swayed and shuddered with its own velocity; its joints creaked and grunted and threatened to start apart. Nothing on rails dared go any faster and still remain on them. But it seemed to go so slow to one, at least, of its occupants. The land was so wide, so vast, so endless. The East never came any nearer. The further toward it you went, the further still you had to go.

The ceiling lights peered down through the blurring layers of to-bacco smoke upon the packed humanity clogging the aisle, swaying and undulating in unison, but in no danger of falling, for there was not room enough to fall in. Passing paper cups of gin and corn along from hand to hand, like relays in a chain, from some far-upward source to some far-downward destination. Singing, shouting, laughing, scowling in momentary quickly dispelled quarrel, comatose but still erect from too many paper cupfuls; blowing a harmonica; playing cards upon the points of their eight knees. The universal cloth and color of the death struggle on every shoulder, except that of an occasional young mother and child, used to this, belonging to it, following the camps around.

The only other non-uniformed individual in the whole carful, the figure huddled in a corner seat, head down, hat brim covering his face, as if asleep; trying to make himself as unobtrusive as possible. He can't be seen, that way; but neither can he see.

Suddenly an authoritative hand came to rest, heavily, with pertinent meaning, on his shoulder, and he quailed and then he froze all over. The way an animal does when it first feels the light touch of imminent capture, and waits, bated, to see which way is the best to try to run.

Slowly his hand went up. Cautiously he raised his enshrouding hat brim. From the corners of his eyes, he sought out the direction of the arrested hand. Expecting to see the familiar olive-drab uniform, the white armband of a military policeman.

Instead, it was dark-blue serge, shiny, with brass buttons. An old man's face beneath the visored cap with a disk attached. All he had in his other hand was a chopper, not a club.

Only the train conductor, asking for his ticket.

"What time do we get in?" he said.

"Eight-fifteen," the conductor said.

———

"What time are you supposed to meet him?" Rusty asked.

"Eight-thirty," Sharon said.

Rusty leaned across the foot-rail of the bed, supported by her elbows, watching her put her things into the open valise that she'd placed on the bed itself.

She didn't say anything more for some time—just watched. Sharon seemed to be, or pretended to be, unaware of her scrutiny.

"So you're going for good," Rusty said at last.

"Good is the word," Sharon agreed. "Good is the word."

"I could think of another," Rusty murmured half audibly.

Sharon raised her head, shot her a look. "What's the matter, don't you approve?"

"It's your business."

"Meaning you don't." She latched the valise down. "That's good, coming from you. Every night a date. Every night a different one."

"Sure, because I know how to handle love, and you don't. I take my love like a man. I may splash it all over the outside of me, but it don't go through. I'm waterproof at the seams, kid. Next morning I'm the same old Rusty. You take it like a woman. Right away you drown and don't come up again."

Sharon picked up the valise, started for the door.

"Why don't you take it easy?" Rusty said, almost pleadingly.

Sharon opened the door. "Talk to my heart. Don't talk to me. My ears'll listen to you, but my heart's tone-deaf."

She raised her free hand and swirled it at her, in parting gesture.

"My share of the room money's on the bureau. You can give my key back to the manager; I've left it there with the money."

Rusty, however, didn't stay behind in the room. She followed her down the stairs, treading almost at her heels.

At the bottom, Sharon turned her head and cast her a slightly impatient look, as though this lengthening of their parting annoyed her. "What's the matter, haven't you got any date of your own tonight?"

"I could've had—two, or three, or four. But it's funny—maybe it's on account of what you're doing—all of a sudden I don't want a date. The game doesn't seem much fun any more."

"Then why don't you play it for keeps, like I do, and not as a game?" Sharon inquired tartly.

"And hit below the belt, you mean."

Sharon was at the front door by now. She didn't answer that.

Again Rusty came after her, even put her hand to the door, to keep it the way it was, if only for a moment longer.

"Is this the best break you can give him, Sharon?"

"Him? Who?" Then she remembered. "Oh. *Him.*"

"I read one of his letters. I didn't mean to, but you left it around the room, and I was fresh out of tissues for taking off lipstick. It wasn't written in ink. Do you have to spill a guy's heartblood that way?"

Sharon plunked the valise down and drew a deep breath, as though there was one point she wanted to get across, once and for all, before she finally left. "Look. I can remember being married to a stranger, once long ago. I can even remember what his name was, too. But it's no use. I can't bring his face back before me. It's like asking me to feel sorry for someone I never really knew."

"These good dames," said Rusty, tight-lipped. "Give me a bum like I am."

Sharon reached down for the valise again.

A telephone suddenly peeled out shrilly at the back of the hall, more like a fire-alarm bell than anything else.

Rusty, almost by reflex action, reached out and gripped Sharon by both arms, as if to hold her fast a moment longer.

A middle-aged woman came out of the back, answered it. Then she went to the foot of the stairs, called up with the stentorian intonation of a train despatcher: "Fay MacKenzie, on the line! Fay MacKenzie, on the line!"

Carpet slippers came slapping down, with a sound like a paddle wheel beating water. A voice cried at the top of its lungs, "Hello, Joe!," then sank into blissful, purring inaudibility.

They both turned their heads away again.

"I've got a funny premonition," Rusty said huskily. "Don't go, Sharon." She kept her hands outstretched to the other's arms, trying to dissuade her.

Sharon laughed at her a little. "What's the matter, have you got the weeping creeps?"

"Look, will you do one last thing for me? I've never asked you anything before. Give me this for a good-bye present."

"Not if you're asking me to change my—"

"Wait half an hour. Give him thirty minutes more. He may phone or something. Give him that much of a chance at least. Don't just walk out cold like this. You'd wait that long for a bus. You'd wait that long for a grade B picture on a Saturday night. You'd wait that long for a table at a crummy greasy-vest feed-mill. Wait that long for the guy you once stood up with, long ago. For old time's sake. For the sake of clean sport. Then go if you have to."

Sharon looked at her. Then she stretched out her foot and shunted the valise over against the wall, just inside the door. "Fifteen minutes," she said inflexibly. "I don't know what for, I don't know what good it'll do, but you've got that tremolo in your voice that gets me. Come on into the company room, we'll sit and put a record on, while I hold my watch across my knee."

She turned her wrist and fumbled with its strap.

"Fifteen minutes' wake," she said, "for a love that's dead and will never breathe again."

————

The day coach stood motionless now, a hollowed-out trough of hazy lights and blurry tobacco smoke and packed humanity, in the middle of the enshrouding blue-black night.

They weren't singing much any more; they were all sung out. They weren't drinking much either; they were out of that too. They were mostly dozing, somnolent, standing up as well as sitting down. The car was strangely quiet. An occasional remark cut through the silence, magnified out of all proportion to its original volume by the complete lack of other, competitive voices.

Somewhere immediately outside there was a continuous clacking vibration going on. It didn't come from the car itself now; that stood still; it was an external vibration that shook its windowpanes, and shook its wheeltrucks, and even seemed to shake the very tracks it stood on. On one side only, on the left, outside on the next track, an endless succession of dark inscrutable cars went flitting by, ghost-like. Not a light showing. A train of death. A cavalcade of doom. Dozens of black cars, scores of them; shaking the rails, shaking the night, shaking the stalled day coach.

All the railroad cars there were in the whole country, all the railroad cars there were in the whole world, going down to death. Like black dominoes on wheels, like litmus paper cut-outs against the stars. Not a light, not a glimpse of the thousands of already dead they were packed with; and all the more awful for that.

The war, the war. The madness of the whole universe.

His foot kept beating a tattoo upon the floor, faster and faster and faster. Trip-hammering his despair, his agony.

"Cut it out!" the man in the seat beside him burst out at last. "I can't stand it any more! You've been doing it for hours. You've got my nerves on edge. Keep your foot still."

"Shut up," he growled dangerously, but he stopped it.

He held his head for a minute, with both hands.

He stood up suddenly, wrenched his way out past his neighbor's knees. Five other men immediately roused from their comas, made a converging dive for his seat. Two of them got it at once; neither one would relinquish it. They split it between them after that, each forcing one hip down into it.

He buffeted his way to the end of the car, momentarily rousing the standing sleepers, breaking up dreams of this girl or that, as he went by—of a turkey dinner at home, or of a bed in some call-house. It didn't matter much; dreams are made to be broken.

He wrenched open the door, and went out into the car vestibule.

The noise rose to a crescendo out here; the side door of the car was open.

"What is it?" he shouted. "How much longer? Forty minutes now."

"What do I know? I'm just the conductor of this train. When it stops, I stop with it. Troop movement cutting in ahead of us, down at the next switch, I guess. They gotta get there first, you know." And then he looked him up and down contemptuously, the battered felt hat, and the greasy mackinaw, and the oiler's pants. "*You* ain't going anywhere so important. There's a war on, you know."

"Shut up!" he yelped, and flung up his hand before his face, and sank his own teeth into the back of it the way you do when pain is unendurable, when you can't stand a thing any more.

Then suddenly he seized the handrail, swung down off the platform into the darkness outside. Was swallowed up, was lost, was gone.

"Well, that's one way of keeping moving," the conductor observed drily to the soldier next to him. "Under your own power."

———

The salesman's black coupe hummed along the highway, its headlights lending the only light there was to the lonely black countryside. Inside it there was silence. The two men sat staring straight ahead, their faces pale ovals against the dashboard light.

The man holding the wheel had the somewhat injured mien of one whose attempts at conversation have been snubbed, and who has made up his mind not to make any more overtures. Paige just had a stony look, as though his face was a gray plaster cast that had long ago set, would have had to be chipped off him to let any expression come through.

"Can't you pick it up a little?" he said suddenly, without moving his lips.

"Sure," was the cold answer. "But I'm not going to. This happens to be my car, and fifty's the ceiling as far as I'm concerned, even in the country at night. I have a wife and two kids. If you want to make better time—" He nudged his head sideward toward the accompanying strip of road.

A smoking sigh hissed through Paige's tight lips. He folded his arms tight across his chest, as if to keep them under control. His hand, slipping under his mackinaw, came to rest on the butt of his service gun. They closed around it.

One word more from him, he vowed, and I'll empty the seat. Keep his mouth closed; I don't want to do it, I'm trying to keep from doing it.

The man at the wheel kept quiet, didn't say anything further.

Paige's fingers relaxed, slipped off the gun-butt.

The speed-clock indicator stayed, quiveringly, at fifty.

The man at the wheel, unconscious of what he was doing, began to hum. Presently he was singing words, in an undertone. "Somebody stole my gal—"

Paige's fingers tightened again on the gun-butt. It jarred a fraction of an inch upward.

He writhed a little on the seat. I'm trying not to kill this man, he pleaded querulously. I don't want to kill *anybody*. I just want to . . .

"Don't," he said, so subduedly that the word could hardly be detected.

Some slight hint of it must have reached his companion, however. He turned his head to Paige in affronted inquiry. "What was that?"

Paige hugged his chest tight. "I said 'Don't.' "

The man gave him a rebuking stare. Then he turned front again. "Touchy, aren't you?" he mumbled.

"Yes," said Paige. "Touchy."

All of a sudden they'd come to a halt.

"What're you stopping for?"

"This is where we split up. Don't you see that intersection in front of us? If you want east, you have to keep on straight along this same road. My territory's down that way. My car and I, we turn off here."

Paige's wrist gave a jolt, and the gun came out, in all its baleful entirety.

"Get out," he said.

"Wha-what're you going to do?"

"Just get out and stand clear."

He accelerated the process by ramming his hip into him. The door opened and the man half fell into the road, had to scramble to keep from going down entirely.

"Wait, what are you doing—? All my samples are in there—! That's the thanks I—I knew I shouldn't have—"

The door slammed shut. The backs of his hands crept pleadingly over its top, trying to hang on to it.

The gun-butt chopped down efficiently, there was a scream, and the backs of his hands weren't there any more.

"You may be going south. But your car and me, we're going east." Paige floored the accelerator. "And mister," he added, "you don't know how lucky you are to be alive."

———

His frantic pounding with both fists stopped short. The door had opened. A girl came out, slowly. She pulled it closed after her, and then she stood there and looked at him, with her back slumped against the door.

She'd had a drink or two and looked like she'd had them alone. She had a lighted cigarette between her lips and talked without removing it. A spare was stuck behind her ear like a pencil.

"You're too late," she blurted out without introduction. "She left just a quarter of an hour ago. You missed her by fifteen minutes."

"How'd you know who I—?"

"Your heart's all up in your eyes," she said gruffly. "I'd know you in the dark by the shine it gives off. Why didn't you get here sooner? Or better still, why did you ever meet her in the first place?"

"She was my wife. She swore that all our lives— Where'd they go? Which way?"

She slumped lower against the door, as if she were tired. Tired of the whole world. "Just call it 'away' and let it go at that. 'Away from you.' You're licked. They may still be in the town somewhere. Or at some motor court on the road out—"

He backed his hand to his skull and screwed up his face into a weazened grimace.

"Tell me something," she said with a curious sort of objective curiosity. "Is it that bad? Does it hurt as much on the inside as it looks like it does on the outside of you?"

She never got the answer.

She was still standing there, shoulders slumped low against the door, tired, tired of the whole world, long after his figure had plunged back into the darkness, the car door had cracked closed, and the red taillight had whirled off.

Suddenly she gave her cigarette a violent downward fling that splintered it into sparks against the ground.

"Jesus!" she exclaimed bitterly. "I hate love!" She turned on her heel and the door slammed.

———

She was alone in there. She had grown tired waiting for him, had dozed off. The tableau spoke for itself. The brightly lighted room in the motor court bungalow, probably reserved ahead of time in her name alone, so he could join her there. And he hadn't come, and she'd slept while she waited.

The shades down on both windows, for she'd undressed before. Her bag open and balanced astride two chair arms, partially emptied. The covers of the bed turned neatly back on a diagonal line.

She was asleep seated at the dressing table, her face resting on her forearm. She was in night attire, a pale-blue negligee over her gown. The hairbrush she had used before sleep overcame her lay there within reach of her hand. Near it stood the little traveling alarm clock she had taken out of her bag. Its ticking was the only sound in there with her. It seemed to point up the scene. Its hands were crossing at five to eleven now, and though no one but she could have told when he was originally supposed to have come, the inclination of her drowsing head showed that time was far past—far past and gone.

And then the knob on the door by which you came in twisted slowly, in subtle noiselessness, as though pressure were being exerted from the outside, secretive pressure. The pressure relaxed, the knob turned back the other way to where it had started from.

No tread, no sound. No withdrawal any more than there had been any approach. But then a window went up softly behind one of the

overlapping, fully-drawn shades. The shade billowed out. A man's leg came down to the floor behind it. A second one followed.

She didn't hear him. Her sleep was too deep and the sounds he had made too hushed.

A hand, the bent fingers of a hand, clasped the edge of the shade, held it taut for a minute, then bent it back in a sharp momentary indentation.

Bucky came out from in back of it, his gun readied in his hand. His eyes were only eyes when they rested on her. When they left her to roam searchingly elsewhere about the room, they became stones, cold and hard, imbedded in his face.

He trod softly. With the terrible softness of oncoming death. He looked into the bath first, fanning his gun in a half turn. He looked into the closet. She'd hung her clothes there, the clothes she'd taken off on arriving here.

There was no other place to look. He put his gun back in his pocket. Those hard stones turned to glance over at her, softened into eyes again. Forgiving eyes. He took down her things from the closet hooks, and carried them over to the open bag, and put them back into it. Even with them, even with her inanimate belongings, because they *were* hers, he was gentle. He folded them over first, so they'd fit in, wouldn't be crushed, wouldn't be harmed.

All but one coat and dress. He left them out for her to wear home with him. Home? Yes, home. Even though they had no house waiting for them, no roof to go over them, home was wherever they were, together.

Then he latched the bag closed and stood it down on the floor, ready to carry it out for her.

Even that she didn't hear, the click of the latches.

Then he went toward her, to wake her.

He stopped just behind her and stood there looking down at her for a minute. If she could have seen his face just then, she would have known she never need fear she'd ever hear a word of recrimination about this afterward. No questions asked, no blame allotted. Just to have her back, that would be enough.

He bent over at last and kissed her gently on the top of the head, to wake her.

"Sharon," he whispered tenderly in her ear. "Sharon, wake up. I'm taking you back with me."

Her head rolled over slightly, along her arm, as a person does who slowly comes back to wakefulness. And she was grinning up at him, sidewise (he could see her profile now). In a sly, elfin sort of way.

But her eyes were still blurry with slee—

His hand stabbed suddenly downward toward the hairbrush, there before her. Snatching, not the brush but what lay under it, held in place by it.

Penciled lines on a square of paper.

You can have her back now, soldier.
Don't say I never gave you anything.

He fell down, first upon one knee, then both, there beside her. He tried to take her in his arms, but every which way he held her, she dangled another way, at cross-purposes to his embrace. Until at last she lay there stretched out on the floor. Still smiling up at him, slyly, elfinly.

With the desperate helplessness of a man beside himself, his hands went slapping down his own sides, seeking to bring something, anything, out of his pockets to help her with. What, he didn't know.

And then they stopped, as one of them felt the gun.

Hoarse with his pain, he crooned to her brokenly, "I don't want it either, Sharon. I don't want it either. If this is what it does to you, they can have it."

He hovered low above her, until he'd reached her tortured, twisted mouth. He kissed it, as a husband does, a husband should.

"Thank you, Sharon. It was nice loving you."

The shot jarred the two of them alike, her dead body and his still living one.

Their kiss only repeated itself as his lips fell athwart hers once more, stayed there. It became permanent.

———

Chance remark during the course of a shop-talk conversation between Detective A and Detective B:

... reminds me of a case we had out our way not so long ago. Found a note saying, "Now you know what it feels like." We couldn't make it out, because they were both dead. Who wrote it to who . . . ?

Chance remark during the course of a conversation between Detective B and Detective C (three weeks later):

... like in that case A. was telling me about a while back. They found a note saying, "Now you know what it feels like." Something like that, I don't remember exactly. . . .

Chance remark during the course of a conversation between Detective C and Lieutenant D (Cameron's chief), six weeks later:

... B told me he heard of a case like that. The note was worded the same way, that's what made me think of it just now. They didn't set too much store by it, just figured it was the work of a crank. . . .

Letter from Lieutenant D to his opposite number at headquarters A (two and a half hours later):

... that MacLain Cameron, at his own request, be attached to your office on a temporary basis, to work along with your men on the deaths of Pfc. Buck Paige and his wife Sharon . . .

Answering telegram from Lieutenant A to Lieutenant D (twenty minutes later):

ONLY TOO HAPPY ACCEDE YOUR REQUEST. SEND HIM ON.

They turned back to the witness again, Cameron and his chief. "Just one more question, Celeste . . ."

The girl on the chair swung her trousered leg off its opposite knee, dropped her foot to the floor with a short-tempered stamp. She took a hitch in her belt. She snapped the ash off her cigarette with a proficient fingernail.

"There you go again! How do you expect me to know who you're talking to? I keep thinking it's somebody else, behind me! Rusty's the name. What do you think I am, a big sissy?"

Cameron and his chief exchanged a look. "Sorry, didn't mean to hurt your feelings," the chief apologized dryly. "It takes us old-timers a little while to get used to the idea you're never, never supposed to call a girl by a girl's name nowadays. Okay, Rusty."

"That's more like it," she relented generously. "Now what can I do for you this time?"

"Sharon Paige had a locket, a thingamabob on a chain around her neck. We want to ask you about that locket."

"Okay, go ahead and ask me."

"She wore it pretty much, that right?"

"All the time. It only came off when she washed her neck. Then it went right back on again."

"Now here's the part we want to ask you about. How did she wear it? Can you tell us? Can you show us?"

"Well, this is the neck of her dress." She yanked out the neck of her own sweatshirt to show them. She pointed, her finger disappeared down the aperture. "Like this see? Down underneath it. All the way down in there."

"Never on the outside?"

"Never once. See, it wasn't for show. It was a personal memento, like, I only knew it was there because I saw her before her dress went on over it."

"But nobody passing her on the street, or even standing talking to her *after* her dress went on, could tell it was there?"

"Only an x-ray machine."

"Thanks. That'll be all, Ce—er, Rusty."

She got up to go. She traced her hand along the wall and a match head flared out.

"Listen—Please—" the chief stammered somewhat helplessly. "Not on our walls."

"What's the matter with your walls?" she said charitably. "They strike matches good."

The door closed after her.

"Don't you see the point I want to bring out? That the poison letters to the husband were written by nobody else but the very guy himself, the one who killed her! Right while he was in the act of seducing her away from Paige, he kept tipping him off as to the progress of the seduction. Giving him a play-by-play account, right as he went along. He used that locket, in one of the letters, as a means of identifying the girl he was seducing as Paige's wife, so there could be no mistake in Paige's mind. Nobody on the street could see it, nobody could see it when she was fully dressed. He's the only one *could* have sent those letters."

"Why should he snitch on himself? That's crazy."

"It's crazy cruel, which isn't the same thing. It's ferocious sadism. He wanted to make him suffer, and he did make him suffer. You heard Rubin on that point."

"All right, but what do we have now? Proving what?"

"That he wasn't interested in the wife; either in loving her, or in killing her. He didn't kill her because he had anything against *her*, he killed her because he had something against Paige. The husband was the target, the wife was just the weapon used to strike him down."

The chief tried to shake his head, fighting off belief.

"Just answer me two questions," Cameron said. "How long did she suffer?"

"Ten seconds. Maybe twenty. Just at the end."

"How long did *he* suffer?"

"Weeks, I guess. Rubin said so. Weeks of slow torture."

Cameron spread his hands. "Which one of them was he really punishing?"

"This," said the chief dismally, "is something new."

———

Cameron had to go all the way out to Tulsa. In Tulsa he had to go all the way out to Dixon Avenue. Along Dixon Avenue he had to go all the way out to its extreme end. Even so, weeks of patient inquiry and research had had to precede this, before he could even find out just where it was he had to go.

He used a variety of methods to get there; train, and then bus, and finally a Tulsa taxi.

Then he walked up a flagstone path and rang the predetermined doorbell. An attractive little housewife of sunny aspect and friendly demeanor came bustling out after a moment or two.

"Graham Garrison lives here, doesn't he?"

"Yes," she said readily. "He's my husband."

"Ask him if he remembers Cameron," he said tactfully. He didn't want to frighten her, he didn't want to tell her he was a detective. There was something so cloudless, so trusting about her.

She repeated it to herself first, the way a little girl does a message entrusted to her, to make sure of getting it right. "Ask him if he remembers Cameron." Then nodding to show she had it, went to deliver it.

Then came back to report, with a candor that was altogether fetching, "He said he doesn't. But he said to come in anyway."

Cameron, thanking her, decided he didn't blame Garrison one bit for remarrying. Or rather, for marrying this particular little person. The wonder would have been had he failed to, once he'd known her. Every man, he supposed, was entitled to his happiness. And the very first look at Garrison's face showed Cameron he had his now, all right, if he'd never had it before.

He'd been listening to a baseball game. It was Sunday afternoon. He politely turned the radio off, successfully concealing the regret that Cameron knew darned well it must give him to do so.

"Are you from the company's eastern office?" he said. "Is that where we met?" Then seeing that Cameron was not quite sure what he meant, amplified, "The Standard Oil Company."

"No," said Cameron. "You didn't meet me in business. I don't know if you recall or not, but—" He glanced around, but they were alone anyway; she'd gone back to some domestic enterprise that held more attraction for her than her husband's concerns.

Garrison's memory suddenly beat him to the punch. He straightened in his chair, snapped his fingers, then pointed one at Cameron. "Oh, *now* I do! Sure. You're the police fellow that came out several times and talked to me, around the time Jeanette died." And then with evidences of extreme satisfaction, though it was probably due far more to his own successful feat of recollection than to Cameron's presence, he urged, "Sit down," offered him a cigarette and wanted to know if he wanted to have a drink.

Cameron got up and closed the door with a precautionary "I wonder if we could talk this over by ourselves?"

"Is it bad?" asked Garrison.

"We don't want your wife to hear it," said Cameron, already her staunch protector after exactly forty-five seconds' acquaintanceship. "The implications aren't too pleasant."

"Nothing'll get her out of the back for hours," confided Garrison with an affectionate pride that shone out all over him. "She's cooking her first Sunday meal all by herself. There's a chalk mark across the back of the hall beyond which I daren't step."

"You're a lucky man, Mr. Garrison," Cameron couldn't resist blurting out.

"I had my loneliness," Garrison let him know.

Cameron reseated himself. "Look, I had to come to you," he explained. "I don't enjoy doing it, any more than you probably will enjoy having me do it. I hate to have to rake up the past. You're out of it now; it's over far as you're concerned. But you can help me. You're the only one who can. You're the only remaining link." Then he added, "*Living* link."

"That sounds pretty grim."

"Well, it has been. It is." He took things out of his pocket, things he'd brought along to show him. "Did you know a man named Hugh Strickland?"

"That bum?" was Garrison's way of answering yes. "They gave him the chair, I understand. He ended up fine, didn't he? I knew he was heading that way."

"You knew him fairly well, in other words."

"Too well to suit me, I dropped him even before Jeanette died. She wouldn't have anything to do with him any more, toward the end. After all, Florence Strickland was one of her best friends. I'm not a puritan or anything like that, but when a man's that open about such things . . ."

Cameron deftly sidestepped the moral aspect of the thing as being no concern of his. "There are two things I'm afraid we disagree on," he said. "But even though we do disagree, you can still help me nevertheless. That doesn't alter things one bit. One is about the death of the first Mrs. Garrison—"

"Oh, you still think Jeanette's death was—not altogether in the course of nature."

"I still do and I always will."

"I don't," said Garrison.

"That needn't hinder us at all. And secondly, it may surprise you, but I don't think Strickland was guilty of the murder of Miss Holliday, for which he went to the chair."

Garrison looked not only surprised, but even rather rebukingly at him for this.

"I interviewed him, unofficially of course, in his death cell some weeks before the execution. He repeated what I'd already heard him say when we first took him into custody—that there was a note lying there beside her body, of a vindictive, gloating nature. He couldn't produce it, of course, so he had no way of saving himself." He leaned forward intently, and indicated his own chest with his thumb. "I happen to believe there *was* such a note. Why? Because it was such an odd, unlikely, you might say pitiful, little detail to cling to, to be the lie of a man trying to save his own life. He never claimed to have seen any shadowy figure of a man slipping out as he got there, nothing like that. Only, and always, he insisted he'd found that note there by her body. He swore to me he had. He quoted from it and his quotation never varied from first to last. And *I* happened to know, which he never did from beginning to end, that you yourself had received pretty much the same type of note a whole year earlier when your wife died. And—*one solid year after he was in his grave*—a third such note turned up, in a third instance, somewhere else. Now do you understand why I've come out here to you?"

Garrison nodded, impressed in spite of himself.

"Now, let's get on with it," Cameron said. "Did you ever know a fellow named Buck, or Bucky, Paige?"

Garrison shook his head, at first tentatively, then as he mulled over it, more and more definitely.

"According to his birth certificate, which I located and looked up," Cameron tried to help him, "his given name was actually Bucklyn. It's on file at Lansing, Michigan. He was born there, nineteen-nineteen."

"No," Garrison kept insisting. "No." And saying it over to himself as a further test. "Paige. Bucky Paige. No."

"You're sure?"

Garrison said logically, "Well, I don't know the name. That much

I'm sure of. I might have known such a person by sight at one time or another."

"Well, let's try it that way, then. Here, look at this. Carefully now."

He passed him a snapshot of two soldiers posing together, arms slung about one another's shoulders.

"Forget this one on the left," he instructed him. "And forget the uniform."

To help him do so, he took two strips of paper and obliterated the headgear and the jacket by framing the face between them.

"Try it with this," he said, and handed him a small magnifying glass. "Now."

Garrison pored. His reaction was not slow in coming. "Yes," he said, "I *have* seen that fellow's face somewhere or other. Now, wait a minute—where? Just where?" He sat back in his chair. He leaned forward again, scanning it some more.

"Keep trying," Cameron encouraged.

"Not in any of the company offices—"

Cameron couldn't refrain from gripping him by the shoulder, as though physical pressure might aid. "Keep it up. Don't quit. Keep it up."

*"Somewhere—some*where*—"*

He closed his eyes briefly, in intensity of effort. Suddenly he jolted from his chair, as though a tack had just been stuck into him. He pounded his fist down on the photograph, making the two strips of paper fly off in opposite directions.

"Why, he was the guide that used to go with us! He was hired by us—! On those trips. The rest of us were all amateurs and he was the professional we took along. He'd find the best places for us to go, and all that. Bucky. Yes, now I remember, we called him Bucky. Gee, I haven't thought about him in years!"

"Went with you where?" said Cameron tautly. "What trips?"

"Fishing trips, camping trips we used to make. Sort of a little friendly sporting outfit we got up. The Rod and Reel Club we called it. We'd all go off, two or three times a year, get away from business and all that. Go up in the woods, roughing it, camping out. You know what I mean."

"That's what I wanted," Cameron encouraged him. "Something like that. That's what I hoped I'd get from you. That's what I came here for. Now we're in the heat. Now, did you have any connection, any contact, with Strickland outside of those trips?"

Garrison nodded. "Yes, previous to them. But not afterward. From then on I stopped seeing him. We broke the club up."

"Paige?"

This time Garrison shook his head definitely. "No, I never saw him *before* those trips, and I never saw him *after*ward. It was only on the trips themselves that I saw him at all. He was there at the airport when we met to take off and we dropped him off there when we landed back and went our ways."

"Then that was the only time you and *both* these men were together? *Both,* not just one."

"That's right."

"You see. I have the three of you linked in two ways. First by a date. And secondly by a note. There's a date touches each of your lives. I don't know why, I don't know what it means. The last day of May, the thirty-first. Your first wife died on May thirty-first. Strickland's, shall we say, close friend met her death on May thirty-first. And finally the bodies of Buck and Sharon Paige were found together on May thirty-first. Twice could be a coincidence. Three times is no coincidence. Not when it happens to three men who already knew each other before it happened.

"And then there's a note. A particularly vicious note each of you got, right when it was calculated to hurt the most. All worded pretty much alike. I saw two of them. And I believe in the existence of a third, because the man who got that, Strickland, didn't know there *were* two others I had already seen when he told me about his. And the wording of his matched the others.

"And now we come to something very important. The crux of the whole matter. Because those notes and that date may recur in other lives, they may not be finished yet. I have no way of knowing until I find out what they mean. So you've got to tell me just who else was a member of that sporting outfit with you. I've got to know their names before we go any further. I've got to know where I can get hold of them and warn them."

"I can give you that without any trouble," Garrison told him. "Because it was a small outfit, only five of us in all." He counted off on his fingers. "Besides myself, Strickland, and this Paige, there were only two other fellows in it. And their names were—"

—

Suddenly, back at the small town where it all began, outside the lighted window of Geety's Drugstore, overlooking the square, the phantom lover, the ghostly drugstore cowboy, is glimpsed again. For just one night. For just one night he's seen standing there again, in his old place, keeping his old vigil. No eyes for anyone but the one who doesn't come.

Most don't know him any more, don't know who he is, don't know the story; the town has changed so. The war came and went; the town swelled up with it and then burst. It's shrunken again now, back nearly to its former size, but the same people no longer inhabit it. They drifted on and others came to take their place. Geety's sign still says "Geety's," but it's just a trade name now, someone else is running it. There's a different cop, and a different girl in the ticket-window of the Bijou; there's a different crew in the trim brick firehouse across on the other side of the square.

But the square's still there, and the same old things go on.

It's June first, it's a Saturday night, and the lights are all blazing and the whole town's out on the hoof. Sauntering by in two's, every boy with his girl, every girl with her boy.

There's nothing disheveled or odd about him. You wouldn't know. His hair's freshly cut, the way a man gets his hair cut before a Saturday night date. His tie's new and colorful. A little colored boy came along before, and he even let the urchin give him a shine. They say purpose in life keeps you alive. Well then his life must be full of purpose. Because there's nothing to show he's gone off on a tangent. A doctor might be able to tell after a few visits. But who's to make him pay those few visits? And doctors don't go looking for their cases; cases have to go looking for their doctors.

The inside of the building may be a charnel house, but the façade is the same wholesome, conventional, commonplace one you see around you on all sides. No one has yet been able to look into the windows of people's souls from a passerby's point of view and see the inside. If they could, there'd be many a scream and many a sudden paling along the streets.

He looks at his watch from time to time, and he even gives a little tolerant, self-assured smile as he does so. The smile of a man who's not put out, who doesn't mind waiting a little; who knows she's bound to come.

Two little bobby soxers, feeling their oats, out looking for escorts (after all, perambulating the square is as good a way as any to get them if you haven't one already) happen by. They glance his way as they come abreast of him and decide even he might do. A new face, somebody new in town. Might be worth investigating.

They smirk and try to flirt with him, and slow their stroll to a snail's pace, to give him a chance to accost them if he sees fit.

"New scenery," one says audibly to the other, for his benefit.

He gets it. (It would be hard to miss.) But he only smiles a little, shakes his head a little. "Waiting for someone," he says. Then he tips his hat to them to soften the rejection and turns his face the other way.

They shrug to one another and go on; plenty of other fish in the sea, especially on a Saturday night.

They'll flirt with many men yet before they grow older and pass that stage. Meaning no harm, down by the square on a Saturday night. They'll never know how close they came to never flirting with any man again. One Saturday night, down on the square, with all the lights blazing. So close death brushes by you in a crowd sometimes.

Then at last the law of averages gets in its work; someone turns up in the crowd, one of the old prewar inhabitants, who knows him from before, knows who he is, or rather who he was. Takes a second look, startles into long-dormant recognition, leaves his girl's side and going over, stops before him.

"Hello, Johnny. Don't you remember me, Johnny Marr?"

Just looks at him, but doesn't answer.

"We used to play basketball together, on the team. Red Washburn. Sure, *you* remember me. Don't you remember the coach, Ed Taylor? Old 'Iron Man Ed'? He died at Tarawa; first man to plant the flag—or one of them places."

Just looks at him, but doesn't say a word. Doesn't even blink.

"What's the matter with you, Johnny? I used to work part-time at Allen's Grocery, after school, delivering orders. I own the store now. Remember old man Allen's daughter, that never would notice any of us? That's her standing right over there. She's my wife now."

Just looks at him, and never utters a sound.

He gives up at last, looks doubtful, looks embarrassed; goes back to her, scratching his head, and they go on together.

"I could swear that was Johnny Marr. Don't tell me I'm losing my memory. Couldn't get a word out of him. *You* remember Johnny Marr; don't he look like him to you?"

"I don't want to look back at him. I never took any notice of that crowd of boys you used to run around with, anyway."

"But then, if he wasn't, why didn't he *say* he wasn't? He just stood there mum, like a ghost. Maybe that story I once heard about him is true after all; that he blew his top and—"

"Oh, forget it, Hartley," she says inattentively, and gives him a slight directional push. "Get on the line and get our tickets; they're all getting ahead of you, and I don't want to sit all the way over on the side again."

Old friendship; youth's friendship.

It gets later, and the crowd thins out, the lights dim out. The movie house empties out, and then the soda parlors, and finally even the two taverns: "Mike's Place" on the square, and the slightly racier "Kelly's" out in the outskirts. Geety's is dark long ago, and the five-and-ten even longer ago. Joe the cabman has put his cab away and gone home to his wife and kids. Even the cop on the beat has clocked out. Even the cats and the dogs have gone in for the night.

One tolls from the steeple. That steeple that's still five hours fast. The square's stark empty now, all the lights are out.

No one sees him go away. No one's there to see him go away. How he goes, nor where he goes, nor when he goes.

But in the morning, when daylight finds the square, the place in front of the drugstore is empty, no one's standing there. And that night no one's there any more, either. Nor the night after, nor the next night.

Just that one night, and then he's gone away again.

But the caretaker of the cemetery up on the hill could tell—but doesn't, because nobody asks him—could tell if he wanted to, how the very next morning, that Sunday morning, when he first made his rounds, he suddenly came upon a fresh wreath of flowers placed on one of the markers, that hadn't been there when he last made his rounds the night before. Flowers in the night, flowers in the dark, that no hands had been seen to leave. Flowers so wistful, so tender, so heartbroken; not storebought, but flowers of the field, assembled, wreathed together, by unpracticed hands.

Against the half-forgotten headstone that reads:

DOROTHY
I shall be waiting.

5.

THE FOURTH RENDEZVOUS

They were all clustered around the clock, thick as bees, waiting for their chosen partners. Their partners of just that one evening, or their partners of every evening. The men waiting for their girls. The girls waiting for their men.

Most of them were young. One or two were a little more mature, but most of them were young, and glowing with their youngness. That is the only time to wait by a clock, for your date around eight, when you're young. When you get a little older, it's a lonesome thing to do. But when you're young, every time you do it it's Christmas Eve and there's a big package coming along any minute for you to unwrap. And even if you don't find what you wanted inside it, it doesn't matter: because tomorrow night will be Christmas Eve all over again, and there'll be another big package coming along any minute for you to unwrap. It's when the packages stop coming and the Christmas-tree lights die down, that you know all of a sudden you're old.

It was the clock at the Carlton Hotel, the clock inside the lobby, the most famous meeting place in town. Custom had made it that, convenience. Everyone met everyone else there. No matter where you were going, you started from there.

The girls were pretty, and the boys were clean-cut and decent-looking. Some of the girls sat while they waited, but a few were standing, because there weren't enough seats to go around. Sometimes, when they knew each other, they split a chair between them, one on the seat, the other perched on the arm, even if they weren't going out on the same date together. The boys, of course, all stood. They acted each according to his temperament and his nature. The restless, the skeptical, the unsure ones, walked back and forth, occasionally went toward the entrance and looked out, came back again, checked their watches against the clock, tapped their feet, drummed their fingers. ("Did she mean it when she said she'd be here, or is she standing me up?") The patient, the credulous, the calm ones stood relaxed, not bothering to move about much, not bothering to consult the clock, except to make sure of their own punctuality. ("She'll be here. She said she would. I can count on it.")

The boy, the one particular boy standing there, was one of the confident, unworried ones. His shoulder was sloped against one of the squared columns that margined the lobby, he was peacefully browsing through his newspaper under a bracket of electric wall candles.

He acted very sure she'd come, whoever she was to be. There must have been a perfect understanding between them, they must have been already in the later stages of "keeping company," just preceding formal engagement when you no longer have to worry about outside interference.

He was about twenty-three. He was a good-looking, husky kid. Good football material. Not overly intelligent, perhaps, no one would have accused him of that. But otherwise wholly prepossessing. The kind of a boy older men would like to take into their offices. The kind of a boy older women would like to have meeting their daughters under the clock at the Carlton. They mightn't know where Mary Jane was, but at least they didn't have to worry about it while they didn't know.

He happened to glance up from his paper at exactly the right moment, almost as if intuition had had something to do with it. He caught her right as she was coming in the entrance.

She'd come. The one for him. His appointee.

The way his paper instantly furled and was discarded gave that away. The way his hand went up and his hat went up. The way his already cheerful face beamed broadly. Before she had even finished clearing the revolving door and the glass between them was out of the way.

The door gave one single complete revolution behind her, empty, and then a man came in on its next turn around. So close behind her you could almost have thought he was following her. If you were the kind of a person who thought things like that. But after all, people were coming in and out every minute through that door. He just happened to be the very next one after her, that was all.

He gave her a single quick glance, from behind, and then he went off to the side somewhere, to the cigar and stationery counter, and began shopping assiduously for a magazine. He didn't just ask for one by name, he looked into one, and turned whole pages of it, before going on to the next. He was a most painstaking magazine buyer.

She'd reached the boy who was waiting for her, meanwhile. Or rather, they'd split the distance between them and met halfway, out in mid-lobby.

Every girl there had seemed pretty until now. Now they all looked plain. A klieg light had just blazed out in the middle of a lot of smoky oil-lamps. She wore her dark hair long, to her shoulders. She had a gardenia in it. Her eyes were gray; or if they were blue, it was so light a blue it seemed gray. She was very young yet, though. At least two years short of twenty, and maybe even three.

The conversation wasn't memorable. But it was vivacious, tinseled with anticipations of an evening's fun.

"Hello."

"Hello."

"Am I late?" She didn't expect any answer. She rushed on without waiting for any. It was, apparently, a form of secondary greeting really and not a question. "Did you get the tickets?"

"Yeah. They're holding them for me at the box office."

"Well, what are we waiting for?" she demanded gaily. "Come on, let's go." And took him by the arm.

They went toward the entrance and out through the door.

The man at the magazine counter, still trying to make up his mind, held one up in front of his face, as if trying to judge its texture.

The door spun around once after them, empty.

He decided he didn't want a magazine after all. He quitted the counter and went out the door himself. The counterman swore at him with noiseless lips, rearranged his display.

The taxi they'd just gotten into drove off.

He got into the next one in line as it shifted forward.

His drove off too. His went the same way theirs had, around the corner. But all traffic had to go that way, it was a one-way street.

They got out a few minutes later and about six or seven blocks away, in front of the theatre. Their taxi drove off. Another taxi came, and another, and another; but countless people always drive up to a theatre in taxis.

The boy got in line, picked up his tickets, rejoined her, and they went in. The next person in the line picked up his tickets, the next one hers. Then a man came along and asked for just a standing-room admission.

"I can give you a good single in the tenth row," the ticket seller suggested. "Last-minute cancellation."

"I just want to stand up in the back," the man emphasized with considerable asperity. "Do you mind?"

The ticket seller looked surprised at the gruffness, instead of gratitude, he'd drawn. He shrugged and sold him his ticket. The man went in.

Between the acts the boy and girl came out into the lobby. But so did everyone else in the audience; the place was thronged, just a sea of anonymous faces around you every which way you turned.

From the theatre, at half-past eleven, they went to a Chinese restaurant and dance spot. Pseudo-Chinese. The waiters were Chinese and the food was the "Chinese" food that China never knew but that Americans think is Chinese. But the band played "The Jersey Bounce" and the biggest seller at the bar seemed to be Martinis. And the man whose money was invested in it was named Goldberg.

The lights, incidentally, were dimmed so low they were almost extinct. Just a faint bluish and reddish tinge to the twilight here and there. This was for purposes of creating a devilish "atmosphere." It was, for anyone under twenty, very romantic. It was, incidentally, very innocuous at the same time. A sheep in wolf's clothing sort of a place. The next stage, in night-life experience, after the corner ice-cream parlor, and coming before the really adult clubs and roadhouses have been arrived at.

They were shown to one of the little booths along the wall, and they sat down facing each other. They couldn't see who came in and stood up at the bar and who didn't. They wouldn't have wanted to if they could.

A man came in and stood up at the bar and ordered a Martini, just to pay his rent, and then he didn't touch it. But he didn't turn around and stare at anyone; he kept his back to the room, so who was to notice that?

They got up and danced, the boy and girl.

Their food arrived.

They sat down and ate rice and fried noodles and foo yung, and things that they didn't even know the names of themselves.

They got up and danced some more.

They sat down and ate some more fried noodles and rice and foo yung. They were having fun.

The party of four in the booth next to theirs got up and left.

The man at the bar with the neglected Martini turned and accosted the head waiter.

"I'd like to order a dinner," he said. "Could I sit over there? That one, over there."

"That's for four, sir. I could give you a nice one down by the edge of the dance—"

"I want that one," the man said grittily. "I'll pay the cover for four." He put something in his hand.

"Yes, sir," the head waiter said reluctantly.

He went over to it and he sat down with his back to them. He ordered dinner.

He sat quietly, waiting for it to come.

". . . I liked the part where she turns around to him and says—"

"Gee, that was good, wasn't it? D'you suppose married people ever really act that way about each other?"

"I don't know. They don't in my house."

"They don't in mine either. My older brother's been married five years now, and I never heard him act that way to Dolores. That's his wife, Dolores."

"I guess they just made it up, for the stage, to make it more interesting."

They brought his dinner, and he still sat quiet. Eating it now.

"...of course I like you better than Charlie Nickerson. I go out with you more than Charlie Nickerson, don't I?"

"Yeah? Well, at Betty's party two weeks ago I counted how many times you danced with him. Out of ten dances, you danced six with him and only four—"

"Well I like that! Now you're blaming *me*. Just because you don't know how to rumba right, I'm supposed to sit on a chair and say 'No' every time anybody comes up to me and—"

The price of his dinner was a dollar and a half. He acted as though it hadn't been worth it.

He started down the stairs—the place was on the second floor—and stopped halfway to the bottom to retie his shoelace. It hadn't come open, but he opened it first himself, and then retied it. They were standing there at the curb-line, hailing up a taxi.

They got one and drove off.

He got one, a moment or two after, and also drove off.

The two taxis went in the same direction.

Theirs stopped outside a large one-family house a considerable distance uptown. Two figures got out and disappeared into the shadows of the entrance.

His stopped three or four houses away. Nobody got out.

There was a wait. A long wait. Ten or fifteen minutes' worth of wait. The doorway didn't light up. Nothing happened. Nothing that could be seen. You couldn't even tell that they were there at all, except that the first taxi, theirs, remained in abeyance at the curb.

Then one figure came back to it. The boy alone this time. There was a brief flickering of orange light as the door opened and closed.

The first cab went on.

The second one too.

"Now get in a little closer," its rider instructed. As though this was the part that really counted.

The lead cab drove north ten blocks, and east another eight, then north again, after waiting for a traffic light, for just half a block more.

It stopped finally in front of a flat building, the third one in from the corner on the east side of the street.

The boy in it got out. He paid it off. He went inside the building.

The man got out of his at the corner. He paid off too. He started down the opposite side of the street, the west side, on foot. He watched the windows carefully.

A single one lit up. On the fourth floor, on the right-hand side of the building.

He crossed over, went into the entryway himself.

He only stopped there a minute, looking at one of the name cards affixed to the letter-boxes. Looking carefully at just one of them, the fourth one on the right-hand side of the entrance. It read:

4-H. Morrissey, Wm. C.

He turned and went outside again, and walked rapidly away from there. That was all.

It was a night later.

The same man had a companion now. A doorway companion. They were both loitering just inside the basement entrance to that same building, which was only a few yards away from the main entrance. It was recessed, and it was set somewhat below sidewalk level; three or four cement steps led down to it. It offered a perfect place of concealment from which to watch the sidewalk and the main entrance to the house. It had a light bulb set above it, to show the ash-collectors their way, but this had either gone out of order or been deliberately manipulated around in its socket so that it no longer conducted current.

The man's doorway companion smelled of cheap whisky and stale clothing, although nothing could be seen of him—there was only the telltale odor to classify him. He fidgeted a good deal more than the man himself. He started to light a cigarette. The man gave a chop of his hand and knocked it to the ground. The would-be user stooped down, located it, and put it back into his pocket, as if he was used to getting them from there anyway.

"Suppose he drives up in a cab?" he whispered hoarsely.

"A guy only does that when he's out with a girl. He was out with one last night. He won't be out with one tonight again. He's a one-girl man."

"Suppose he chases me himself and catches up with me?"

"Hit him in the belly, then," the man said grimly. "Foul him so that he can't. I thought you said you were an ex-pug. You ought to be able to take care of that."

"Okay, I will. I'll double him up like a pretzel."

"Make sure you get the wallet, now."

"I'm not new at this. It's the first time I'm doing it for somebody else, and not myself; that's the only difference."

There was a blur of lights down at the corner as a bus halted momentarily, then went on again along the lateral avenue that intersected there. Three people had been deposited at the stop, started going their diffuse ways. One was a girl, two were men.

"See the one with the floppy topcoat, hanging open?" the man coached. "That's your boy."

"It won't work," his companion said tautly. "The girl's heading the other way, but that other guy's coming right along behind him on this same side of the way. I can't do it with him there, he'll jump in and help him—"

"There's two chances out of three in our favor," the man said, equally taut. "He may turn in one of those first two houses. If he doesn't, then we'll put it off until tomorrow night."

The anonymous second man passed the first house.

"Even odds, now," the man in the doorway breathed.

The anonymous second man turned, went in the second house, as he came up to it. Morrissey remained alone on the sidewalk, striding for the third house, his own.

The man in the doorway let out his breath. "It paid off." He gave his companion a push, out and up the three short steps. "Get going before he gets the door open."

The shabby, hulking figure accosted Morrissey just as he reached the band of light flaring out from the doorway, said something to him in a whining undertone.

Morrissey half reached into his pocket, about to hand him something. Then he changed his mind. "No—beat it," he grunted. "You're no good, I can tell by looking at you."

He turned to go in.

The panhandler brought the edge of his hand down like a cleaver, across the back of his neck, in a devastating rabbit-punch. Then as the boy swayed and went staggering off-balance, he swung him around forward and drove his knee brutally up into his intestines. The boy gave a deep, shuddering groan and collapsed to his knees. His assailant spaded a hand deftly around to his back pocket, extracted his wallet, then let him tumble in a writhing heap. He turned and fled, disappearing around the lower corner where the bus had just stopped.

The man in the basement entrance now jumped up, as if on cue, and reached Morrissey at a run. He bent over him solicitously.

"What happened? What'd he do to you?"

Morrissey lay there helpless, hugging his stomach and gagging. He was still conscious, but unable to pick himself up yet.

"Stop him—took my wallet—" he panted.

The man ran on in pursuit. He turned the corner. There was no one any longer in sight. He ran down that way for a block, and then turned the next corner and ran up the adjoining side street beyond there. He dove suddenly into a basement entryway, highly similar to the one he had just quitted, as if he knew ahead of time there would be someone in it. There was.

"Okay, give me back the wallet," he breathed heavily.

"Here. Don't forget the rest of what's coming to me."

"Here's your second ten." The man took it out of his own pocket, not the thefted wallet. "Now, on your way. Make yourself scarce." He gave him a push to get rid of him.

He waited until he was alone in the doorway. Then he jerked at his own necktie, pulling it awry. He scoured his palms against the brick wall, getting them good and grimy, then he transferred the dust in streaks to his own face and the shoulders of his coat.

He was punching and swatting at his hat when he came back in sight of Morrissey a few moments later, as if it had been knocked off and he'd had to pick it up from the ground.

Morrissey had managed to stagger erect now against the wall, and was standing there with both hands against it to support himself, and with his head held low between them, looking down at the ground.

"Did you lose him?" he said weakly.

"I latched onto him around the corner, but I couldn't hold him. I tried to tackle him, but he got away. But I made him drop the wallet. Here it is." He dusted off his shoulders ostentatiously, and felt tenderly of his jaw, as if to see whether any teeth had been damaged.

"I was sick all over the place just now," the boy said ruefully. "Thanks for helping me, anyway." He took the wallet, leafed through its contents.

"Did he get anything?"

"No, it's all here. I only had seven dollars in it, anyway."

"Feeling better now?" the man asked solicitously.

"Yeah, I guess so. I'm still a little wobbly inside. Gee, I sure appreciate your giving me a hand like that—"

"Anybody'd do as much," the man said disclaimingly. "I couldn't just stand still and watch, could I? Glad I happened along when I did."

"There's never a cop around when you need one," Morrissey said.

"No, there's never a cop around when you need one," the man agreed. "Sure you're feeling okay? You still look a little white around the gills. Want to go to a drugstore and have them look at you?"

"No, it'll be all right."

"How about a drink, then? That'll straighten you out. I could use one myself." He looked vaguely up and down the street as if in search of some bar they could adjoin to.

"Swell," the boy said heartily. "That's more like it. There's a nice place down the line I know of." He held out his hand in new-found friendship. "My name's Bill Morrissey."

The man took it, shook it. "Mine's Jack Munson."

———

Munson came in and went up to the bar. He ordered a Martini, just to pay his rent. There wasn't anything Chinese about the place except the waiters. The band played "The Jersey Bounce" and the operator's name was Goldberg.

Munson turned around and faced the room, this time; he kept his back to the bar. He kept looking steadily over at the booth where Morrissey was sitting, until finally their eyes met, as they were bound to sooner or later.

Morrissey quickly took a second look to make sure, then raised his arm in greeting.

Munson raised his in answer.

Morrissey beckoned him over, both with a nod of his head and a sweep of his hand.

Munson picked up his drink and sauntered casually down that way. Then as the booth came into frontal perspective, a girl was revealed, sitting facing Morrissey. A girl who made every other girl in the place look plain. She wore her dark hair long; she wore a clasp of brilliants in it. Her eyes were gray, or if they were blue . . .

"Hello, Jack," Morrissey greeted him warmly. "What're you doing here, all by your lonesome?"

The girl looked at him. With polite interest, no more. Such as was due the friend of an escort. She didn't smile. But she didn't frown.

"Hello, Bill," he answered. They'd been calling one another by their given names ever since their third stag meeting, approximately.

"Miss Drew, this is Jack Munson; good friend of mine."

They chatted for a few moments.

Then, "Aren't you with anybody, Jack? Come on, sit down," Morrissey invited. "There's room enough on the bench."

"Thanks, but I don't want to intrude." He looked at the girl for her permission.

"Do," she said mildly.

He sat down.

———

Again the clock at the Carlton.

The two of them were waiting now, together, side by side, running-mates on an evening date.

"What do I owe you for my share of the tickets?" Morrissey asked. "Better let me fix it up with you before I forget."

"You mean while you still have that much on you," Munson ribbed him.

They both laughed.

"Here they are."

She'd brought another girl with her. That had been the arrangement.

Less lovely, less radiant, but then anyone would have been. Still pretty enough in her own right.

The introductions were made. They paired off. Morrissey with Madeline Drew. Munson with Miss Philips.

They took a taxi to the theatre.

They came out, formed a momentary little island in the eddying current of the audience streaming past them on the sidewalk.

"Shall we go to the Bamboo Grove again?" Madeline suggested.

"Sure, that's our old standby," Morrissey answered, more particularly to her than to the other two.

Munson danced with Miss Philips first.

Then the next time the music played they changed partners. He danced with Madeline, and Morrissey with the other girl.

"How do you like Harriet?" she asked him.

He looked at her, at her, herself, and only smiled.

That was all that was said while they danced.

She hummed the tune a little, lightly under her breath. Not very surely, almost self-consciously.

Then the dance was over.

———

He danced with Miss Philips, first. Then the next time the music played, they changed partners. He danced with Madeline.

She looked up at him presently.

"Why so quiet, Jack? You haven't said a word all evening. You're not as good company as last week, or the week before."

"And you should be good company," he said somewhat bitterly.

"Harriet thinks you don't like her. In the ladies' room at the theatre just now she told me she thought she oughtn't to come along with us any more. You should really be more attentive to her, Jack. She feels hurt."

"I haven't thought about her once the whole evening," he admitted.

She shrugged reproachfully. "But you're her escort. Then who—?" She stopped that before she'd said it.

He didn't answer. He looked her straight in the eyes, deep in the eyes.

They didn't say anything more, either one of them.

Then the dance was over.

———

Morrissey was waiting alone by the Carlton clock this time. It was late. The crowd had thinned out. They were going to miss the show. He fidgeted; went to the entrance to look for her, came back disappointed;

went to the entrance, came back agonized. He looked at the clock too much, he looked at his watch too much. That didn't help. They gained a minute, every minute, and that was all they could tell him, either one of them.

It was the death-watch of a date; that final stretch when it's about to expire into a full-fledged stand-up, give up the ghost. You can't keep it alive just by waiting there: it takes two to keep it alive. But you wait there anyway, trying to give it adrenaline.

He smoked too much, and he used up all his cigarettes; then he bought another pack, and he smoked them too much. And didn't half finish what he began.

A hundred thousand men before him had been through what he was going through now. But that didn't help; to him it was just like the first time. It was excruciatingly brand-new.

Then suddenly—a whirl of leopard collar, of flaring green coat, spinning around in the wings of the door—and there she was.

She was forgiven, it was over; it was all right before she'd even reached him, even opened her mouth.

She came in alone. Well, naturally; this had been rigged as a single date. Miss Philips had dropped out, piqued. And that had made Jack de trop.

Her mien was sober. A little wan, you might even say. When she greeted him she smiled, but the smile soon died.

"Gee, I didn't think you were coming any more! What happened?"

She couldn't get up much vigor. "Oh, I don't know—" she said lacka-daisically. And then: "I'm here." As if to say, What more do you want?

He didn't press her further. They had headaches sometimes, he'd heard vaguely; they weren't like men. They were more variable, they went up and down like barometers.

The curtain had already gone up when they found their seats.

"Like it?" he said between the acts.

She wasn't explosively enthusiastic. "It's sort of cute," she said tepidly.

Then the show was over. "The Bamboo Grove again?" he suggested. "How about it?"

"No, no Bamboo Grove tonight," she said. "I'm not in the mood. I think I'd rather go straight home."

"But—"

She gave him a look, and he saw danger in it. He flagged a cab.

On the ride back she said two words. "Thanks," and then "Thanks." To a cigarette, and to his lighter.

When they got out, he took her over to the doorway. But when he tried to kiss her, she turned her head slightly—looking to see if she had her key—and her lips evaded him. You can't *stretch* in a kiss, or it loses all grace, all spontaneity; it has to descend where you directed it, or it's spoiled. His was spoiled.

He caught on at last, three hours late. "What is it, what have I done, Madeline?"

"You haven't done anything, Bill." She looked at him, almost as if she now realized for the first time that it was he who had been with her all along. She added, "And believe me, that's the truth."

"Then why is it—? You're acting different."

She had her key in, as though that was the main part of it to her. He put his hand over hers, the one with the key in it, and held it that way, to keep her a moment longer.

"People change," she said pensively.

Her hand squirmed, under his, trying to free itself so it could work the key.

"But Madeline, Madeline—you're breaking me up, you're doing things to me. Don't leave me out here like this—give me something to hang on to—"

She freed her hand, and turned the key, and got the door open. "What can I do?" she said pessimistically. "Say I love you?"

"Can't you?" he said, suddenly frightened pale.

She shook her head, very slowly, a very little. And that was her good night.

She closed the door, and went up the stairs disheartenedly.

She went to her own room first, and took off her things as though they weighed a thousand tons and dragged her whole frame down.

Then she looked at herself in the glass, and looked away again, as if she was ashamed of *that* girl.

She went out into the hall, and up front to her mother's room. The sitting room part of it, anyway, where her mother usually remained up reading after her father had gone to bed.

It was lighted and cheery and her mother was up reading. Her mother looked thirty, and Madeline looked thirty-two. Or acted it, anyway.

"Hello," she said leadenly. "Back."

"How was the show?" her mother asked.

"*Was* there a show?" she answered dully.

Her mother gave her a quick knowing little look; then held her peace.

"Well, now that I've made a station announcement, I guess I'll go to bed."

She turned around and went out.

She halted, turned, came in again.

"Well, good night," she said lamely.

"Good night, dear," her mother said readily.

She turned around and went out.

She halted, turned, came in again.

"Yes, dear?" her mother said patiently.

Madeline bit her lips, as though she knew they were about to waste their time. Then she relented, and let them have their say anyway.

"Nobody called, I suppose;—did anybody?"

"Yes, a young man did. He didn't leave any name. Just asked, 'Is Madeline there?' and before I could ask him who he was he'd hung up." Then she added, not very wittily, "Somebody you know, I guess."

"Yes," Madeline agreed. "Somebody I know, I guess."

Her hand made a little start toward the region of her heart, but didn't complete it. Suddenly, she wasn't old, she wasn't tired any more. She was a child on Christmas morning. Her eyes lit up as though a switch had been thrown behind them. "Oh yes," she said, "somebody I know! Somebody I know!"

She seized her mother, unaccountably, and hugged and kissed her feverishly. And she laughed as she did so—laughed with a curious sobbing effect. Then she turned and fled like one possessed out of the room and down the stairs to where the phone was. She dialed a number. She made the wheel go around so fast it sounded like rain hitting a tin bucket.

A voice answered.

She said, "Was it you?"

"Yes," he said.

"Oh, I knew it was, I knew it was!"

"I didn't want to," he said. "I tried not to. But Madeline, I can't hold out any longer."

"Oh, Jack, I can't hold out either. It's no use, no use. Everything was so still all night long. And now all I hear is music, coming from everywhere at once. Oh, Jack, for the first time in my life, I think, I'm falling desperately in love—" Then she begged piteously, "Jack, don't hurt me too much, will you?"

"The clock at the Carlton," he suggested softly.

"Yes," she said, half deliriously. "Oh, yes—yes. Any time you say, any night—from now on."

———

She came down the stairs ready to go out, and she found that her father had somebody closeted with him in the library. She could hear the voices. Some stranger. Some man he'd brought home with him. Some business friend or associate, perhaps. She caught a glimpse of him as she passed the doorway. Someone she'd never seen before.

She shrugged the matter off. It held no interest for her.

Her mother suddenly appeared from nowhere, stopped her as she'd reached the front door and was about to open it. Her mother acted frightened. Well, awed by something or about something. Taut.

"He wants to see you. He wants you to go in here."

"I'm just leaving. Four-star date. Tell him I'll see him when I come back."

"No, it's something important. You'd better go in, Mad. I promised I'd send you to him the minute you—"

Whether she would have or not, she wasn't sure herself. But suddenly he'd heard their voices and appeared in the library entry.

"Madeline," he said. "Come in here, please." And he wasn't smiling. She went in.

Her mother attempted to follow at her heels.

"Not you, my dear," he said inflexibly, and closed the door in her face. The other man got up.

Her father was taking it big, whatever it was. His color wasn't good, and he kept mopping his brow in one place, right over one eye, though it needed it elsewhere as well.

"My daughter, Mad, this is Inspector Cameron."

A detective, of all things! She was annoyed at being detained like this, by such an oddity. They belonged in newspaper items. The sort of items you didn't read. Not in the library of your own home—acting like actual people.

"Sit down," her father said. "This is important."

They looked at each other, he and the interloper. As if to say, Do you want to ask her or shall I?

Her father was the one who did, finally. "Have you met anyone new lately?"

She pushed her brows up until they were center forehead. She let that serve for her answer.

"That's a perfectly simple question, Madeline. Don't fence with us. We're dead serious about this."

The detective rephrased it. "Have you met anyone lately whom you didn't know previously, who wasn't included before now in your circle of friends, Miss Drew?"

Something warned her, Say no. "No," she said.

"You're sure, Madeline?" her father insisted anxiously. "At anyone's house, at some party, in some restaurant—?"

"Through somebody else," the detective put in. He spread his hand. "Like, say, introduced to you by somebody you know already. A very close friend or—"

She turned her head his way, briefly, and flattened him to a run-over dime. "Oh, should you be introduced? I usually walk along the street and drop my hankerchief."

He turned all colors of the rainbow and tried to screw himself into his chair.

"Who're you meeting tonight, Madeline?" her father asked appeasingly.

She'd been ready for that since the question before. "Someone whom I was *not* introduced to," she said. "He sat down in the seat next to me, and some of my belongings were on it, and he apologized, and that's how we became acquainted."

The detective stiffened, leaned forward. She loved it.

"Oh, I forgot to add that I was fifteen, and he was sixteen, and we were both in first-year high. Bill Morrissey." And she rose to leave.

They both slumped. She loved that too.

Her father looked at the detective inquiringly.

"You'd better tell her, Mr. Drew," Cameron said quietly. "I think you'd better tell her."

"Tell me what?" she challenged.

"You're in some danger from a man, Madeline—"

"What man?"

"Well, we don't know exactly who he is—"

A derisive note sounded from her. "If you don't know who he is, then how do you know I'm in danger from him? Well, what sort of danger? Oh, I suppose the usual kidnaping-for-ransom routine. It's getting so you haven't *arrived*, you're really nobody at all, until you've been kidnaped for ransom at least once. It's like being listed in Bradstreet's."

"Danger of your life, Miss Drew," the detective said patiently.

She made a gesture of mock melodramatic dismay, crossing her arms over her shoulders and stepping back. "Well, if I see anyone peering at me from under a broad-brimmed black hat, I'll let you know."

"You won't know him, Miss Drew."

"*I* won't even know him when I see him? Really, Inspector—"

"Madeline—" her father started to say, but she'd opened the door and eluded them.

Her mother was still hovering around outside. "What did they want, dear? What was it? They wouldn't tell me."

She had to curb herself. They'd come to the library entrance after her and were both standing there at her back. She simply shook her head at her mother, incapable of speaking. Or afraid to trust herself.

It was only when the front door had closed behind her that she let herself go. She emitted a whoop of laughter. She fairly staggered. That was the funniest thing she'd ever heard.

She was laughing so hard she could hardly see to get herself a taxi. It was a death on her make-up, the way her eyes were tearing.

It took the better part of the ride for it to wear off. She laughed nearly the whole way to where she was going.

———

He refilled her glass. "What else did they say?" he prompted. He was enjoying it as much as she was. That was the nice thing about him, he always shared your moods with you. When you were giddy, he was giddy too.

She sputtered so she blew nearly half the champagne out of her glass. "They sat there with faces this long." She gestured across her midriff. She dropped her voice to a mock basso profundo. " 'Have you met anyone new lately, Mad?' Tell the truth, doesn't that sound just like the end man in a minstrel show throwing a straight line?"

He nodded. He showed his teeth straight across, from corner to corner of his mouth, and his shoulders went up and down in a risible palpitation.

" 'You tell her, Inspector.' 'No, you tell her, Mr. Drew.' Then after all this build-up, when they finally got to what it was they wanted to tell me—" She hid her face behind outspread fingers and shook with hilarity. "They didn't know who he was, or what he looked like. *I* wouldn't know him either, even when I saw him. Really, either my father has lost his sense of humor completely or—"

He was enjoying himself so hugely that he became downright silly in the effort to prolong their mood still further. "Maybe they mean me. After all, I *am* someone you've met only lately. You'd better watch out, I'll bite." And he pretended to snap his teeth at her, like a dog.

That was all she needed. She threw her head back and fairly screamed. "Oh, don't start me off again," she pleaded. "My ribs ache. I can't take it any more."

On his side of the table, his own head went back and he brayed right along with her.

"Murder," he gasped.

Everyone in the place was looking their way, with half envious smiles of sympathetic approval.

"Not a care in the world," someone said. "I love to see a young couple enjoy themselves like that, while they can. They've got plenty of time for heartaches later."

———

He was just finishing up with his dressing for the evening when there was a knock at the apartment door.

He dropped the necktie he was holding as suddenly as though electric current had just shot through it. He made a swift dive over toward a chest of drawers. He shot the middle one out of it. A gun momentarily flashed into view, then disappeared again. His hand came away from his back pocket, empty.

He went toward the door and he said batedly, "Who's there?"

"Bill Morrissey," a voice answered curtly from the other side.

He let out his breath slowly, with a sort of silky sound. Then he unlocked the door, opened it.

Morrissey came in. Morrissey gave him a rather long-drawn stare, that started from over the threshold, went all the way around him in a long arc, and ended up on the other side of him, in the center of the room. His eyes never once quitted him during that whole time.

"I'm sorry, Bill, I'm going out."

"With my girl."

Munson didn't answer for a minute. He tried a half smile. But it was for himself, not for Morrissey. It wasn't extended to Morrissey; it wouldn't have been accepted if it had been. "Are you sure you've got the straight on that?"

Morrissey's eyes never flickered. "I'm sure."

"I don't think you have. You just said, 'You're going out with my girl.' I'm going out, all right. But not with your girl. That's the part you're balled-up on."

"I'm balled-up-hell," Morrissey said in a cold sing-song. "You're going out with Madeline Drew. If you say you're not, you're a liar." The adjective he used to modify the noun was unprintable.

Munson nodded slightly. "I'm going out with Madeline Drew," he said. "Now we've finally got it straightened out. Where does the 'your girl' part come in?" He waited a moment. "And you've come here to do what about it?"

"I've come here to punch your head off."

"All right, Bill," Munson said mildly. "All right, go to it. If that'll get her back to you." He gave another of those smiles that were for himself again.

"It may not get her back," Morrissey said, narrowing his eyes wickedly, "but it'll make me feel a lot better than I do now." He backed toward the door from where he was. With hands behind his back he felt for the key, and when he'd found it, turned it and locked the door.

Then took it out and shunted it into his pocket. His eyes had never left Munson's while he was doing this, and his teeth were bared, but not in a smile.

"Put up your hands," he prompted with a misleading appearance of geniality. Probably suggested by the fact that his teeth were showing so widely.

"Don't let's be formal," Munson said ironically. "If you're going to sock me, then sock me with them down."

He made no move to defend himself. Nor yet to retreat either. He stood there half lounging, with his elbows supporting him against the top of the dresser.

Morrissey's face was yellow with bile. His coat rippled down him to the floor, somewhat like an up-ended snake shedding its skin. "You think you'll take her away from me? Well I won't let you!"

Munson shook his head slightly, almost as if he pitied him. "You fool," he said softly. "You can't take people away from someone, unless they want to be taken away. Don't you know that yet?"

Morrissey strode in close, swung at him viciously. It caught him on the side of the face, and since the bureau was supporting him at his back, he cartwheeled sideward into a crumpled heap.

"You're yellow! Get up!"

"Oh, never mind the etiquette," Munson said almost wearily. "You don't have to have a set-up. Take me from here."

Morrissey, almost crazed by rage, reached down and hauled him bodily to his feet. Then he hit him again, so that he went down again. And went stumbling after him himself, with the violence of his own blow. Then straightened, and readied a third one. But there was nothing for it to come up against, no opposition. And that undid him. He faltered, stood there at a loss.

A change came over his face suddenly. He slapped both hands, open now, flat against it, as if to keep the other man from seeing it. "What good are my fists?" he groaned smotheredly. "They won't get her back! And I don't know any other way."

He sought the door as if half blinded, then when he'd found it leaned against it for a moment, inert, frustrated, spent. Then took out the key, unlocked it and went out, leaving it open behind him.

Something that sounded like a gagging cough, but might have been a male sob, came drifting back along the hallway after he'd passed from sight.

Munson picked himself up painfully. He took a handkerchief and wet it and held it where his face was bleeding. He had to keep moving it around to catch all the different places. But he was smiling, distorted as the smile was; still smiling that smile meant for himself alone.

He went over to the door, walking a little unsteadily, and pushed it closed.

He took the gun out of his pocket and tossed it back into the drawer where he'd originally got it from. It had been on him the whole time. He could have shot his assailant with it a dozen times over. It was as though he hadn't wanted to. It was as though he hadn't meant it for him in the first place.

And he was still smiling.

——

And now it was she, waiting there alone under the Carlton clock. Something she, at least, had never done before, no matter what other girls did. The men in her life had always been waiting there ahead of her, well ahead of her.

But now it was she.

She was sitting there in a chair and everyone that came in looked at her, but the only one she would have looked at didn't come in.

If it had been anyone else she was waiting for, she would have got up and gone long ago. But if it had been anyone else, she wouldn't have been here in the first place.

She wanted to go—and yet she couldn't. She was held fast, bound, trapped. It was as though there was a rope around her, lashing her to the chair. What was that song—"Prisoner of Love"—that was she.

She got up from the chair at last, unable to endure the ogling, and the circling and the maneuvering that seemed to be going on about her, with herself as the focus. That expression so plain to be read on all their faces, "Wouldn't I do, instead? *I* wouldn't treat you this way. Just give me a chance and I'll show you. Won't you let me meet you—instead of him, whoever he is?" She went over to the side and took refuge by one of the thick, fluted columns. That way they couldn't get at her so easily, they had to walk all the way around the column, like a huge Maypole, if they wanted to stalk her.

She opened her compact and looked at herself. It didn't look like the face of a girl who got stood up, who let this happen to her. And yet, even now, rather than the annoyance, the humiliation, the wounded pride, she would have felt if it had been someone else, her main feeling was one of uneasiness, of chill foreboding; of worry, rather than resentment. Because it was he.

"What is it? What's wrong? Has he gone and left me? Won't I see him again? Oh, I must! He has to come!"

She knew in her innermost heart, though she kept telling herself "This is long enough. Not another minute. I'm going to walk out of here right now," that she'd still be here an hour from now, still waiting like this. And even at midnight, with the lobby empty and the lights turned down, she'd still be here waiting.

She couldn't help it. It was something stronger than she was. It was love.

And then suddenly a bellboy bawling, "Miss Drew. Calling Miss Drew."

She almost ran across the lobby toward him, she went so fast. Shot out from alongside the column.

"What is it? What?"

"There's a call for you. You can take it in the Three Booth, over there."

If she didn't actually run toward the designated place, it was only by exercising the utmost self-control. Her hopes ran and her fears ran; it was only her feet that didn't.

She picked up the phone-piece, dropped it in her haste, regained it.

Then he said contritely, "I've kept you standing there all this time.... Will you forgive me? I couldn't help it. I tried my level best—"

"It doesn't matter, it's all right— Only, what was it?" she said in staccato.

"I'm a little beaten up."

Her breath siphoned sharply inward. "Were you held up? Were you—"

"It was more of a social call. One of your friends paid me his respects."

"Bill Morrissey," she said instantly.

He confirmed it with an indulgent little laugh, without any direct answer.

Again she drew her breath in, this time in exasperated anger. "That does for him. That finishes him with me. Are you bad? Are you—"

"I could get down there in a taxi, I suppose, but I don't look so good. Court plaster here and court plaster there. I'm not sure that you'd want to be seen with me in public."

"Where are you?"

"Up at my own place."

"But are you sure you're all right?" she kept saying. "Are you sure you're all right? Not badly hurt?"

"I hate to call it off like this. Unless of course— Would you want to come up here instead?"

She hesitated. Whether it would have been prolonged or not, he gave it no chance to be anything but momentary. He answered for her.

"No, of course not. I understand. I shouldn't have asked that, should I?"

That decided her, inversely. "I'll come up," she said firmly. "Where is it? You've never told me where you live."

He was now the reluctant one, rather than she. "I don't want you to do anything that's against your—"

"Jack," she said. "Don't you understand? I love you. I *want* to come."

———

The door swung slowly inward, his hand upon the knob, and the rectangular opening revealed them clinging together in a final embrace just inside it, outlined in gold on one side by the lamplight, outlined in blue on the other by the shadows.

Reluctantly they separated and his encircling arm dropped away.

"Now you see? You're leaving just as—just as unharmed as you arrived."

"Are you quite sure," she whispered, "I wanted to be?"

"There's always tomorrow."

"But this was tonight."

"Never mind, tomorrow will come. Tomorrow, the thirty-first of May."

"When a girl's not in love, she hates it if you're not a gentleman. When she is in love, she hates it if—you are."

"Mad," he said, crushing her to him. "I didn't want to get you up here under false pretenses. Not you, Mad, you're too lovely. That would be cheap and sneaky. But that was tonight only. Now the period of grace is over. Now I'm giving you fair warning. Mad, if you ever come here again . . ."

She looked at him. She understood and acquiesced. She gave him one last kiss.

"Till tomorrow," she said.

"The clock at the Carlton?" he suggested.

She shook her head. She tapped her index finger downward toward the floor. Then she turned and fled away from him down the stairs.

———

She was still in a state of exaltation, beatification, stars blinding her eyes, golden pinwheels blurring her senses when she opened the door of her own bedroom half an hour or so later.

The lights were on full blast, but even this did not register on her intoxicated faculties at first. She could almost have walked into a raging fire without realizing it, the state she was in.

Then little by little the fact that all her dresses, her lingerie, in fact her complete wardrobe, was strewn about in varying ordered piles, on chairs and on the bed, penetrated her awareness.

Her mother came in suddenly through the communicating door between their two rooms, further articles overlaying her arms.

"What is it? What are you doing?"

"Packing your things for you. I waited as long as I could for you to get home, but it seemed as if you were never coming and I thought I'd better begin it myself. We've got an early start to make tomorrow."

"An early start to where?" Madeline demanded warily.

"We're going down to the shore place."

"But why tomorrow? Why not next week, next—?"

"We were told—" Her mother stopped short. "We were told to make it tomorrow, at the very latest. It's essential that you—that we leave here tomorrow."

Suddenly she understood. "That man. The one that was here with

Father when I went out the other night. Has *he* been around here again?"

Her mother didn't answer.

"For heaven's sake, Mother! I like a good joke once in a while myself, but this one's getting stale. Is that what they pay him for, to intimidate people?"

"He's convinced your father, and that's good enough for me."

"Well, he's not running *my* life for me! He's not ordering *me* about, telling me when to come and when to go!"

"Sit down here. I want to have a serious talk with you." She moved some of the things aside. "I'm your mother. We're alone now."

"You're my mother, and we're alone now," Madeline said dryly. "Both those facts are self-evident."

"Is there anyone *new* you've been seeing lately? Anyone *besides* the boys you grew up with?"

"Are *you* starting in now? *They* asked me that the other night!"

"Who were you out with tonight?"

"Isn't that going backward a little? About ten years?"

"Madeline, who were you out with tonight?"

"Bill Morrissey." She looked her mother unflinchingly in the eye. "What am I supposed to have been guilty of?" she asked coldly.

"Madeline, this isn't a mother's strictness asking you this. It's a question of your own *safety.*"

"*He* told you to," she flared accusingly. "*He's* the one."

"Madeline, who were you out with tonight?"

"That's the third time you've asked me that. And this is the second time I'm telling you. Bill Morrissey."

"Madeline. *Bill called up here a little before ten tonight and asked for you.*"

The cleansing tissue she was rubbing off her face cream with never missed a stroke. "Certainly. We had words and I got up and walked away from him, left him sitting there in the theatre. I suppose he thought I'd gone home. That must have been when he called. I sat by myself in the lounge through the whole second act. Then I went back to my seat just before the final curtain."

"Oh," her mother said, in a faint, relieved little voice. "Oh." When you want to believe, you believe. She reached over and patted Madeline's hand.

"Have I ever lied to you before?" (But, she thought, have I ever been in love like this before?)

Her mother kissed her appeasingly on the forehead. "Good night, dear." She moved toward the door. "And you *will* let us take you to the shore place tomorrow? You won't make any fuss about it?"

Madeline looked at herself inscrutably in the mirror. "I won't make any fuss about it," she promised docilely.

———

They started early, the sun still only high enough to lie in slanting slats on the streets, like a fallen yellow picket fence—almost as if afraid to let the full, baleful light of the fatal day find them still in the zone of danger. The servants and the greater part of the household impedimenta had already gone on ahead the night before (Madeline only now discovered); there was, nonetheless, great to-do and commotion with the hand luggage, repeated false emergences and reentries into the house on the part of her mother before they were at last ready to make off.

Madeline, through it all, sat there in the back seat of the town car in complete indifference, a cigarette in one idling hand, an overnight case in the other, almost as though she were an onlooker at this whole proceeding, it had nothing to do with her whatever. She even looked the other way, out the opposite side of the car, away from the house.

She only showed rancor at one point, when, after the driver was already in his seat and just as they were about to start, Cameron suddenly opened the forward door, got in beside the driver, and closed it again. He had not come from their house; it was as though he had suddenly appeared from nowhere.

"Does *he* have to ride with us?" she demanded in a quite audible voice. "What is this, a deportation?"

"Sh-h-h," her mother urged tactfully.

Only the back of his neck seemed to have overheard her; that took on a slightly deeper tinge.

When they arrived at the shore place, he disappeared again as abruptly as he had first appeared. Got out, and suddenly wasn't around any more, was nowhere to be seen. You wouldn't have known he had come down with them.

Madeline had a sardonic smile indenting one corner of her mouth; perhaps elicited by this, or perhaps due to her thoughts in general.

Just before lunch, however, while she was stretched in a deck chair on the grounds some distance from the house, he materialized again, as though he'd been wandering about making a tour of inspection. She pretended not to be aware of him although she could hear the grass rustle under his feet and see his shadow on it, coming from behind her.

He just stood there and looked at her, very unobtrusively.

Her head suddenly went up and she gave him a thunderously dark look.

"I'm reading a book," she scowled. She held it up grimly to show him. "See. Book. You know what they are, don't you? You do this to them"—she bent over it—"and then some jailer comes along and gawks—"

"I'm sorry, Miss Drew," he said mildly. "You seem to resent having had to come down here."

"I happened to prefer it where I—" she began incautiously. Then stopped short.

"*Was* there some association that's been interrupted?" And he gave her a needle-like look of speculation.

She fell suddenly silent; turned her shoulder, went back to her book. As if realizing she'd almost made a tactical error just then.

At lunch she was suddenly someone else again. The stiff mouth was gone, the sullen mien was gone. She was gay, talkative; a little too high-strung perhaps. But she seemed to have accepted the change of scene with good grace, reconciled herself to it. She only made one indirect reference to it and that was a favorable one. "It *is* lovely down here; we should have come down earlier other years, not waited." And even toward him, Cameron (he lunched right at the table with them), she was more amiable though she did not address him directly. Let a brief smile fall athwart him once or twice in passing it on to someone else. As if to say, "See? I'm perfectly happy here. I'm content. No other place holds any attraction for me. You were mistaken."

Again she only got needles of speculation from his eyes.

They went down to the beach in the afternoon. He was in the background again, sitting on a sand hillock. He didn't seem to watch her; he was always looking off the other way. She didn't seem aware of him;

she was always looking an opposite way, in all her frivoling in the water and cavorting on the sand. But there was a heightened pitch to her behavior, as when one is performing before an audience. (And it isn't natural for two people *never* to happen to both look the same way at one time and meet one another's glances.)

Two boys and a girl she knew down there joined her and she invited the three of them back to the house with her for cocktails, and to have dinner, and to spend the evening.

"I'm sort of in quarantine," she laughed. "It'll help me out."

They all went back together in the same station wagon that had brought them down.

They had their cocktails right away, as soon as they'd got back, she still in her beach clogs and robe of white toweling. They even passed him one, but he shook his head and sent it on by. She was strident, she was high-pitched, she was raucous; almost as though they'd been made too strong, or she'd had one too many. She even did a little informal dancing about the room, first with one of the boys, then with the other, to the throb of the battery radio. There was a lot of laughter, there was a lot of chatter, there were a lot of wisecracks and horseplay.

It showed signs of going on indefinitely, but suddenly her mother came down the stairs, dressed for dinner, and inquired a trifle sharply, "Madeline, are you going to stay that way all evening? We'll be sitting down in a few minutes."

Madeline stopped short, glanced down at her own person, as if only now recalling what she had on, smote herself ingenuously on the forehead, and exclaimed, "Oops, I clean forgot! I *thought* I felt kind of draughty." Then, to the accompaniment of her friends' laughter, she fled up the stairs, losing one clog on the way and hurriedly turning back for it.

Presently the spanking water from her shower could be heard plainly, all the way down below in the living room where they were. She must have left both doors, her own room door and the bath door beyond that, wide open.

"That child," her mother murmured, with a little helpless shake of the head.

A maid appeared in the dining-room entrance and looked in interrogatively.

"Yes, we're ready," Mrs. Drew answered.

She rose and went out to the foot of the stairs. "Madeline!" she called up. The torrent of water continued unabated.

"She waits until the last moment," she complained. "She knows how I detest to have dinner kept waiting— She was *in* the water all afternoon—"

"But that was salt water," one of the boys chuckled. "First you have to get it in your pores, for your health, then you have to get it out again, for your health."

Mrs. Drew had started up the stairs by now, to overcome the acoustical impediment of the raging shower.

Cameron, who had been sitting where he could command a view of the stairs ever since Madeline had left the rest of them, abruptly got up and went after her.

Mrs. Drew was calling her from the bedroom doorway now. "Madeline!" She still failed to hear her mother because of the thunderous crash of the water, made even more resonant by the tiling around it.

Cameron reached the bedroom entrance in turn, glimpsed the discarded clogs and toweling robe, and that held him back for a moment.

Mrs. Drew was at the very entrance to the bathroom by now, still trying to make herself heard. She finally ventured toward the vibrating curtains, drew one of them gingerly aside.

"Madeline," she shouted exasperatedly. "I've been shouting my head off! Are you going to stay in there all eve—"

The water was gushing down in crystalline emptiness behind the curtains, reflecting nothing pink but only the bluish-white of the tiles backing it. At the same moment the flirt of a breeze-stirred curtain dangling vacuously over one of the wide-open bedroom windows caught Cameron's eye.

———

In the gasflame-blue smoothness of the vivid sky, a single splash of silver stood out, the evening star that Tannhäuser sang about. Its rays seemed to stream, elongated, down toward the earth, like wet paint, running because it hasn't yet had time to dry. Under it, along the luminescent road that reflected the sky's brightness upside down, like a steel rail, her eager little roadster coursed along, throbbing as though it were in love itself. Little friendly roadster, smuggled out to a nearby

garage with connivance of one of the servants, bedded there in hiding throughout the day, tuned up and waiting for the moment of flight. Little roadster that no detective in the world could overtake now any longer, because its mistress was in love, and love has wings, doesn't bother reading speed gauges.

Hurling like a bullet along its concrete trajectory toward the city, toward the bridges leading into it, toward the supreme rendezvous.

Neckscarf streaming out flat behind her like a pennant on the bosom of the wind. Hair trying to do likewise around all its unbound edges. She was like a latter-day Valkyrie cresting the curved surface of the earth, into the black fastnesses of night. She looked back once or twice, but in derision, not in any real misgiving. The wind tore her laughter from her teeth.

Once an intersection held her up—there were such things, even love had to pay heed to them or risk the consequences of more successful pursuit from closer at hand—and she stood erect in her car, full length, and shook her fist at the sullen red light that impeded her until it blanked out, as if in astonishment at such defiance.

There were two bridges to choose from, a near one and a far. Shrewdly she chose the far, the one that meant turning out of her way and then retracing it, knowing he might have sent word ahead to the likeliest one, she might be halted and held for him there, at its approaches.

She crouched down low in her seat, averted her head as she trundled by, caught in the interlocking mesh of traffic and slowed to a more sedate pace now. But the bridge traffic policeman, there on his little shallow concrete island, close enough to have touched her door-handle, never even glanced at her.

That had been the last hazard. Nothing could stop her now; nothing more.

The city's serrated outline crept up into the sky, in gun-metal, smoked pearl, dark-purple and charcoal-black, and she went rushing down the long descending arc of the bridge to entomb herself at its feet.

———

The others were waiting for him at the bridge approaches, where he'd signaled ahead for them to join him, when he came lumbering in in

the unwieldly Drew town car, too big and heavy to be risked at the rate of speed her roadster had attained.

He jumped out of it, changed into the faster police car they had there. The siren wailed out and the bridge traffic ahead shored over to the side, in a long, curley-cued, frontal breaker, to give them clearance.

"Nothing doing?" Cameron asked. The answer was obvious, or she would have been there in their custody when he arrived.

"Not a sign of her. We've checked every car going through for the past twenty minutes. She may have got through just ahead of us."

"She couldn't have made it that fast. She took one of the other bridges, then, and beat the dragnet through."

"What's she being stopped from?" one of them asked him.

"Stopped from being killed," he answered tersely.

—

Her demented, love-smitten little roadster came sluicing around the corner of his street on a kiting turn that almost swept it up onto the sidewalk, straightened out for the final heat and bore down toward the opposite curb on a long diagonal that finally closed in directly opposite his door.

It shuddered and jarred her, with the wrench she gave its brakes.

Sudden silence. She'd arrived. She was there.

She sat there for a moment, as though she were as spent as the car from the long race. Turned her head and looked at the doorway, waiting there for her, so shadowed, so inscrutable, yet somehow so batedly expectant. As if it were holding its breath to see whether or not she intended to come into it.

It needn't have taken pause; no power on earth could have kept her outside of it.

I'm here, my love, her heart murmured. Did I keep you waiting? Am I late?

She flung open the door, and letting it swing idle behind her, skimmed across the sidewalk and inside. A diagonal edge of shade, like a knife blade, sheared down her back and took its brightness off.

The stairs were nothing to her winged feet. She stopped outside his door and quirked her head a moment, listening. There was no sound, no sound at all. But she smiled in a surety, a confidence, that could not be gainsayed.

She touched at her hair, at her scarf, at her coat, to make what he saw look better, to make him love her more.

Then she raised her hand and knocked.

There was no answer.

But she only smiled that smile again.

She thrust her face closer to the door, the better to be heard.

"Open," she coaxed in a throbbing, low-toned voice. "It's me. Don't you remember me? I have a date with you."

The door swung slowly open, without there being anyone visible behind it, not even the hand that turned and held its knob.

She spread her arms wide for the embrace that was to come. She went in that way, arms outstretched at their widest.

The door swung slowly shut.

—

The whole stair structure from top to bottom throbbed and pounded, like the rolling drumbeat accompanying an execution, and one by one they came hurtling off it, Cameron in the lead, and slammed to a stop in front of the door.

Sudden silence, then, for a moment only.

A streak of flame spit from Cameron's hand, a shot raged out thunderously, and the decrepit lock splashed into particles.

Cameron moved the toe of his shoe, and the door was wide open.

Again silence; but this time not for just a moment. Long, long silence. Nobody moved. There was no more need to. Nobody said anything. There was no good saying anything.

A couple of them drew their breaths in lingeringly; like you do when something hurts you pretty badly. It did hurt them; it would have hurt anybody.

She was alone in there. Half propped and half lying on a sort of settee there was in the room. Almost like in life, when you feel too indolent to straighten up as the door opens and someone comes in. Except that one leg was out a little too far, as if it had delivered a spasmodic death kick and then never quite dropped all the way back to rest again.

She seemed to be looking out at them, from in there, just as they were looking in at her, from where they stood huddled. Almost as if to say, "Come on in and close the door, don't just stand there."

But her face was what was worst about her. He'd kept the blood from going down, and now it never would any more, and it had turned . . .

The face that they'd all looked at under the Carlton clock ("*I wouldn't treat you this way; won't you try me?*"), they would have gagged at, and backed away, and run from now. No one would have wanted it now, nor even recognized it.

Cameron walked quietly in and turned his head the other way as he went past her. A detective, but he turned his head the other way; that was his parting homage to what she'd once looked like.

There was a calendar on the mantel, the numerals "31" in jumbo black digits on its topmost leaf.

Cameron tore the leaf off, let it flutter to the floor.

Then his head went down limply, in abject defeat.

———

It was the yellowed, faded, almost blanked-out snapshot of a young girl, that must have been taken years ago. Of a young girl, standing on a porch step, one foot raised to the step behind her, smiling into the sun.

Cameron found it on the floor in back of the dresser when he shoved that bodily out of the way. Not even *on* the floor, but partially in it, imbedded upright in a crack, so that only the top rim of it peered forth.

It might have been originally inserted into the frame of the dresser mirror and been shaken loose at some violent dislodgement the entire piece of furniture received. Such as one man hitting another a blow to the jaw and sending him sprawling back against it. Or it might have been berthed inside one of the drawers themselves and fallen through a gap in the back of it, down to the floor, at some swift movement of opening or closing. Such as an unexpected knock at the room-door could have brought about.

Anyway there it was. And it belonged to no predecessor of the last tenant, they established that. The floor had been scraped and the room painted just prior to his occupancy, the landlady told them.

"Find this girl," said Cameron grimly, "and we find him."

He broke that down still further. Everything in police work must be broken down; there are no generalizations.

"And to find her, we have to find out two things. When it was taken and where it was taken."

He had six enormous enlargements of it made, about the size of a window pane. Every shadow, every detail stood out. And where the lines weren't firm enough, they were retouched. But nothing was added. Then he took one to each of the head buyers of women's apparel in the six largest department stores in the city.

"I want your opinion on the date this was taken, as closely as you can give it to me, on the basis of what the subject is seen to be wearing."

The analyses came back in from one to five days. A composite of them, with repetitions eliminated, ran as follows:

Lack of shoulder padding in coat: 1940. Shoulder padding was first introduced by us in our 1941 models.

Straight up-and-down lines of coat (trade term "box coat"): no later than 1939. Fitted coats began to appear 1940; caught on by 1941.

"Rolled" lapels: out by 1940. Deeply-notched, flat lapels, such as in men's wear, after that date.

Fullness of skirt: before 1942, when wartime restrictions on material came in.

Closed-toe shoes: before 1940, when open-toes swept market.

Hair-do: introduced by the actress X—in picture Y—. Release date of picture, summer 1940.

Costume jewelry: one strand of pearl beads, such as subject is wearing close about throat, in vogue late 1940, early 1941. Following season, two and three strands. Previous to that, long strands, lying on bosom.

But they all alike added this note of warning: "Make allowance of one entire season (that is, spring to spring, or fall to fall) for the sake of probable accuracy. Background in exhibit appears to be rural, and subject not ultra-smart or clothes-conscious. It takes from six to twelve months for vogues launched by us in key cities to attain full acceptance throughout country."

Most of it was Greek to him. But they were experts, he took them at their word.

Boiled down (and with the aid of a tendril twining one of the porch posts in the background) he got this out of it. Early spring, no earlier than mid-March, no later than mid-April; no earlier than the year 1940, no later than the year 1941—the snapshot had been taken.

"Now we only have to find out where," he said.

And when he looked at the two white porch steps, the two white porch posts, the skimpy dab of clapboard house front, and the extreme edge of a window with a lace curtain showing in it, which was all the snapshot gave him (three million square miles of the United States, and every hamlet in every county in every state could have produced pretty much the same vignette if called upon to do so!), he was ready to give up in despair then and there.

But instead he just buckled down and went ahead working on it.

6.

The Fifth Rendezvous

Cameron shrugged. "How do you go about finding out who the best-loved woman in a guy's life is? Ask him?"

His chief shrugged back. "Do you know of any other way? That's your problem."

Cameron held his jaw as though it ached. "It's not an exact measurement, you know. You can't go to anyone with a scale and *weigh* it out."

"I know," his chief said drily. "It's tough, it's a stickler. I don't want to hear how tough it is. I just want to hear the answer. The *correct* answer. So when you've finished squirming and wriggling, will you kindly go out and bring it back to me?"

Cameron writhed, executed a sort of rotation from the waist up, then brought his torso back to where it had been before. "But *how*? Just by watching him. That might take weeks. It's something that's kept on the inside, anyway. Sometimes it doesn't even show on a guy's face."

"Then *get* on the inside and get with it!" Cameron's chief bounced his knuckles down on the desk and up again.

"There may be nobody."

"Everybody likes somebody, some one somebody, just a little better than he likes anybody else. It's put into them. It's nature. With men, it's a woman. With women, it's a man."

Cameron sighed dismally. "It's an impossibility, Chief."

"I admit," his chief said stonily.

"But I'll go out and do it."

He didn't get any thanks. "Of course you will. Only, why didn't you get started five minutes ago, instead of sitting here wasting both of our time, cringing away from it?"

"Have you got him pretty well card indexed?"

"Thoroughly. All the preliminary work's been done."

Cameron leaned forward. "Then give me a list of *all* the women in his life. Can you do that? Have you got one?"

"I can," his chief said. He thumbed a lever on his desk. "And one is about to come into being now although it wasn't in existence in just that form until this minute." He gave the order, he shut off the lever again.

"And let me advise you," he said while they were waiting, "not to go at it in reverse; not to go to *them,* the women, and try to find out from that direction. Because every woman in a man's life thinks, or would like to think, she's the best-loved woman in that life. It has to come from the man himself."

It came in the form of a very small, neatly typed list; five names on it.

Cameron studied it carefully. "Not many women in his life."

"It may not be on there. That isn't holy writ. *You* were the one asked for that. Remember, this is just from external observation—and at a respectful distance. It didn't get inside him. So watch yourself."

Cameron put it away in his billfold, stood up. "I'll find out," he promised. "I've thought of a way."

He didn't get any praise. "What a delayed departure," his chief remarked astringently. "If everyone took as long when I sent them on an assignment, we'd still be working on the Rosenthal case."

Cameron was at the door now. "He mayn't know himself. May never have thought about it before. But he'll tell me. I'll know."

———

The receptionist combined the perfect grooming of a mannequin and the icy manner of the headmistress at a girls' finishing school. She had no doubt been hired for just those qualities, or else she would not have displayed them so copiously.

"Do you have an appointment?" she said down her nose.

Cameron shook his head.

"Well, I'm sorry—" she started to say. "Does he know you?"

He gave her a look. "When your house is on fire, do you have to know the fireman before you let him put a ladder to your window?"

Her brows went up. "This has to do with fire ladders, then?" she sneered.

"That was just a figure of speech, as you are perfectly well aware."

"Well, what *is* the nature of your business?"

"Police business."

Her brows went up once more, but this time without the accompanying sneer. "Oh. Is there—is there something I can do? I mean, if it's about a ticket or a violation—"

"There is nothing you can do except to get me in there to see Mr. Ward. I realize what your duties are, but there is a time and place for everything. And, believe me, this is not the time to try to keep me out of his office."

"Just a minute," she said, almost hastily. "Come in," she said, when she had returned, and held the door for him. Then closed it on the two of them.

Ward was standing up behind his desk. He had on a very light-colored gray suit. He had been handsome up to about five years ago; now it was slipping away. His hair was still richly dark, but there was a lighter tipping, a frosting, beginning to glint here and there, as on a silver fox fur. His eyes were extremely intelligent, but it was a kindly, forebearing intelligence, not the shrewd hardness of a typical business-man.

"I'm Cameron, of the police department," Cameron introduced himself.

Ward shook hands across the desk. He looked politely blank and not very interested.

"Miss Koenig tells me—" He didn't finish it. He hadn't meant to.

"I don't like to come here to your office like this, but after all, it's the kindest way. The telephone is pretty heartless at certain times. . . ."

"Kindest? Heartless?"

"I have bad news for you," Cameron said bluntly. He took out the typed list, held it so that it lined his own hand.

Ward came around from behind the desk, then stopped short.

"There's been an accident," Cameron said. "Someone's been hurt. We're not sure what relationship *she*—" he deliberately emphasized the word, "bears to you."

He was holding the list in such a way that only he, not Ward, could read it.

"Is it Louise? Is it Mrs. Ward?"

Ward's face was strained and pale, but steady. Cameron watched it closely. He murmured something hesitant, purposely indistinct.

"It's not my mother, is it? Not Mom—?"

His face grew whiter still. It flickered tearfully while he strove to hold it still.

Cameron watched it closely.

There were only three more names on the list: two married sisters, both younger than himself, and his partner's daughter, a girl of twelve or thirteen. Cameron shook his head to himself.

"I don't believe—" he said blurredly.

Ward took a staggering step toward him, then another. He caught hold of his lapels in supplication. His eyelids drooped, half-covering his eyes.

"Martine—" he whispered expiringly.

"Who's Martine?" Cameron answered.

He didn't answer that. "Oh, my God," he shuddered convulsively, his knees dipped limply, and he would have at least slid downward, if not fallen, had not Cameron caught him under the arms and held him for a moment until he got his own powers of support back again.

"What's her other name? Her last name?" Cameron had to put his mouth close, aim the words directly into his ear, to get him to understand them at all, acknowledge them. His faculties were so clogged with shocked grief they would not, it seemed, have penetrated otherwise.

"Jensen," he moaned, in mechanically extracted answer.

Cameron led him over to a chair, helped him down into it.

"Take a drink, Mr. Ward," he said.

Ward nodded, pointed. Cameron got it out for him, poured it, handed it to him.

"There has been no accident. No one has been hurt." He wrote the name down on his list: "Martine Jensen."

He had to repeat the statement. "No one. Miss Jensen or anyone else."

Ward's reaction was slower this time, but as thorough as it had been in the first case. When it had completed itself, he rose to his feet. He dashed the half-finished brandy in the paper cup full into Cameron's face. Little straw-colored drops stood out on his white shirtcollar.

"Get out of my office." He shook with the effort of dislodging the words.

He came closer, swung, and hit him in the side of the jaw.

Cameron staggered, kept his balance by putting his hand out to something behind him.

"I won't hold that against you," he said. "I would have done that to anyone too, who did what I did to you."

Ward kept his arm from delivering a second blow only by sheer muscular contraction which made it tremble as it held itself back.

"What'd you do a thing like that for?"

"I had to find out whom you loved most. There was no other way."

Ward didn't ask him why. "Get out," he said through his clenched teeth.

Cameron opened the door. "I'm getting. I'll be back—shortly."

Cameron went back and showed the chief his list. Three names had been crossed off. Three remained, one of which had not been on it originally, had been added during the interview itself. They read:

1.   3. His wife.
2.   2. His mother.
3.   1. Martine Jensen.

The chief was annoyed. "Well, which is which? Why the double sequence of numbers, what do they mean?"

"That's what I wanted to ask you. They mean: one is the sequence in which he mentioned them. In other words, the speed with which they came to his mind. The other is the degree of emotion he showed. Now, which is it? Is it the one that first came to his mind, his wife? Is it the one he showed the greatest emotion about, his Martine Jensen? (Whoever she is.) I'm not a psychologist."

"We agree," the chief added parenthetically.

"I thought it would be clear, it would be easy to tell. It isn't clear, it isn't easy to tell. That's the trouble with these tests of behavior. When human nature is involved, it's never predictable, it always—"

The chief had been pondering. He stopped pondering now, nodded in arrival at a conviction. "The one he showed the greatest emotion about," he said, speaking with great deliberation.

"But maybe it was *cumulative* emotion, the result of increasing strain. Maybe the first in mind was the right one, but he still had enough self-control at that moment to keep from showing it fully. It was only later that his control finally wore out. In other words, the emotion was for his wife, but it was carried over, past that point, and only showed itself by the time we'd reached the third name, *externally.*"

The chief didn't bother arguing with him. "The one he showed the greatest emotion about," he said doggedly.

"But will *he* figure it out that way too? The Danger? If we, the police, can't be sure, how can he, on the outside, be sure? We may protect the sweetheart and *he* may go after the wife."

"The one he showed the greatest emotion about. Look, try not to think, will you, you only get in trouble. Just be the machine you're supposed to be. A little logic gives us the right answer and that's all I've used. The mere fact he has a sweetheart in addition to a wife, shows he loves the sweetheart more. If he loved his wife more than his sweetheart, he wouldn't have a sweetheart at all. He wouldn't need one. She would be superfluous."

He took his pencil and he took Cameron's list. He crossed out "wife" and "mother."

"Now go to work on this," he said.

There was left only: "Martine Jensen."

———

Cameron went back again next day.

The receptionist was no longer icy. She was hot, she was flaming with resentment, even though it was vicarious.

"Mr. Ward will not see you," she said sultrily. "I will not take your name in to him. I have standing instructions from him. This is a law-abiding private office and it's protected by civil rights. Whether you're a member of the police department or not, you cannot force your way in to him, you cannot compel him to see you. If you try to, he'll get in touch with his attorneys at once and bring a civil suit for damages against the police department itself. Now go ahead and try if you think you'd care to."

Cameron knew he couldn't. He turned around and walked out. From the lobby of the building he telephoned the chief. The chief telephoned Ward. Then called Cameron back, in the lobby, where he was waiting.

"Go on up," he said. "He'll see you now. I've thrown my weight be-hind you."

The receptionist was already au courant by the time he got up there again. She was still resentful, but it was a passive resentment now, no longer an active one. She didn't say "Come in." She merely held the gate for him. Then Ward's office door, beyond it.

Ward was still resentful too.

"Sit down," he said, frowning.

Cameron sat. "May we have this talk without being disturbed?"

"The order's already been given," Ward said curtly.

"It's essential that you believe every word I tell you."

"I'll reserve judgment on that."

"You are on a death list. Not your name itself, but, by proxy for you, the name of Martine Jensen. If you give us your fullest co-operation, I think we can promise you that no harm will come to her. One advan-tage we have is: the exact date of the danger is known to us. The attack will come during the twenty-four hours beginning midnight, May thirty-first, and ending midnight, June first, or not at all." Ward had said something under his breath. "What did you say just then?"

"Fantastic."

"You don't believe me, I see."

"I haven't an enemy in the world."

"No man can safely say that until after his death. You may not have an enemy you *know of,* but that's not the same thing."

"What's the motive? Blackmail?"

"Money wouldn't ward it off. Money only has power over the sane mind. Maniacs don't have motives. I could call it revenge, but even that wouldn't be correct; because where the injury has been unintentional or unknowing, revenge can be reasoned with, turned aside. About the closest I can get to it would be: a revenge-mania."

"Who is he?" asked Ward satirically.

"You wouldn't know him, because—" He hesitated, and then he added reluctantly, "We don't either."

"You know what motivates him, or fails to. You know that money would not influence him. You know he's a maniac. You know the date he'll strike, down to the last twenty-four hours. Yet you don't know who he is. Great police work. How do you go about it, in reverse?"

"Sometimes it has to be done that way. Sometimes it happens that way. Not often, thank God. But this time it did."

He waited for Ward to say something. Ward didn't say anything. There was a treacherous mobility, however, to the corners of his mouth, as though he were having difficulty restraining his risibilities.

"You've got to help us," Cameron said.

"I'm a little old for games."

"You've got to give me all the information you can, on Martine Jensen—"

"Such as?"

"Well, we don't even know where she lives."

Ward's face darkened. "So that you can go to her, question her, and pester her, and frighten her? I'll do no such thing. Come to me with all these cock-and-bull stories you want, but keep away from her, leave her out of it! Do you understand that?"

"She *can't* be left out of it," Cameron said patiently, "because she's the center of it, she's the object, she's the target. It's not you, it's she." He groped to find the right words. "We'll be tactful about it. We police-men understand many things, we come across all sorts of things. We know there are sometimes certain—certain relationships in a man's life, that he doesn't want— We'll try not to tread on your toes, Mr. Ward. . . ."

Ward sat bolt upright, as though some point of honor had been touched just then. He was deadly serious now, intense.

"You don't understand. You don't understand at all. You think I'm carrying on a cheap affair behind my wife's back?" He cleared his throat disgustedly. Then he sank back again, as if in futility. "A man doesn't tell another man his personal history."

"But to a police official, trying to protect the life of someone very close to him?" Cameron prompted tactfully.

Ward nodded at last, dully, after some moments of thought. "Yes, I guess you do," he admitted. "Although I never had to before."

"It's just the general background we want," put in Cameron persuasively, and held his breath for fear the other wasn't going to talk.

He did at last, in that almost trance-like state of contemplation in which one reviews factors in one's life, forgetting before long even the auditor, in one's absorption.

"I knew Martine first, long before there *was* a Mrs. Ward. She was my first love, she was my last; she was my only love." He kept balancing a pencil on its point on the desk top, and watching it as he did so. Then he broke off to ask, "Is this a matter of life and death?"

"Of life and death," Cameron assented, keeping his own eyes down out of consideration.

"I've never loved Louise. It was a marriage of second choice. No choice at all. I don't know what to call it. Before then, it had always been Martine, with me. All my life, Martine. But we waited, like fools. We were so sure that it would never be anybody else but she for me and me for her, that we waited. Next year; it was always going to be next year. That 'next year' that never comes. Then all of a sudden, it was too late. She wouldn't have me. Something happened that—came between us. She thought it did, anyway. She said, 'I can't let you, now.' She wouldn't have me. I waited around and waited around, and she wouldn't have me. The 'next years' kept coming along thick and fast, and there we were, each alone. She told me to marry someone else. That was her wish for me. She said she didn't want me to be alone any more. She said it would make her a little happy if one of us, at least, wasn't alone. And I had always done what ever I thought would make her happy. So I did it this time too; this last time of all. I married Louise, who'd come along later."

"Does she——?"

"She doesn't know about Martine. She knows there *was* a Martine. She doesn't know there still *is* one. Martine is no rival to her, on one plane. I've been faithful to my wife since my marriage. But she's no rival to Martine, either. Martine is my love and no one else ever can be."

He stopped balancing the pencil and put it away in his pocket.

Cameron didn't look up at him, and he didn't look over at Cameron. They were both thinking about it, their eyes at cross-trajectories of contemplation.

"Now I've talked about it," Ward sighed at last. "And I feel cheap about it. It was like a beery bar-room confession."

"No," Cameron said. "It's a matter of life and death. There are two times when you tell things. When your peace of mind is threatened, you tell them to a priest. When your safety is threatened, you tell them to a police officer. And you just did."

Cameron took out a notebook, prepared to jot things down. "Now, if you'll just give me some of the necessary details—where she lives—"

"No," Ward said. "I don't want her disturbed. I don't want her intruded on and frightened. I won't have it."

"But we're only trying to protect her. We *have* to take certain precautions—"

"You haven't made out a very convincing case to me. You don't know who it is, or where he is, or what he is, or even what he looks like. It's the funniest thing I ever heard of. On the thirtieth of May, she's safe all day, but on the thirty-first of May, she has to watch out all day. Then on the first of June, she's safe again. It sounds more like a weather forecast than a—"

Something about it struck his risibilities. He began to laugh, and he couldn't stop. He threw his head back and brayed. He slapped the top of his desk.

Cameron didn't try to curb him. "It'll take a little while, I see," he said. He stood up to go. "That's all right, there's still time."

————

He came back the next day.

Ward grinned again when he saw him. "Are you going to start that boogie-man stuff all over again?"

"I just wanted to show you these," Cameron said quietly.

He took out some clippings, newspaper photographs, a couple of "stills" from the morgue, spread them on his desk.

Ward looked them over, still chuckling slyly.

"You knew him, didn't you?" Cameron pointed.

Ward nodded.

"His daughter died."

Ward gazed up at him calmly. "I'd already known that. Heard it in a vague, roundabout way. Too bad; but it does happen, you know. What connection has that got with me? I have no daughter. And Martine is not an adolescent who has had the misfortune to lose her head over a degenerate. That's all it was."

Ward pointed again. "You knew him, didn't you?" he said accusingly.

"Very slightly. And I've also heard that one. Combat fatigue. He took his wife's life and then his own. If you're trying to protect me from a suicide pact—" He swept the clipping aside. "That was years ago, during the war."

Cameron brought it back center again. "Notice the date line on it."

He wasn't impressed. "I see. That's where you got that idea from. Just a coincidence. These two things are two years apart."

"And in between, there was this," Cameron said patiently.

Ward shrugged. "He murdered his mistress. He was electrocuted. Well, that's what the law says shall be done to you when you do such a thing. Why make hocus-pocus out of it?"

"The date line."

"This time is completely out of kilter. You've slipped up."

"Of the crime, not the execution."

"Now, please . . ." He was good-natured but firm. He wouldn't hear any more.

Cameron got up to go. "All right, there's still a little time."

"Here, take these with you."

"You don't want them?"

Ward shook his head. "You're wasting your time."

"No, I'm not. There's no such thing in my line."

Ward was still grinning when he left the room.

———

And the next day again he came back.

This time Ward only smiled a little when he saw him; not very surely.

"Look, you're beginning to get on my nerves, Inspector. I'm a businessman, I have a job to do here. I can't be thinking about things like—"

"Are you sure it's me that's getting on your nerves, or is it— something else?" Cameron asked softly.

"Well, after all, you come stalking in here each day with the regularity of a radio time signal, and turn my place into a chamber of horrors."

"I just want you to look at this report."

Ward read a line or two.

"This is a death certificate," he said impatiently. "And moreover, it has to do with a woman whom I never knew, whom I never set eyes on while she was still—"

"But you knew her husband. Notice the name."

"So I did. But according to this, she died of— How many people die of that every year, Inspector?"

"They contract it accidentally. She was infected with intent to kill."

"Were you able to prove that?"

"The case would have ended then and there if I had been able to," Cameron admitted.

"If," Ward said dryly. He handed the certificate back. "Will that be all for today?"

"You'll have to answer that."

"Very well. Then I'm afraid it will."

He wasn't smiling any more when Cameron closed the door after himself and left.

———

The elevator didn't immediately stop by to pick Cameron up on his way down. While he was standing there waiting, the ground-glass door at the end of the corridor suddenly flared open and the receptionist came running out after him.

"Mr. Ward wants you to come back," she said breathlessly. "Right away!"

Broken down, thought Cameron, with a sigh of satisfaction.

Ward had just finished a drink. He looked as though he still needed a second.

"Close the door," he quavered. He slumped back into his chair. "I don't know if this is what you wanted to do to me, but you've sure done it," he said accusingly. "I'm frightened now. Good and frightened."

"But you're also being smart, Mr. Ward. At last you're being smart."

"How much time is there?"

"Enough."

"Why did you let me waste all these past days?"

"What have I been coming here trying to do?"

Ward mopped his brow. "My God! If anything happens to her—"

"Nothing will, if you'll just put yourself in our hands. Will you take me to her now? Are you finally willing?"

"Right now. We'll leave right now."

He stopped Cameron for a minute just inside the door. Took him pathetically by the sleeve. "Does she have to know? Do we have to tell her? I've always tried to save her from every shadow—I don't want her to know about this."

"We'll do our very best to keep it from her," Cameron promised him. "If it's at all possible."

———

It was a private house. Cameron hadn't expected that. He'd thought it would be one of these flashy luxurious apartments in which men so often tuck away their outside loves. It was wholesome and home-like and well-cared-for; a pleasant-looking limestone front, windowpanes polished to invisibility, spruce gauze curtains behind them, window boxes with plants on every one of the upper sills. It matched the terms in which Ward had spoken of her to Cameron: not an undercover affair, the love of his life.

A motherly woman in her early fifties opened the door at their ring. A sort of housekeeper-companion evidently, though she wore no apron nor distinctive uniform of any kind, simply a neat flowered indoor dress.

"Why, Mr. Ward!" she exclaimed happily. "Martine will be delighted!"

"This is Mr. Cameron, a friend of mine," Ward said a little nervously. "Mrs. Bachman."

"Come in. Let me have your things." She bustled about them.

"You're staying to lunch, of course?" She addressed the two of them alike.

"I don't know. . . ." Ward said doubtfully, and gave Cameron a questioning look.

"I'll run up and—"

"No. Where is she, upstairs? Let me go up and surprise her."

"Well, let me run down and tell the cook, then. Now, you're *staying*." She put her hand commandingly on Ward's arm for a moment. "Why, it's already five to twelve. Do you think we'd let you go out of here? Martine will love it; it will make her so happy."

On their way up, Cameron cautioned him, "Pull yourself together now. You're a little jumpy. If you don't want her to notice anything—"

"Help me," the man said pathetically. "Help me."

Cameron slung his arm briefly to Ward's shoulder, then dropped it again. He felt sorry for him. He hadn't met love much, so far. He'd heard it existed, but he hadn't been any too sure.

Ward knocked on a door. He knew which door to knock on.

A lovely, melodious voice, already thrilling because it had guessed his presence by the very knock, said, "Come in."

He opened the door and Cameron saw her.

The sunlight was falling on her from the front window. She'd been sitting there beside it. It made a sort of halo all around her. Or no, maybe it was *she* made the halo, and not the slanting sun.

She turned her face toward them. She was beautiful. So beautiful. No wonder she was the love of his life, Cameron thought. The keynote of her beauty was youthful purity. Not lush ripeness, not exoticism; the wonder and trust of the eternal child peering through just beneath the surface of the young woman.

She was looking at Ward. Cameron was right beside him, they were standing shoulder to shoulder. But it was Ward she was looking at.

"There's somebody with you," she said.

She was totally blind.

———

Cameron reported back to his chief on the measures that had been taken up to that point.

"I have four of our men right in the house with her. They work in shifts of two each, they're on duty night and day, twenty-four hours a day. One takes the place of the furnace man who used to come and regulate the heating for the house. The original furnace man is no longer admitted, he's been paid off. All the locks have been changed and we're putting in an electric alarm system throughout, back and front. No delivery men are admitted. No one gets past the front door without my personal okay, with one exception: Ward. And even he's been restricted to two periods a day in which to make his visits; he can't just drop in any more whenever he feels like it, particularly after dark."

He waited for commendation. He didn't get any. "Through?" was all he got.

"Not quite. Now I also have the house under observation from the outside, or at least the street in front of it. Whatever cars come along, or if anyone should loiter about— I couldn't get any of our men into houses opposite because it's not a neighborhood in which they take roomers. However, I have two of them on a roof across the way, doing a fake repair job that they'll keep stringing along until the deadline's past. They commanded a full view of the entire street, from corner to corner. They have a two-way radio up there, they can signal down immediately. Also a pair of high-powered lights they can train down."

"You'll have to watch the food going in. Remember Garrison's wife. You'll have to watch out for mailed packages; they may contain explosives."

"The local branch post office has been ordered to hold all mail for that address, to discontinue deliveries until further notice. The cook was dismissed ten days ago. Even though they had a woman cook, who had been with them for years, I thought it better to get her out of the way. She might, in all innocence, have had some outside male associate, or even relative, that couldn't be vouched for. I have a police-woman in there now as cook, attending to all the buying and preparing of the food for them."

"And what about the companion? This Mrs. Bachman the girl's so attached to?"

"Mrs. B., as the girl calls her," Cameron said, "is the only member of the original household I've left in there undisturbed."

"You can guarantee her?"

"I can vouch for her with my life; there's no shadow of a doubt attached to her. I've had a whole battalion of people checking on her exhaustively, all the way back to her original birth certificate in city hall. They haven't missed a childhood case of measles on the way, nor what buildings she attended grade school in, nor who her teachers were. She has no surviving relatives, not even a fifteenth cousin; her husband died of yellow fever during the Spanish-American War, within a year of their marriage. She's lived under the same roof with the girl since she was a child; I don't even think she's been out of the house without her for ten or twelve years. She has no life of her own; the girl's her whole life. Even so, I would have removed her for a while, just temporarily, but I consulted with Ward about it and we both agreed it would do more harm than good; not only shock and frighten the girl unnecessarily, but even be a disadvantage from the point of view of security. The woman is so devoted to her she makes a better watchdog even than our own people. This way we've got one more person working for us."

"That's the whole set-up?"

"That's the whole set-up," Cameron concluded. "The outside is guarded, the inside is guarded. There's no one at all in the house with her now except our own people and Mrs. B. I tell you, I've turned the place into a regular fort. No one, and nothing, can crack it."

"So far so good," was all he got. "Only, remember one thing: a fort's only as good as the guys standing behind it." And he looked straight at Cameron.

———

When Ward woke up at eight—that was his usual time—on Thursday, he still didn't know he was going to do it. Thursday was the 15th. The decision came on abruptly. Rather, it came to the surface abruptly. It had been there latent for days. It must have been. Growing stronger all the time. Day by day, hour by hour.

He shaved. He showered. He dressed. He selected a foulard tie, blue background with gray flowers. He decided against a regimental-striped silk. "I'll wear that one tomorrow," he said to himself. Showing that he still didn't know he was going to do it.

He went downstairs. His breakfast was there. His wife was there.

His newspaper was there. The latter interested him more than the first, and the first interested him more than the second, but he was polite enough to conceal this, giving his attention to all three in equal amounts, with the newspaper perhaps having a slight edge on the other two.

He kissed her and they made small talk. Friendly, pleasant, not very sincere. There was, at least, no animosity. There was no appeal either. They were just two well-bred people, not very interested in one another.

He left for his office. He took his newspaper, he took his briefcase with him. He said, "Good-bye, Louise," from a room away. He didn't know he would never see her again. If he had known, he would still have said, "Good-bye, Louise," from a room away, in that same voice.

He still didn't know he was going to do it.

He got into his car which was waiting for him at the door. On the way to the office he went ahead reading his newspaper.

The date line struck his attention for some reason. It hadn't the first time. Sixteen days away. And tomorrow it would be fifteen. Why just sit here waiting for it to happen, when there was the whole world to hide in? Trapped, like a squirrel in a cage.

Suddenly he knew he was going to do it.

He rapped on the glass. The driver turned his head. Ward motioned him to pull over, then and there, and stop.

He got out, closed the door again.

"That's all," he said curtly. "Don't wait." The car was a hindrance, might be recognized, might betray him. For all he knew, he was being watched at this very moment.

The driver looked surprised, but he drove off.

Ward changed to a taxi. He drove to his bank. He went down a flight of steps to the vault. He signed for identification, his signature was checked, and he was admitted. These precautions made him doubly grateful now.

Alone in a little private booth with a safe-deposit box before him, he ransacked it hastily but methodically. Louise's jewelry; he didn't want that. Engraved sheaves of orange-colored General Motors stock; he cast them aside too. Too long to convert. Sheaves of chocolate-colored American Tel. and Tel. shares; too long. Goodyear. General

Electric. They all went into the discard. An insurance policy for seventy-five thousand dollars, his wife Louise the beneficiary. (He shuddered, as though the very sight of it frightened him.)

Then the Government bonds turned up, underneath everything else. These were what he wanted, what he'd come here for. He pocketed them. Fifty thousand dollars' worth. Convertible on demand, at sight, instantaneous. Good all over the world, anywhere, everywhere.

He hurried upstairs, he asked to see the bank manager in his private office.

Ten minutes later he came out of the bank again, a letter of credit for fifty thousand dollars in his pocket. Sixteen days. The whole world to hide in. When a turkey is awaiting death, it cannot get out of the coop it is penned in. When a man is awaiting death, he can flee to the ends of the earth; for he knows what death is. God gave him that knowledge.

He took another taxi. He got out at a travel agency. He gave the clerk in there a fifty-dollar bonus, with a promise of an equal amount to come. He would, however, give no name or address or telephone number, as was customary in such cases. He said he would stop in in person the following day. The clerk was to use his own name, Breuer, in whatever transactions he undertook. And though the clerk did not know it, he had then and there become a godfather.

Ward then went to his office. He canceled all his appointments for the day. He ignored all matters that were pending or current and concentrated on completing those which had already been in progress for some time or were in arrears; affairs which because of his familiarity with them he was in a better position to complete than anyone else would have been.

He worked straight through his lunch hour and half into the afternoon. Then at three he finally stopped, through sheer exhausted inability to accomplish any more. The last thing he did was lock his office door on the inside, turn on the recording machine, and talk a message of resignation to his partner, turning over his share and interest in the business to him. ". . . And God bless you, Jeff." There were tears in his eyes when he turned off the machine. Men can get sentimental in business too.

At 3:15 he left for the day. Or rather for the rest of his life.

He was more devious now than he had been during his progresses earlier in the day, for his destination lay closer to his heart, there was more at stake. He took three taxis, and interspersed them with concealed waits in stores and such places, to break the continuity of his trip.

He had brought his briefcase away from the office with him through sheer habit and nothing more. When he first noticed this, he tried to deliberately discard it, leave it behind in the first taxi.

The driver foiled him, called after him, "You forgot your briefcase, mister," and handed it out to him.

Had it been something that he was desperately trying *not* to lose, it occurred to Ward ironically, it probably would have remained in the cab undetected.

He tried again in the second cab and this time a woman, clambering in at his very heels, was the one who shrilled her discovery from the window and forced it back on him.

The third time he hid it under the seat cushion, and at last was rid of it.

The taxi let him out at Martine's house and he hurried inside, doing his best to keep from looking fearfully up and down the street, for he realized that even were he being watched, he would have no way of discovering it. He wasn't used to such things, and his watchers, presumably, would be.

Mrs. Bachman did her usual crowing over him, but he silenced her with whispered instructions. "I have to be with her alone. There's something I want to talk to her about. Stay here at the foot of the stairs and see that none of *them* come near us."

She nodded, always willing to champion him against outsiders.

Martine was sitting reading a book with her fingers, her head tilted at a slight angle, almost as though she were listening instead of feeling.

She wore a yellow dress, a black ribbon drawn through its neckline, and just over her ear Mrs. Bachman (probably) had cocked a pert little yellow bow.

"Allen?" she said, as the threshold throbbed his footfall. And the sun came out in her face. Not on it, but within it, shining from the outside in.

"My little Marty," he half sobbed.

He held her to him first, good and tight, for a long time. Until she knew by that alone something must be wrong.

"What is it, Allen?" she coaxed. "What?" And caressed the outlines of his face with her knowledgeable fingertips that told her so much.

"I'm going to have to frighten you a little."

She sat down in the chair once more, to brace herself, and he, without releasing the double clasp of her two hands within his, knelt beside her to bring their heads close so that they need not raise their voices.

"Are you leaving me? Am I going to be all alone in the dark?"

"Never; not so long as I live. That's a pledge I gave myself years ago, and it'll never be taken back."

"Then what—?"

"There's—there's someone trying to take *you* from *me*."

"In what way? How can they?"

"In what way could they? What is the only way? Think."

"Death," she breathed, appalled.

"In that way," he admitted. "That's the way. The only way they could."

She thrust her face violently forward and hid it against his bosom; pulling at the revers of his coat, at his shirtfront, as if to draw them still closer about her and hide herself further still. Her breathing was quick and frightened, and though he held his arms tightly about her and tried to calm her, he could feel her shivering in spite of that.

"No," he kept pleading over and over, with the automatic intonation one uses in a terrified child. "No. No. No."

"Even in the dark, life is better than—not living. Why must they try to—take even that little away from me?"

"No. No. No," was all he could say.

"What have I ever done to anyone?"

"It's what I've done, not you. And I never knew I'd done anything. But..."

"Who is it?" she asked presently.

"I don't know. They don't either. I've never seen him. They haven't either. Some man—no, some murderous thing that once was a man. Some diseased affliction that needs a mercy death. He must be that; who else could hurt Martine?"

Presently she grew a little calmer; still lay there with her face upon his breast, but grew a little calmer. He left her side then, for just a moment; a glass stopper gave a chord-like pluck; then he came back again.

"Drink this. And then I want you to listen to me very carefully."

"What is it?"

"Just a thimbleful of brandy."

He held the minute draught to her lips.

"Now listen to me very carefully. I'm going to whisper in your ear. I don't want anyone to hear. Wait, I'm going to lock the door first."

He went over and turned the key. Then he unfolded a pocket handkerchief and hung it from the knob, so that even the little slit of vision the keyhole might have offered was blocked.

Then he came back to her again, crouched down on one knee beside her and put his lips close to her ear.

She began to nod her head presently.

"Yes, I do," she murmured. "I trust you with my life. You *are* my life."

Again she nodded while his whispering continued.

"Yes, I will. I'll do just as you say. Whatever it is. No, I'm not afraid. Not with *you*."

His own voice rose a trifle, presently as the secret message reached its conclusion. A scattered word or two became audible.

"Our only chance . . . no one . . . not a word to anyone . . . not even Mrs. B."

And then at last he kissed her. On the forehead, on the eyelids, finally on the lips, in dedication to their resolve, whatever it was.

"They won't have you, love," he said fervently. "They won't harm you. I'll put the whole wide world between them and us."

—

She combed her hair carefully. She could do that herself. And strangely enough, she always did it standing directly before the mirror. From old habit. Though for her there was no mirror.

Then she went to the chair where Mrs. Bachman had laid out her things. By feeling, she knew it was the black wool dress Mrs. B. had selected for her to wear today. Her fingers told her. This was no marvel, this was elementary. She knew the weave, she knew the self-covered buttons, she knew the sleeves, the collar. She knew all her clothes by heart—by finger-touch—of course. She only had to take the word of another in one respect: the color. Mrs. B. had told her this one was black. She put it on.

She was dressed now. She could have even put on lipstick if she had wanted to, and made a good job of it. But she never used lipstick. She went to the room door—without a hesitant step—opened it, and went out. She found her way unerringly to the breakfast table, to her own chair at that table, and drawing it out, sat down to the breakfast Mrs. B. had ready for her on the table.

She could do all these things.

She reached, found her orange-juice glass, raised it to her lips. Mrs. B. left all containers of liquids only two-thirds filled for her; there was less danger of her spilling them that way. That was the only concession either one of them made to her disability. It was a matter of pride, to the two of them alike.

She found her toast and buttered it herself. Mrs. B. filled her coffee-cup for her (but this was even done for people with sight), but she added the sugar and cream for herself. A delicate sense of weight and balance aided her in the two latter procedures. Uncanny as it seemed, she could tell fairly accurately how much a spoon held; whether it was heaped or leveled; how much was emptied over the spout of a pitcher, in the latter case by the downward *pull* of it in her hand.

They chatted desultorily as they did every other day. Mrs. B. read to her from the morning paper. Then breakfast was finished.

He'd located (after a great deal of trouble) and bought for her a unique clock that softly chimed off each hour with the appropriate number of strokes. It followed the European, and military, time system, progressing up to twenty-four for the post-meridian hours instead of falling back to one again. It did this quite cleverly by giving a double stroke instead of a single one for each hour-count past twelve. Thus the time required to count was not greatly increased. Its uniqueness lay in the fact that it was not a grandfather clock, but a mantelclock that could be carried, even by her, from room to room at will.

It struck off ten times now. She counted. Then—as if this had been a cue prompting her—she said to Mrs. B., "I'd like to take a walk. I'd like some fresh air. Let's do it now instead of waiting for this afternoon."

"Why, of course, dear," Mrs. B. agreed readily. She must have glanced from the window; there was a tiny spaced pause. "It *is* a beautiful sunny day out."

"I know," Martine said simply. "I can tell." She could. Without having to glance from a window.

They separated, to make their several preparations apart. She went into her bedroom alone, went to the closet, took out her jewel case. Several rings she knotted into a handkerchief and thrust into her handbag. The Tiffany pearls he had given her, she put around her throat. The neckline of her dress, which was rather high, effectively concealed them. She took out one more thing. The rest, a number of clasps, brooches and bracelets, she left in the case. She found time to pencil a hasty little note: "These are for you, Edith dear. Preserve this slip carefully, it's a form of will." And put that in with them, closed the case up, and thrust it away.

The one remaining thing she'd taken out, she had to have help with, couldn't manage alone. It had a complicated safety catch. He'd given her it too, of course. Therefore it had a sentimental, though no longer a utilitarian, value to her. It also had a tremendous intrinsic value, but this did not enter into it as far as she was concerned.

She called Mrs. B. in. "Will you fasten this for me?"

"Why, you're wearing your diamond wristwatch!" Mrs. B. gasped.

"I want to look nice," Martine said quietly. "It's such a nice day. It's that kind of day."

She could have broken it up into its component stones and scattered these along the sidewalk one by one, like pebbles, as she walked, and Mrs. B. would still have let her have her way; they both knew it.

They left the house together, Martine's hand tucked under her escort's. Two well-dressed women, one young, one mature; you could not have told that one was sightless. And if you had, you might even have mistaken the elder one, with her glasses, for the disabled of the two.

Mrs. B. said quietly, "Good morning."

There was no answer, but when a hat is raised, it makes no sound.

Then, within a few paces, Mrs. B. said again, "Good morning." And again there was no sound.

But to the rearward of them now, from this point on, came a soft double tread, like an echo, a smothered bass accompaniment, to their own.

"Where are we?" Martine said presently.

"Around the corner. We're boxing the block."

"Let's—let's go somewhere special. There's only cement and dusty stone here. Let's walk along the outside of the park. From Seventieth, in the downtown direction."

Mrs. B. didn't demur.

Presently Martine spoke again. "Are we there now?" Then answered her own question. "Yes, we are. I can smell the grass and the leaves of the trees. Isn't it sweet and fresh?"

Mrs. B. inhaled enjoyably.

Martine lowered her voice a shade. "Are they still behind us?"

There was another of those spaced pauses. Mrs. B. had turned her head. "Oh, yes. They should be, you know."

"I know they should," Martine answered dryly.

She spoke again after a while. "Tell me when we get near the statue of Lafayette."

"We're near there now."

"Are you sure we're walking in the downtown direction, the same way that the traffic is going?"

"Why, of course, dear." Mrs. B. was amused. "Why would I want to mislead you?"

She asked another question. "Is it twelve yet?"

A spaced pause. "About three to."

"Here comes the statue," Martine said. "We're in front of it now, I can tell. The pavement has changed. It's smoother, ornamental flagstones all around the base."

Suddenly she said, "Let's walk along the outside edge of the curb."

"That's not safe, dear. Cars come along, and they're liable to graze us."

"Let me do it." Then she said, *"Please."* That word, from her, that Mrs. B. could never resist.

They shifted over; Martine took the outside position. Mrs. B. must have glanced back. "They're motioning us to stay further in," she reported.

Martine tightened her hold on her arm playfully, in secret conspiracy. "Let's pretend we don't understand. They can't *make* us if we don't want to, can they?"

"No, I don't suppose so," agreed Mrs. B. dubiously. "But why don't we want to?"

"I want to try something," Martine said. "When I was a little girl, there was a game I used to love to play. A way of walking. I used to love to walk along the exact rim of the curb, and balance, and see if I could keep from stepping down into the gutter."

"Not here, dear."

"Yes, here. I want to remember that feeling, from when I was a child. You're right beside me. What can happen? Look, I'll hold on to your hand."

A male voice said suddenly, from directly behind them, "What's she doing?" One of the plainclothesmen must have closed in.

Mrs. B.'s maternal instinct was aroused. "Leave her alone, can't you?" she retorted brusquely. "Don't watch her like a hawk every minute."

"Make them keep back," Martine urged in a plaintive undertone.

"Go on back with your friend," Mrs. B. ordered none too gently. "Stop treading on our heels."

The slight aura of tobacco breath and flintiness of personality that had interjected itself into their own immediate atmosphere (noticeable to Martine alone) was withdrawn again. It had been almost extrasensory, anyway.

"Is it twelve yet? I'll stop at twelve," she promised.

"Just like a child," said Mrs. B. with a tear in her voice. "One minute to."

"I've only missed my footing once," she gloated. "I'm still good at it after all these years. And now my heels are high, and I have no—" She didn't finish it. She seldom used the word "eyes" any more.

"Your hand is shaking, dear," Mrs. B. noticed.

"That's because my whole body is shaking, trying to keep my balance. It must be twelve to the minute now." Suddenly she said in a hurried voice, as if the one thing had some connection with the other. "I love you very much; you've been like my own mother to me; always believe that, I love you very much."

"God bless your heart!" the sentimental Mrs. B. immediately reacted, with profuse emotion.

She had to release Martine's hand for a moment, to plumb for and bring up a handkerchief, to maintain the effectiveness of her own sight.

There was an incurving hissing rush of tires. Martine was suddenly swept up bodily in a double grip, an arm about her waist, a hand riveted to her own (which she had carried extended out toward the street by the act of "tightrope-walking"), by some blurred form leaning out above a running board.

For a moment she had a dizzying sensation of being carried along in thin air, clear of the ground. Then she was drawn inward, deposited onto an upholstered seat. A car door cracked shut. There was the vertigo of a vehicle making a violent out-curve again.

Outside, to the rear of it, there was Mrs. B's heartrending scream of despair. Somewhere even further back, a man's alarmed shout. Then a crashing report, as a revolver-shot was fired for warning into the air.

Inside, there was a momentary silence. A lull. The vibration told her they were picking up speed, hurtling along.

Her hand reached out tremulously and found the side of a man's face. She explored it with gossamer sensitivity, came to the lips at last, traced their shape.

They contracted slightly, delivered an impalpable kiss against her questioning fingertips.

She gave a deep sigh of unutterable relief.

"It's you," she murmured. "For a moment I wasn't sure."

———

The chief's rage was something Homeric, and he wasn't a man given to displays of ungovernable anger as a rule. He raised his office swivel chair from the floor, not once but repeatedly, and brought it crashing down until one of its pediments splintered and flew off. He was prevented from throwing the desk telephone from him only by the fact it was attached to an extension bracket which limited its range. Likewise the water cooler, which was too heavy to lift above it base. At least by a man wearing a truss.

"The fool!" he roared. "The fool! The blazing fool! He's taking her straight to her death. *We* try to save her life, we work for weeks at it, taking every possible human precaution, and he snatches her away from us, takes her straight to her death! They won't live an hour on their own! They haven't a chance! Jesus, if I had him here this minute—!" And he gripped the outside edges of his desk with his bare hands until the knuckles showed through like white operation scars.

He not only demoted the two unhappy plainclothesmen who had had her in charge, who had been on that particular shift, but insulted their parentage and was prevented from dismissing them from his presence with actual blows only by Cameron's restraining grip on his wrist.

That attracted his wrath to Cameron himself.

"And you!" he yelled, turning on him. "What were you doing? Where were you? A *blind* girl he takes away from you! A *blind* girl, in broad daylight! Twelve o'clock noon! *She's* not the blind one; *you* are! You should have told us you need a seeing-eye dog, I would have made arrangements."

"Do you want my badge now?" Cameron asked respectfully. "Or shall I wait until I'm officially noti—"

This did nothing to assuage the tirade.

"Oh, a quitter as well as an incompetent! The easy way, hunh? Lie down flat on your back the minute— You're not only stupid, but yellow!"

"I wouldn't take that, sir, from anyone but—"

The chief's voice rose to an exasperated scream. Or at least as much of a scream as a basso is capable of. "Well, what are you standing there for? Do you want written instructions? Do you want me to take you by the hand and show you the door? They've already been gone over an hour and forty minutes!"

He raised both arms high overhead, packed two massive fists, and brought them down upon the long-suffering desk with a crash that went echoing all up and down the corridors outside, and made people think a steam-pipe had burst.

"Go after them! Catch up with them, no matter where they went! Bring them back here! I want them back here, in protective custody, before the thirty-first of May!"

One of Cameron's unfortunate characteristic fits of indecision seemed to strike him, then of all times.

"If they went west, by train, maybe I can still overhaul them," he mumbled. "But if they went east, by water—I'm sunk."

The chief flung himself, suddenly, over toward where his coat was hanging upon a clothes-tree. He might only have been in search of a handkerchief, to staunch his perspiring brow. But he also had his holster hanging by it.

"So help me," he intoned in a hollow, gasping voice, "I'm going to be brought to trial, yet, for shooting one of my own men in my own office!"

Cameron didn't wait to find out what he was looking for.

—

And now they were on a train. Locked in a room within a train. The never-ending darkness was not still any more, stable, as it had used to be for her; it hummed like a low but constant wind; it whined a little, and there would be a slow, curving shift of the equilibrium. Around toward the right. Or around toward the left. Then the whine would die down and motion would straighten itself out again. There was a continuous, even accompaniment; like dice being rattled in a dice box. But very even, not syncopated. Once, everything became hollow for a brief while, and her ears wanted to close up; that must have been a tunnel. Then the various sounds lost their resonance and they were out in the open again.

(For me, she thought wryly, but without complaint, all life is a tunnel; a long, never-ending tunnel, which has no other end.)

The sensation of rushing was there, except that, without vision, it was impossible to tell if you were going forward or backward. At times she'd even grow confused and think they were rushing backward, instead of ahead. But she knew that the way she was sitting, the way he'd placed her, she was facing the same way the train was, so that feeling was just an illusion, a mirage, of the senses.

Everything jittered a little; it gave her the sensation of mild "pins and needles" in her feet as they rested on the floor.

She sat there with her head resting on his shoulder.

"Read the scenery to me," she said.

She felt his outside arm move past her, and the shade went up a little, then clamped fast at its new position.

"It's green," he said. "And wavy. It undulates a little as we go by. The basic color is green, but in all its different shades. Some of it is dark, and some of it, way over there, where there are meadows in the sun, is light, like apples."

"I know, I know. I can see it."

"There was a cow, by a fence, just now. It was looking at the train with such a dumb, questioning expression; its head up and its grazing interrupted. Red-brown, with a white streak on its forehead."

"Poor cow. Dear cow. Lucky cow."

"A little creek just went by. It went by so fast. I bet it never moved so fast in its life before. Ffft—and gone. It didn't look like water, it looked like silver plate; the sky was reflected in it."

"I remember," she said. "Little creeks used to look like that. They haven't changed, have they?"

"They haven't changed. A little white house just went by."

"I wonder who lives in it? I bet they're not afraid of dying, like we are."

"Now here come some trees. They're very dark green and their shadows are slanting away from the sun. They're even hitting the windowpane, and making it dark, light, dark, light, dark, light. . . ."

She reached out and put her fingertips to the glass. "Am I touching their shadows?"

"Yes. Light; now it's dark; light again."

"I can't tell. But it's sort of nice. Like being out there with them."

There was a sudden knock on the door, and fright blotted out all the colors in a swirl of inky-black.

The shade came down with a snap. He got up and left her. She could tell he was standing over where the door was, but there was no unlocking sound. She knew he'd taken out a gun, though the woolen fabric of his clothing made not the slightest whisper.

"Who is it?"

"It's the steward, sir. With the tray you ordered."

"Say something else."

"What do you want me to say, sir?"

"Say 'mulligatawny.'"

"Mulli-gaw-tanny," came through the door.

She nodded to him; he must, though she could not see him, have nodded back to her.

"Hit something on the tray. Make it sound out."

Silverware clashed faintly against crockery.

"Put it down on the floor, right by the door."

A pause. "It's down, sir. Down flat."

"Now go to the door at the end of the aisle, go out, and let me hear it close hard after you."

"Your change, sir. You got nigh fifteen dollar' coming back to you out of that twenty you pushed out to me under the door before."

"Keep it. I want to hear that end door close good and hard."

The slam even penetrated to where they were.

Then, and only then, he unlocked their room door.

———

She woke up and the strange noises of a strange city were in her ears. She opened her eyes; the darkness remained, but the lids of her eyes nevertheless went up. To lift them was instinctive.

Noises, street sounds, told her so much more than other people. To them, the hum of traffic was the hum of traffic anywhere in the world. To her—

There was a sharp, brittle edge to them, so the atmosphere was cold. There was a certain grating squeak to them, so that told her the place was hilly, vehicles had to climb up, had to coast on their brakes going down. Cable cars keened unmercifully every now and then, going round a turn. The air had a certain tang, a tingle, an aliveness, to it. It made you want to do things; it made you get them done. She didn't imagine they loitered going along the streets; she didn't imagine they were downcast or depressed. It was a good place for a city to be.

San Francisco, they called it.

So she had seen San Francisco, as much as many people, and more than some. Cool, hilly, brisk, and stimulating.

She had seen San Francisco, but yet she couldn't tell if she were alone in this hotel bedroom or not.

"Allen," she said softly. "Allen, are you in here with me?"

There was no sound of breathing, other than her own.

It frightened her a little, to be alone in a room in a strange city. But she quickly forced herself to calmness, kept from crying out his name wildly, as her first impulse was.

He'd be back soon. He hadn't gone far, nor for long. He wouldn't do that to her. She trusted him.

She found the silk wrapper at the foot of the bed, put it on, and got out of the bed. She tapped one foot about on the floor, in a circle, as if she were doing a little dance step sitting down, and found her slippers.

She got up and moved carefully about the room. She found a door and opened it. Hollow sounds from a distance reached her. It was the outside door. She quickly closed it. She found another, opened that. A beaded chain tickled her nose; the empty sleeve of a coat met her fingers inertly. It was a closet door. She found at last a third, cold and slippery to her fingers. A mirror panel in it.

She contemplated taking a shower. She'd better not. The fixtures were new to her, and she might scald herself unmercifully. Back home she knew on which side the hot was and which the cold.

There was imminent disaster about her all the time, but the thought never even occurred to her. She'd never been inclined to feel sorry for herself. No matter what they took away, you still had so much left.

She went back to the main room and dressed herself.

A key turned in the door, and the door opened.

"Up, dear?" he said.

But there was someone with him. The rustle of entry was double.

She stood still and kept her head turned the other way. He'd warned her never, if possible, to let others know or see she was blind. Knowledge of her total helplessness was liable to increase her danger; that, she supposed, was what he feared. And when she looked at anyone, they could tell as a rule, and when she didn't, they couldn't.

"Put it down there," he said.

Then he said, "No, never mind; I'll do that myself."

Change clinked. The door closed. They were alone.

"All right, Marty," he said. "He's gone."

She came toward him, knowing unerringly where he was, and answered his kiss with her own, and he held her in his arms for a moment.

"I brought up some coffee for you," he said. "There's a little table here he opened."

They sat down together.

"Careful, dear," he said. "The sugar lumps have jackets on them."

"I know," she said indulgently. "I can tell."

"How nice you look, how lovely; so fresh and sweet."

"Is my hair all right? Sometimes the part gets away from me; that's one thing I have to guess at."

"Like an arrow."

She heard a match scrape, and smelt the fragrance of his cigarette smoke. "I have our tickets for"—he dropped his voice—"a ship. I don't think we should stay on, even here. Trains keep coming in, all the time, from back there. Would you be afraid to—leave your own country, go to the other side of the water with me?"

"No," she said almost inaudibly. "You're my country, now."

He lowered his voice still further. "It sails tomorrow, at noon. But I've made arrangements for us to go aboard tonight, around nine or ten. We can keep the suite locked during the night. That way we won't be seen coming aboard in the daytime. We'll stay here where we are, in the hotel, until after dark. I had to have our visas sent on airmail, there was no time to wait for them; but they got here, I picked them up just now. There's a doctor coming here later, to give you shots for cholera. I'll take mine with you. You won't be frightened, will you?"

"You'll hold my hand," she promised him, "and I won't be afraid." As though she were the one reassuring him, and not he her.

Presently she asked him, "Was I alone in here last night? The last I knew you were sitting over there in a chair. I fell asleep."

She heard the tender smile in his voice; yes, heard, that was the word. "Do you think I'd leave you alone in a room in a strange city, after bringing you here? No, I slept right in here with you. The sofa opens as a daybed. But I had a hard time doing it quietly; the springs creak so. Then I made it up myself when I first got up, and put the extra pillow back on your bed without waking you. We're registered as man and wife, you know."

She thought for a while, smiled a little. "How strangely unimportant propriety becomes when you're down to elementals such as life and death."

"Propriety's what's in the mind," he said. "Two people can be a thousand miles away from each other, and still be guilty of all sorts of derelictions. Two people can share the same hotel bedroom, as we did last night, and still be completely decorous."

He took her hand. "Martine," he said, "I want to marry you some day when this is over and we're safe again. This time will you let me, will you have me? All those years we threw away. Louise will be only too glad to let me go, she doesn't care enough one way or the other."

"Yes," she said softly. "This time I want you to. I'm ready now." And then she added, "If I live."

"You'll live," he said huskily. "Oh, I swear you will. If I have to take you to the ends of the earth. If I have to keep running with you until there's no breath left in us."

At three or thereabouts, the phone rang. For a moment it struck fear into her, and she knew it did into him too, by the way he held back, refrained from answering it at once.

Then when he had, she knew he was still afraid by the low, cautious sound his voice had.

"Hello?" he said. Then he listened. Then he released his breath in relief. "Yes, of course," he said then, and hung up.

"The doctor's on his way up," he told her.

"I'd forgotten him!" she exclaimed.

"I had too," he admitted.

There was a three or four minute wait. They were both extremely nervous.

"It seems to take him a long time to get up here," he remarked.

"The elevator may have kept him waiting."

She heard him go to the door, open it, knew he must be looking out expectantly.

He closed it, came in again.

Coins jingled, as if he were holding one hand in his pocket, shaking it impatiently.

"I'm going to find out what's hap—" he started to say impetuously and strode over to the phone. She heard him pick it up.

At that moment the belated knock sounded at the door.

She took two or three quick steps, found a chair, sank down upon it; she clutched the seat of it in a sort of desperate intensity, holding it *underneath* at the sides.

"Does he know? Did you tell him?" she whispered.

"I had to. Otherwise he would have made you go to him, instead of coming to you."

The door opened.

"I got off at the wrong floor—" a sonorous voice began.

She heard a catch to Ward's breath.

"Oh—you're somebody else."

"I came in Dr. Conroy's place. He found he couldn't get away after all. You know how it is, he's got plenty of work on his hands."

There was no answer from Ward.

The would-be entrant must have caught something from the look on his face, however. There was a trace of stiffness in his voice as it next sounded. "I'm just as experienced at giving these shots as he is. There's nothing to them really. Here are my credentials." And then in implicit reproof, "You know, we don't do this sort of thing as a rule. You have to come and get your shots where everyone else does. We made an exception in your case, because of the circumstances."

"I appreciate that," Ward said a trifle sheepishly (she thought). "Come in, doctor."

The door closed. The weight of leather went down on a chair seat, with a sort of creaky squash.

"This the young lady?"

She tightened her grip on the underpart of her chair.

"Yes, doctor, this is my wife."

"How do you do?" she said, and aimed her eyes directly at where the voice had last come from. She must have misled him. He must have come closer, passed his hand before her eyes, testing her. Something like that.

She heard Ward say quietly, "Don't you believe me, doctor?"

"I beg your pardon," the doctor answered him contritely. As if he did now. A latch clicked open. He resumed his professional briskness of manner. "Is there some hot water here? I want to wash first."

He left the room. Ward came closer, put an arm to her shoulders, drew her head to him momentarily, as if to instill courage.

"It's all right," she whispered. "I'm not frightened. Not a bit."

The doctor's tread sounded again. Ward stepped away from her. "I'm going to take mine first, doctor." He must have bared his arm.

"I understand," the doctor said. "But don't you think it's kinder not to make her wait?" Whether he made some sign to him, implying he would do it suddenly and spare her the suspense of anticipation she could not tell. Whether Ward nodded his head in agreement, she could not tell.

"Give me your hand, dear," Ward said quietly. It was given relaxed, but then he held her arm slightly bent, so that it was taut. The sleeves of her dress were almost nonexistent. Cool moist cotton dabbed at her skin. She only had time to promise herself, "I will not show anything." Then there was a sudden shooting pain. The pain was not too much, it seemed to be the violence of the thrust itself that was harder to bear. As if he'd been unnecessarily rough, though probably he hadn't, it had to be done that way.

Then pain a second time, going in the opposite direction. Another dab of grateful cotton, this time left on. "Just hold that there for a few seconds."

"Did I show anything?" she whispered vaingloriously to Ward, as he bent to touch his lips solicitously to her forehead for a moment.

Ward took his next. She heard him give a sudden, small-boyish yelp of pain. She wondered whether he'd done it purposely, for her to hear, as an oblique compliment to her on her own courage. Or whether, like many another man who can be capable of great stoicism in meeting physical torture when it's required of him, he was at the same time afraid of little hurts. Whichever it was, she loved him for it equally.

"You're worse than she was," the doctor chuckled. She smiled a little. Ward may have winked at him. Perhaps that was the effect he had wanted to achieve. "Now I'll just sign this, it's yours. You'll have to show it before they let you go aboard."

The door closed, the doctor was gone.

The fear that struck them both was strangely dilatory; it didn't manifest itself for another ten minutes after he'd left.

He was sitting perched on the arm of her chair, his own arm about her. "How is it?" he asked. "Do you feel anything now?"

She didn't answer the question. Almost as though she hadn't heard it.

He reached for her hand. At its touch, his voice rose in alarm. "What is it? Martine! Your hand's like ice." He sprang up from the arm of her chair, but without releasing her hand. Then he stood there stock-still, as the same thought struck him, whether transmitted from her or born of itself.

"But you're shaking too, as you hold my hand," she remonstrated. "I can feel it."

"Are you thinking the same thing I am?"

"I'm afraid so," she winced, trying to control the nervous shudders that ran through her. "That he— That he may have been—"

"So am I," he admitted strickenly. "Now that it's too late."

—

And now they were on a ship, coursing deep water, crossing an ocean between two worlds. The eternal darkness was still all around her, but there was a sense of spaciousness with it now, of emptiness, of remoteness. The air smelt of salt and iodine. There was a very soft but continuous hissing audible outside the windows, like water falling from a garden sprinkler. From the opposite direction, fore the door, the chary times it was unlocked and briefly allowed to open, came the rather brackish odor of rubber corridor matting. And once in a while, but not very often, there was a creak from a joint of woodwork. Above all, there was a slow, rolling motion from side to side. Very soothing, very restful, not at all abrupt. You soon grew used to it and forgot that there was any other way for things to be: perfectly rigid and unyielding and *still*. This was better by far. You let your body go with it, slightly over, and then come back with it, slightly back; and it was like being in a very gentle, very lulling, swing.

And there was always Allen, close beside you, scarcely leaving you at all. With every knot came greater safety until finally safety would become the absolute and not the comparative any longer.

He took no chances, however. Though death had missed the boat, though this little floating iron world was cut off from the other world, and no harm could come to them here, he took no chances. They had come too far, and been through too much, to foolishly throw away their gains now.

The door, the one door to their suite, stayed locked all night while she slept in the inner room; and he stayed in the outer one on a bed that came down out of the wall. Then at nine there would be a knock from the steward, but no steward was ever let in. He would wait for him to go away again, and then draw their breakfast tray in himself after careful reconnoitering, the way he had on the train.

At eleven or so, another knock. This time the stewardess. They admitted her; she was the only member of the ship's personnel they gave entry to. But she never saw Martine. He'd have her retire to the private bath that went with their suite before he let the woman in. She would only emerge again after the outer door had been locked behind the stewardess. And in the interim, he always lingered close beside the bath door, ready to forestall any attempt at sudden entry. The stewardess must have known there was a woman occupying the quarters with him; there were enough mute evidences of that lying about every day. But she'd never yet set eyes on her. She couldn't have described her. Above all, she had no inkling that the phantom in question was blind. No one on the entire ship did. He'd brought her aboard in the dead of night; and from that moment on no eyes but his own had fallen upon her.

She could not even persuade him to leave the suite himself; to go up on deck for a breath of air or to stretch his legs. He would not leave her side for a single instant. "Not," he said obdurately, "until after—a certain date has passed."

She knew what date he meant. She didn't have to be told.

He'd brought along a little battery radio, picked it up in San Francisco just before they left; cleverly contrived, as they were making them now, to look like a piece of luggage. That helped them pass the time away.

The weather got warmer, and then it was Honolulu. She woke up and the ship was motionless. She missed the soothing sway. There was a good deal of trampling about audible in the corridor outside, as baggage and people were readied to disembark. Then after a quarter of an hour or so, things settled down again. The ship became still with that unearthly stillness of ships in port. It was like—death. Or waiting for something to happen.

They were both more tense and keyed-up than they had been while out in the open sea. Danger was nudging the ship here. Danger was a pier thrusting itself out from shore to meet it. Danger was a bridge that could be crossed over to it.

It told on him finally: "I'm uneasy," he admitted. "I'm going up for a minute and look around. I can't stand this. I won't go far, and I'll be right back." He left his gun with her this time, instead of taking it with him.

He locked the door after him and took the key with him.

It was just as well that he'd made the excursion.

Within a very short time she heard his key clash hurriedly in the lock and he'd come in again.

She could tell he was alarmed.

"What is it?"

"Hawaiian police officials," he whispered. "They've come aboard and they're making a cabin to cabin search for you. Cameron must have wired a warning from the coast."

"What'll we do? We're trapped in here. Where can I hide?"

"You can't hide. That won't do. We're both down on the passenger list and must be accounted for." He raked fingers through his hair distractedly, and glanced around at the door. "We haven't much time either. They're already at the upper end of the corridor, working down this way. The steward let the cat out of the bag; I happened to run into him out there luckily. I've been tipping him well and he's the talkative kind anyway."

"Then the moment they set eyes on me—"

"No," he said. "They have no exact description to go by. Cameron evidently figured we could change that too easily. They don't know *what* you look like. The steward tells me he overheard them admit that to one of the officers. They're just relying on the one main thing; he must have thought that would be sufficient, that there was no way we could get around that. They're looking for a man and a sightless woman traveling together. They're not even sure of the ship, it could be any ship coming in right about now. They've been searching every ship that's come in within the past twenty-four hours. So we have that much of a chance."

He plunged his fist into his opposite palm like a tormented baseball catcher.

"They must see you, but they *mustn't know you're blind.*"

She stood up, suddenly resolute. "Then they shan't!"

"Can you do it?" he asked doubtfully.

"For you," she said, "I can do anything. To stay with you— To keep them from taking me away from you. Hurry! you've got to help me. Did you see them at all? There are things I must know."

"The steward pointed them out to me just as they were going in two doors down, and I had a chance to make a good quick study of them."

"Then these are the things you've got to tell me. And be sure, because you won't have time to tell me more than once. First, how many?"

"There are two of them, accompanied by two policemen, but the two policemen won't come into the room."

"And the two who will?"

"One of them's Hawaiian, dark-skinned, short, stocky. The other's a Saxon-American, tall, lean, fair. His skin's peeling a little from sunburn, I noticed."

She made a hectic grasping motion toward him with both hands. "Their voices, quick—so I can place them."

"The Anglo-Saxon's is barrel deep. About like this—" He dropped his own. "The other's considerably higher, just short of piping."

"Their clothes, now quick!"

"The islander's all in white. Spotless. The other in gray, and pretty wrinkled. He seems to perspire a lot, not used to the heat."

"He takes a handkerchief to his face?"

"The back of his neck."

"Then clear your throat when you see him do that in here. Only the first time, not after that. Their neckties."

"The Hawaiian has on a loud green thing. The other's I didn't notice."

"Then it's quiet. Were they smoking anything? What?"

"The short one, no. The Yank emptied out a pipe just before he stepped into that other stateroom, and I saw him stick it into his breast pocket up here."

"Stem showing?"

"Stem showing."

There was an indistinct murmur just outside their door, as if several persons were gathering there in that one spot.

"Can you do anything with all that?"

"I shall," she promised. "I have to. Help me; put everything out on this dressing table, all the cosmetics from that travel kit I never use."

"What are you going to do?"

"Make-up. It will keep me seated in one place and it will keep my eyes fixed on one place, the mirror." She sat down.

The knock had already come on the door.

"Can you get away with it?" he breathed. "Suppose you put the wrong thing on, or too much in one place?"

"My fingers know all the little jars and pencils by heart. Men can't follow the intricacies of it, anyway. A woman might catch on, but men won't."

The second knock came, more insistent.

"Don't be frightened, love," she whispered. "Just do your part, and I won't let you down. Forget about me; I'm Louise, or somebody else." *She,* instilling courage into him! She raised her voice suddenly, to a stridency he had seldom if ever heard her use before. "Joe!" she wailed, as if summoning him from the adjacent bathroom. "Somebody at the door! See who it is for me, will you please?"

The door opened. She took a deep breath, raised her eyes into the impenetrable darkness, and carefully began to stroke the tip of her little finger across her upper lip, then taste and tongue it, then stroke some more.

A high-pitched voice said, "Mr. Breuer?"

Allen said, "Yes?"

"Sorry to bother you. We're from the Honolulu police. Just checking up on the passengers."

"Come in," Allen said. A chair crunched very slightly. A second chair crunched quite heavily.

A very deep voice, from the second chair, said, "You're Mr. and Mrs. Joseph Breuer?"

"Yes."

"You embarked at San Francisco?"

"Yes."

"Your destination is—?"

"Yokohama, first of all. Then we may go on to—"

There was a sudden silence. They were watching her with typical masculine awe. She had taken a small crescent of isinglass, somewhat resembling a half optical lens, inserted it carefully under the lower lashes of one eye, and was carefully stroking them black with a small paint brush.

"Cigarette?" she heard Allen offer.

She didn't give them a chance to answer. "Never offer a pipe smoker a cigarette, Joe. You're wasting your breath."

Allen gave an impressive gasp. "How do you know the man's a pipe smoker?"

"I can see it sticking up in his breast pocket from all the way over here."

Pause, while the owner must have looked down at his own breast pocket in surprised confirmation.

She said suddenly, speaking as if via the mirror, "You haven't been out here long, have you?"

The deep voice said, "As a matter of fact, no. How'd you know that?"

"I can tell your skin's still sensitive to the sun."

"You're very observant, ma'am."

Allen cleared his throat a little.

She turned her head slightly, toward where the second chair was. "I don't see *you* mopping your neck," she said playfully. "You don't seem to mind the heat as much as your colleague does. Why doesn't he wear white like you?"

"An' look like a bottle of milk?" the deep voice from the other direction growled half audibly.

"I can also tell you're an islander by that cheerful tie you're wearing," she went on. "Sunny climate, sunny necktie."

Almost at once, as though the remark had had the effect of a lever on them, she heard them both get up. "Let's go," one murmured to the other. The tone used was the rather flat, disgusted one of two men who find they have just made a complete waste of their time.

Allen shepherded them toward the door. "Were you looking for anyone in particular?" she heard him ask as he prepared to close it after them.

"Yes. A blind woman. We have orders to take her into custody for her own protection."

"Joe," she called out sweetly just then, from the depths of the stateroom, "tell the gentleman he dropped the rubber band from his notebook."

Steps came forward again toward one of the chairs, stopped—"Much obliged, ma'am; here it is, I see it here"—withdrew once more; the door closed and the key went home.

Allen hurried back to her, dropped down beside her on one knee, tipped her chin with his fingertips. "How did you know?" he marveled. "How?"

"I heard it snap when he stretched it and took it off the notebook. I didn't hear it snap a second time, so I knew it had never gone back on again. I took a wild guess and figured it had fallen either to his chair or to the floor without his noticing it. It was a gamble, too. He might have just stuffed it into one of his pockets, or wound it around a finger. But I won my gamble."

He clasped her hand in both of his.

"Swell performance," he congratulated her ardently.

———

Later in the day he made another brief investigatory foray. She was safe now, she was immune—at least as far as *they* were concerned—but he wanted to confirm it.

"They've gone," he reported on his return. "They went ashore fifteen minutes ago. One of the big President liners is just coming in past Diamond Head, and they received a radio report there's a blind woman accompanied by a seeing-eye dog aboard. Or so my all-knowing friend the steward tells me. By the time she's cleared herself we'll be miles at sea. Out of reach. With the next stop Yoka.

"Funny thing, though," he added. "They left one of the two policemen behind. I just happened to see him now, on my way back. He's standing there on duty at the upper end of the corridor. Very inconspicuously."

They got under way again at five that evening. The grinding and pulsing of the engines, always more noticeable in still water, came on again and a slow gliding motion became perceptible, as steady at its inception as that of a train leaving a station. The breeze freshened, the clanking of dockside machinery faded off.

He made another quick trip out and back that happened to almost synchronize with this slow-moving process of departure.

"Is that policeman still posted there?" she asked him when he came in again.

"He still was when I went out," he said, "but when I went by the second time just now, on my way in, I didn't see him any more. He must have gone. I've brought you down a lei. I wanted you to have one. They're given to everyone who leaves Hawaii and you weren't up there to receive one for yourself."

But the pulsing and the gliding and the commotion of departure had just preceded, not followed his issuing from the stateroom. They were too elated to notice the discrepancy, if there was one, in the rearguard policeman's quitting of his post. Or perhaps, for all they knew, his orders had been to remain aboard until the last moment, until the outermost limits of police jurisdiction had been reached outside the harbor, and then to be dropped off by a pilot boat or some such.

All that mattered, all that counted, was: she was safe, she'd been rescued. She'd been saved from—safety. Rescued from rescue.

———

Midnight on a chromium-plated sea. They were together in the semi-darkness, their heads pressed together, each with an arm about the other's back, waiting, tense, immobile, breathless, starry-eyed.

They had all the lights out in the suite. But chromium gleams would glide across the walls, and then ebb back again, from the moon-glowing sea outside the windows.

Two small flecks of light marked where they were and these too were constantly turning over, turning back again out of sight, though in a different, quicker way than the liquid gleams upon the wall. One was a red dot, and one was a cluster of pale-green dots. They moved together each time, one just above the other. A cigarette in his nervous hands, and the radium numerals of the watch upon his wrist.

And in the silence the tiny whispers of two babes in the woods. Babes who are at the very edge of the woods now, almost out.

"Now what is it?"

"Eleven fifty-eight. Sh, be patient."

Back go the red and the green glints.

"Is it—now?"

"Not yet. Eleven fifty-nine. Just a minute more. Just a minute. Don't breathe, don't speak."

Like children cautioning one another, "You'll break the spell."

Her hand goes up and seals his mouth. His hand goes up and seals hers.

Their hearts go tick, tick, tick, tick, sixty times; not his watch, but their hearts. Together, in perfect time, as one.

His hand drops away from her lips. He raises the little diadem of luminous numbers.

"Now?" she whispers.

"Now!" At first he whispers it. Then he speaks it. Then he shouts it. "Now! *Now!* NOW!"

They jump to their feet together in the dark.

"Twelve midnight. The first of June. The *date* is past. He's missed the date. Marty, Marty, do you understand? Do you hear what I'm saying? We're safe. It's over. We've won. We've won."

He runs all around the place, touching here, touching there. All the lights flame up, every light in the place, kindling into a blinding blaze of incandescence.

They kiss. He drags into view a little gilt bucket of ice, hidden until now behind the settee, waiting for them in case they—lived. He hoists a bottle of champagne. They kiss. He brings two glasses. They kiss. He twists the cork. They kiss. The cork pops. Foam trickles down the sleeve of his coat. They laugh. They kiss, and kiss again, and laugh, and kiss again.

They touch their glasses high above their heads.

"Here's to life!"

"To life! Lovely, lovely life!"

They crash their glasses in the corner, fill two more. She's crying a little, but out of joy, sheer ecstasy. "We're having a party. Just you, just me. Like living people do."

"We *are* living people now."

"I know, I know." She holds out her arms toward him. "Dance with me. It's been so many years.... Any step, I don't care how hard, and I'll follow. Dance with me, like the living do."

He turns on the little battery portable. Faintly, on short wave, from some far-off shore, faltering music comes in, strengthens, steadies. Voices are singing in chorus, in a hymn of gladness. The waltz from *Traviata*.

He sweeps her around and around the room in his arms in delirious abandon, her unbound hair flying loose. Then without stopping, catches up her half-emptied goblet, hands it to her on the wing. On the next time around, catches up his own.

They renew their toast, clink glasses in mid-waltz.

"To life! To the long, long years that lie ahead!"

"To the long, long years we have waiting for us!"

———

And the next day life began, the world began. No more locked doors, no more passwords, no more smuggled-in trays of food. They were out of their suite the live-long day, from earliest morning to swift ocean twilight. In perfect immunity, now, they roamed about, went where all the others did. Nodded, smiled, passed the time of day. She was a poor sailor, she'd been ill, she fibbed, when anyone mentioned not having seen her about until now.

They went up to the topmost deck and watched the lush sunrise spill over the sea, like the emptying of a bottle of chili sauce. He watched, and painted it for her in words. They breakfasted in the dining saloon. They requisitioned deck chairs and lolled all morning long in the sunlight. And since all the other women wore dark glasses against the glare, you couldn't tell the difference with her.

They only returned to the stateroom at dusk, to dress for dinner. They were to sit at the captain's table, it had been arranged; no inconsiderable honor in itself. She had brought no party clothes with her, but there was a dress shop on the ship, and that afternoon he'd bought her a gala gown for the event. It had been altered to fit, had been delivered during their absence, and was now lying packaged on the bed waiting for her.

She was like a child. She picked up the carton and held it pressed to her. She wouldn't open it in front of him; he must see it on her, and not before.

"You go outside," she said. "I don't want you to see me until I'm all ready. I want to surprise you."

"I'll go up and have a Martini at the bar," he agreed. "That be all right?"

"About half an hour. Then come back to me."

He placed his lips tenderly to hers. She put her hands behind her back, still like a child, and waited to hear him go.

She heard him lock the door on the outside and draw the key out. From sheer habit, probably. There was no more need to. But it was probably just as well to be careful.

She began her preparation. She opened the box. Tissue hissed and spit at her. She took the dress out and spread it on the bed. He'd bring her flowers. Though he hadn't said a word, she knew that was one of the reasons he'd gone up. They had them on the ship. Gardenias or orchids to wear pinned on her shoulder.

She took off her outer things, changed hose and shoes, did her hair over. Then she put the dress on. It was a simple matter; the woman in the shop had rehearsed her. Just two fastenings far over to the side, and then you had to be sure the tiers fell straight. Her fingers saw to that for her. It was cut a little low above, though. Scarcely anything to hold it but two strips of lace. She'd need something to go over her shoulders and back; it got cool on the ocean after dark. And they might go out on deck afterward when they'd grown tired of dancing, and listen to the music from there.

Too bad she didn't have a shawl or a spangled scarf. No, wait. She knew just the thing.

She felt for the closet door with her fingers. They found the slippery, ice-like surface of its mirror panel. They shifted, found its hexagonal glass knob. She opened the door, reached inside. Her fingers told their way along the hanging garments one by one, until they came to what she wanted, almost at the far end of the closet. A little silken jacket, diminutive as a page boy's.

She took down the hanger it was on, took it off the hanger, then reattached the empty hanger to the rod, careless just where she put it.

Then she pushed the mirrored door back again, but didn't keep her hand on the knob the whole way, so that it fell somewhat short. The latch tongue didn't quite connect within its socket. The door touched the frame (she heard the little clout it gave as it did so) but didn't sink entirely into it. It didn't matter.

She drew the jacket over her shoulders, shifted it, turned this way and that, just as a seeing woman would have, getting it to fall just to her satisfaction. That would do. It was warm enough, and yet not too heavy.

She sat down once more at the dressing table for the final touches. Found the little bottle of cologne, took out the stopper, touched that to the tip of each ear.

Dressing-up for the evening was so nice. Frivolity was so nice. They were going to live like other people now. No more fear, no more hiding away. They were going to dine at the captain's table, laugh and chat and have wine with their dinner. They were going to dance. They were going to stroll the deck afterward in the starlight, and stand by the rail. Unafraid, unafraid. A footstep passing would be just a footstep passing, something to turn and nod civilly to, or to ignore, as you chose.

Unafraid, unafraid.

The hanger that she had replaced a while ago lost its grip, slipped off, and fell to the closet floor with a trifling little clack.

She knew what it was, the sound was self-explanatory, so she didn't even turn her head. They were apt to do that. If you didn't set them quite straight, or if they swung too freely after you took your hand off them.

She was considering lipstick. Whether or not to use it. Tonight was gala. She knew she would suit him as she was, but they would be in public tonight. It was a social convention to use it, nowadays, rather than an attempt to mislead the onlooker as to the coloring of one's lips, as it had once been. On that ground, she decided to put it on. No one would have believed that she, a blind woman, could have successfully applied it without producing an overlapping smear, but she already had in the past and she knew she could.

A few careful moments and it was done.

She stood up now. All through. Nothing more to do. Nothing but wait for him.

She recalled the fall of the hanger she had heard before. She went over to the closet to pick it up from the floor and put it back in place, simply from the age-old feminine instinct for tidiness, having things back in their right places; simply from not having anything else to do for the moment.

The door stood out at right angles from the frame, as she had left it just now, when she was last there. She reached down to the floor, just inside it, and within a moment had found the recumbent hanger, restored it where it belonged.

Then she closed the door tightly, so that the latch tongue clicked into place, the knob recoiled slightly in her grasp, as it was supposed to do.

She turned and started back toward her dressing tab—

At right angles from the frame, as she had left it.

But she hadn't. Her fingers had pushed it back, then let it go. She had heard it graze the frame, stop there.

Night came on in her heart. One by one, all the lights went out. It got cold, and a wind from nowhere knifed at her. Her step didn't falter; outwardly there was nothing to show that, within her, the whole world was going down into blackness. Her hand found the back of the dressing-table bench, and she sank down upon it, rather too heavily, that was all.

In here with her. There was somebody in here with her. *It, he,* was in here with her at this very moment. He hadn't come in, he had been in already, from the very first. First in the closet, now out in the very room itself.

But where? Over which way? Not a sound. Not a stir to show.

Her lips flickered tremulously. "Allen," they murmured without voice.

The door? The outside door, in the next room? Perhaps if she could get near enough to it, be near enough to it, Allen would suddenly unlock it, come in again in time to—

She was putting on cologne again. Too much cologne. A thin trickle of it ran down the side of her neck, from just under her ear.

Not a sound. Not a stir. She bowed her head, held it that way, very intently. Listening with every fibre of her being. Every fibre of her trained faculties, that could hear things others could never hope to.

Uncanny cleverness, not even to draw breath. Or draw it so subtly that it left no trace upon the sound waves reaching her. Yet somewhere within this room, this square of space, another heart was going. Another, beside hers.

Where was he standing? Where?

If he wouldn't move, if he wouldn't come to her, then she must go looking for him, she must find him. There is a certain form of suspense so terrible, so pitched above ordinary range, that it cannot be borne passively. This was of that kind. If its source would not reveal itself to her, then she must find it.

She went looking for it.

As the filing is drawn toward the magnet. As the bird is supposedly drawn to the snake.

She rose, went toward the wall first. When she had reached that, she began to follow it, with her left side, her heart, nearest to it. Tracing it with her hands, hand over hand; making circular wheel-like patterns upon it.

Tears were in her sightless eyes, and spilling slowly, one by one, down her cheeks. Her lips kept fluctuating. Saying low, over and over, the same one word. "Allen. Allen. Allen." She could not scream. Something had happened to her. She knew she would not be able to even at the end, if there was to be an end. Fright, like a searing flash of flame, had short-circuited her vocal cords, burned them out.

She had a strange feeling, and it might have been true she was already dying, slowly, even before a hand had been laid to her. Was already in the earlier stages of expiration; the process was already under way.

A chest of drawers broke the continuity of the wall, the one with Allen's things in it, and she went out and around it, and then back in to the wall again. Swimming, swimming with her hands; a dying swimmer who knows she will never make the shore.

Beyond, just ahead, there was coming the door to the bath, and though she had not thought of this before, it occurred to her now that if she could get in there quickly enough and pull the door to—

Air fanned past her face, and the door crunched shut. It must have just missed the tips of her oncoming fingers, in its arc. Hope had a miscarriage, and left a residue of pain gnawing at her vitals. A key wrangled, was taken out of it. When her hand had found the knob, it was still slightly warm against her skin. Warm from some other hand.

Her tongue flickered, moistened her searing lips. "Allen," they breathed quietly.

She extended her arms full length before her now, trying to discover him. He must be within a foot or two of her, to have closed that bath door that way.

But he must be retreating as she came on. Her twitching fingers kept finding only empty space.

Danse macabre, with the partners keeping an even distance, never joining. Saraband of death.

On she went, step by step, along the wall. She boxed the corner of it, and started out along the new side.

Halfway along it the bed broke its straightness of progression, jutting out head to wall.

She came to that, and arms out before her like a sleepwalker, turned to follow and to round it.

And it was then, midway along the length of the bed going from head toward foot, that two other hands, reaching across from its opposite side, joined themselves to her own at last; claimed them, as it were; clasped and partly enfolded them, and began to draw her with them, almost gently yet with remorseless insistence, causing her to veer in her direction so that now the bed lay directly before her, and the pull came across it from its far side.

It was like a grisly game of London Bridge Is Falling Down, with the bed between them.

Yet somehow she wasn't even frightened any more, didn't recoil nor cringe nor stiffen. All that was behind her already, far behind her, back in life. To know fear, you have to be still fully alive. It was as if she knew that this must be, and no struggle could evade or alter it.

Listlessly, her lids dropped shut over her eyes. She knew that Allen wouldn't come in time. That was her last thought, as the darkness changed only to another darkness.

———

When the needle had stilled his hoarse cries at last, and just before sleep came to release him for a while, he caught at the sleeve of the ship's doctor, and pulling and dragging at it as if he were trying to tear it off him, whispered hopelessly, "But they told me—Cameron, the police—they *promised* me it was only the thirty-first we had to watch out for, he only did it then. And the thirty-first ended last midnight—

I stopped watching her, got careless—Why did they fool me? What went wrong?"

"I don't know what you mean," said the bearded ship's doctor as gently as he could. "I know it was the thirty-first all day yesterday, from midnight to midnight. But today it was also the thirty-first, all day long, from last midnight to this coming one. The date repeated itself. You see, as we sail westward toward the International Date Line we gain a day. We hit it exactly on the thirty-first. So the thirty-first lasted for forty-eight full hours. Didn't anyone tell you that? Didn't you know?"

———

Cameron expected rage, a volcanic upheaval, bellowings, thunders and lightnings, a smashing of the office furniture. Instead he got— invisibility. He simply couldn't be seen. It was as though something had happened to the chief's eyes.

It took him twenty minutes to summon up enough courage to approach the office door. This included standing across the street from the building before crossing over, loitering out on the front steps before going in, monkeying around with the water cooler in the hall and drinking water that he didn't really want before approaching the dread door.

Finally he knocked.

No answer. Whether the chief knew he was due to report, or recognized the knock, or had an uncanny sixth sense that told him who it was, no answer.

Cameron knew he was in there, because he could hear his voice on the telephone.

He waited, then he knocked again.

No reaction. It was like being a ghost.

Finally he opened the door, went in.

The chief was there big as life, scanning reports.

Cameron closed the door, stood waiting.

Somebody came in, somebody went out. The chief spoke to *him* all right, had no difficulty seeing or hearing him.

Cameron cleared his throat.

The chief's eyes just wouldn't go up, he couldn't hear a thing.

Cameron went over to the desk and stood there right in front of him.

The chief snapped on a desk light. "Gets dark early," he mumbled indistinctly to himself.

Finally in desperation Cameron said, "Chief, I'm standing here. I'm waiting to speak to you."

The chief got through with one report. He rummaged looking for another, found it, started on that.

"Chief," said Cameron, "you've got to hear my side of it at least."

The chief stuck the tip of his little finger in one ear, and shook it out, as though something in the air bothered him.

"There was a slip-up, that was at least as much the fault of the Honolulu police as mine! I was in Frisco, I wasn't even there. When the ship got to Yokohama the captain wired back a report to the Honolulu authorities, but it was too late by then. They forwarded it to me. Two police detectives and *one* policeman boarded the ship at Honolulu at nine A.M. that day to search for her. Fifteen or twenty minutes later a *second* policeman showed up, as if to join them. He wasn't stopped, wasn't questioned, they thought it was just police routine. When the detectives went ashore again, they still just had one policeman with them. The second stayed behind in full sight of everyone, on guard duty. It was done so openly it never occurred to anyone to check up on it. He was never seen to leave, but then once the ship was under way, he was no longer seen aboard either, so everyone thought he'd left."

The chief didn't hear a word. He was signing something. Now he was blotting it. He looked right through Cameron at the clock on the wall, then he looked down again.

"A new mess boy was signed on at Honolulu. I went out there myself and checked, and he was a legitimate replacement. *But*—here's the angle, Chief—several of the other crew members claimed later that he looked different to them afterwards than when he first came aboard. Like two different people. Nobody investigated, nobody did anything about it. There was a half-breed Hawaiian mess boy's name down on the list, and there was a half-breed Hawaiian mess boy to match up with the name, and that satisfied them. Then he jumped ship at Yokohama anyway, so it was too late to investigate by that time. Chief, a *second* murder occurred on that ship, and a police uniform was quietly dropped overboard, somewhere between Honolulu and the International Date Line. I knew I made a hash of it. But all I can say in my own defense is—"

He brought his hand down on the desk despairingly. "Chief, say *something,* will you? Cuss me out if you have to! But don't just let me stand here like this—"

"Harkness!" the chief called stridently.

A desk sergeant stuck his head in.

"Harkness, what's the matter with you?" the chief bawled him out roundly. "Don't let people walk in here unannounced. This is a police station. Don't let just anybody walk in off the streets that feels like it. The first stranger, the first passerby that happens along. The public at large isn't supposed to be admitted, you know. You should take care of that down at the desk at the end of the hall. Now will you please clear this place out for me; I've got a lot of paper work to do and I only want members of the division in here."

Cameron's head went down, way down, as if he'd never seen his own feet before and was trying to make out what they were.

"You heard the chief," Harkness whispered ruefully, as if he hated to do this himself.

"I'll be back," Cameron muttered doggedly, and he turned on his heel and went out.

"Harkness," said the chief, "there's an old saying. They never come back."

———

Letter from Garrison to Cameron, originally postmarked Tulsa, addressed to Cameron's home station, forwarded to San Francisco, reforwarded to Honolulu, returned to San Francisco, returned to Cameron's home station, readdressed to Cameron's home address with notation in chief's handwriting, "Wrong address!"

. . . unable to help you when you were out here in July of last year, even though you hung around here for ten days. Well, anyway, to get to the point. Last night my wife and I were returning from the theatre in our car when a staggering drunk standing on the street corner threw a liquor bottle almost directly in front of us. I wasn't able to brake quickly enough, we got a flat. I had him run in for disorderly conduct then and there, but it was a full three-quarters of an hour before I could get repair service and we could get under way again.

We were both pretty put out, as you can imagine, and my wife exclaimed bitterly, "People like that are dangerous! Imagine looping a liquor bottle up into the air like that! Why, it could have come down on someone's head and killed them!"

I said, "I used to know a fellow that had a habit of dumping them out of planes," and I went on to tell her about Strickland doing that on one of those plane trips we took when we both belonged to that fishing club. And then suddenly right while I was telling her, I realized that that might have been the very information you wanted when you were out here that time, and which I wasn't able to give you then.

You may not want the information any longer. It may be stale by now, or maybe it was not what you were looking for in the first place, but ever since last night it has been bothering me, and so to get it off my mind . . .

Hope this reaches you, etc. . . .

Telegram, Cameron to Garrison:

Information still vitally important. Imperative you answer these questions without delay. Wire me collect. One. What was date of trip on which he did that? Was it May thirty-first? Two. What was plane's destination on that trip? Three. At what time did plane leave airport? Four. Any idea what time bottle was thrown out? Five. Can you estimate plane's average speed maintained during flight?

Telegram, Garrison to Cameron (sent prepaid, not collect):

One. Pretty sure it must have been Memorial Day. He always did his heaviest drinking on holidays. Two. Lake Star-of-the-Woods, near the Canadian line. Three. Six P.M. Can be positive of this because we always met at airport at the prearranged hour for take-off. Four. Impossible say exactly. Remember lights were already on below us, yet could still see by daylight, so must have been at onset of dusk. Five. Was an old crate. I'd give it 100 m.p.h., but this is sheer guesswork.

The rest took him ten minutes. Not even that. A large-scale master map of the entire state that showed every hamlet, every crossroads, almost every farmstead. Then a ruler-straight line from airport to lake, with the overall air-mile distance marked alongside it. Then an almanac for that year, the year of 'Forty-one, that told him the exact time of the sun's setting, the exact time of nightfall along these latitudes, that day, that year.

Six P.M. marked off first of all at departure point. Then a succession of notches stroked across the main distance line at hundred-mile intervals, to give him the plane's theoretical position at subsequent hours, seven, eight, nine. Then each one divided in two again for the half-hours. Then again for the quarter-hours. Until he had it down to five-minute notches. All this only valid of course if the plane *was* maintaining an even hundred mile per hour speed. If the pilot had gone faster at certain times, slower at others, good-bye. But that was a chance he had to take.

Then a slashing arc, between the 7:50 and the 7:55 notches, to mark the setting of the sun. Then a second arc to mark the fall of darkness. And in the space enclosed between these two arcs, like parentheses, he had his bull's-eye.

Within that whole immediate area, there was only a single hollow circle printed on the map, the customary symbol for a town. With its accompanying name. No other anywhere near it.

That was where. He knew now the "where" that went with the snapshot. At last—one life, two lives too late—he'd found out where.

———

The old lady sat in the rocking-chair beside the window and stared fixedly out to a great distance. With one hand she held back an edge of the lace curtain. The same lace curtain that had once crept into the background of a faded yellow snapshot, taken long ago.

"She's dead now," she said. "Was it yesterday? Was it many years ago? I don't know, I'm not sure. My heart doesn't tell time so good any more. I only know I'm alone. I only know she isn't here."

"Yes, there was a boy. A boy she loved. She only knew one boy in all her life. She only wanted to know one. Yes, she was going to marry him. She had to marry him or die, I guess." She stopped a moment, abruptly, as though she'd just recalled something. "She died."

She rocked a little, stared out to that great distance.

"She used to meet him every night at eight. Down by the drugstore, down by the square. Well, nearly every night. Once in a great while, when it was raining too hard, or I was cross with her, I wouldn't let her go. She was a good girl, she obeyed. When I wouldn't let her out, he'd come up here instead, stand under her window and whistle, and she'd open it and talk to him, and they'd see each other anyway. I'd let them; I'd hear them, but I'd let them.

"He had a funny little whistle, just for her. I can hear it yet. Not loud, not bold. A gentle, pleading little thing. Like a—like a baby owl that's gotten itself lost. 'Tweet-hoo. Tweet-hoo.' Like that it went.

"A funny thing happened, once about a year ago. One night I was sure I heard it again. Under her window, where it used to come from. It was the middle of the night, and I was lying awake in bed. It kept on, and kept on, so coaxing, so heartbroken. Finally I got up and went in there, to her room. I went to the window and opened it, and he was standing down there. I could see him in the moonlight standing down there. He looked up at me, and I looked down at him. He kept looking up, eyes all hopeful and shining and young. Then he tipped his hat just like he used to, long ago when they were kids, and he said, 'Can Dorothy come out?' Just like he used to, like he used to long ago.

"I forgot that she was dead.

"I said, 'Not tonight any more. It's too late. Tomorrow night.' And I swept my hand at him to show him he should go away. The way you do with the boy that loves your little girl. You know: kind but firm.

"Then I closed the window and turned away. When I got halfway across the room, suddenly I staggered and I thought I was going to faint for a minute. I could see the empty frame of her bed there, all hidden under a big dustcover, the way I'd left it years ago. I ran back to the window, but there was no one down there; I couldn't see him; he'd gone.

"Was I dreaming? Or was he really there?

"I don't know," she went on presently, "I don't know what this love was. It was bigger than I could understand. Sometimes I think it was bigger than she could or he could, too. I don't know how it came to them. A simple girl like my Dorothy. A plain boy like this Johnny."

The man, the detective, stood there quietly without answering her. How could a thing that was so good become so bad, he was thinking; how could a thing that was so right become so wrong?

She kept staring fixedly out to a great distance, the old lady in the rocking chair beside the window.

7.

REUNION

A shabby room in a typical small-town hotel. A room of the vintage of about 1916; unchanged since then. The woodwork, including the insides of the window casings, stained an ugly dark walnut. Wallpaper with blisters, where air has crept between it and the plaster; faded red flowers crawling all over it. They look like bugs parading up the walls in symmetrical lines. A light fixture in the center of the ceiling with bell-shaped glass domes over the bulbs.

A young girl and an elderly man are in it. His hair is touched with gray, he has on thick-lensed glasses, he is wearing a white smock to protect his clothes. She is seated before a self-lighted make-up mirror that shines up into her face like a spotlight. She has on a bib to protect her clothes. A towel is pinned back over her hair, concealing it entirely. Strewn all around her, cosmetics such as the theatrical profession knows. He is the one working with them, not she. She sits with her hands folded on her lap. On the floor, on a small stand, a wig waiting to be used.

Before them, propped upright on the dressing table, two things: a yellowed, faded, almost blanked-out snapshot of a young girl that must have been taken years ago. Of a young girl, standing on a porch step, one foot raised to the step behind her, smiling into the sun. That's on the left of them. And on the right of them, an oversized enlargement of the same subject. But this time of the girl's head only; her body, the porch steps, and the background, left out. A gigantic head, larger than life, craftily restored. Notations penciled perpendicularly down its edge, as a sort of a guide chart.

> Hair parted on left. 14" bob.
> Brows three shades darker. Chautun #3.
> Three or four light freckles beside outside corner each eye.
> No make-up, lashes.
> No make-up, cheeks.
> No make-up, lips.
> Sand-colored coat, brass buttons.
> Light-blue neck scarf, worn open.
> No hat, habitually.
> Low-heeled shoes.

The man is working with flesh-colored clay or putty, kneading it into her cheekbones, along her jawline, changing the contours of her face. He takes off a little excess here, adds a little surplus there.

Then he takes a large, pancake-like puff and carefully touches here and there dulling the shine, blending the whole thing into one. Then he steps back and consults the head on the photo-mat; looks from it to her, from her to it.

"Turn this way a little.

"Now turn that way a little.

"Look down.

"Now look up."

He nods. The two are one. She is facing a reproduction of herself. Photography first copied life; now life has copied photography.

He carefully unpins the towel from her head. The dualism shatters; five hours work is apparently thrown away. The hair is dark, almost black.

He takes the wig up from the stand. He unpins from it something that is at first invisible. A swatch of sample hair, scissored from some-one's head. Perhaps even from a head that already lay in a casket, ready for burial; a last memento.

He carefully adjusts the wig over the subject, and the dualism springs back into being; the two are one again.

She gets up and takes off the bib. From a box he takes a light-blue scarf, and carefully, with careless effect, drapes it about her neck, con-sulting the smaller model, the snapshot, this time. Then from a larger box, a sand-colored reefer. From this, again, he unpins a small jagged sample, taken from some coat perhaps, that hung in a closet for many years, its wearer dead and gone.

She puts this on.

In the snapshot, one of the brass buttons is a little loose, tilts down-ward on its thread. On the reproduction, one of the brass buttons is a little loose, tilts downward on its thread.

"Open," he cautions her. "Never buttoned. Always open. Even if the wind freezes your tummy."

Then he goes over to the door, knocks on it, as though he were on the outside, not the inside.

A key is put into it from the outside, and a little old lady is ushered in, faltering, by a man behind her.

"Ready?" the latter asks.

"Ready," the expert answers. "I've done all I can. I can't do any more for you."

The girl turns slowly, to face them.

A stifled scream escapes the old lady. She presses her hands to her mouth.

"Dorothy!"

She cowers back against the man who came in with her, tries to hide her face.

"That's my Dorothy—!" she sobs incoherently. "What did ye do—? How'd she get here—?"

The man guiding her pats her head and shoulders consolingly.

"That's all we wanted to know," he says soothingly. "I know it was heartless, but there was no other way. If she can fool your eyes, she can fool..."

The man is Cameron.

He turns her over to someone waiting outside the door and they lead her gently away, whimpering and mumbling and trying to look backward at her dead. Her long-lost dead.

The expert has packed up his things, taken off his smock, he's ready to go.

Cameron shakes hands with him. "You did a good job."

"I never did police work before. But I've made them up for the cameras and the klieg lights for twenty years, and I think she'll pass."

Cameron hopes she will; because there won't be any retakes on the scene she's set to play. Either she's letter-perfect the first time, or she's dead.

The door closes and they're alone, he and the bit-player. The player for an audience of one.

He takes out a .32 calibre revolver and places it on the dressing table.

She puts it into her handbag. Fits it into specially prepared clamps that hold it at firing position. So that it can be used from where it is by dropping her hand to it, without extracting it from the bag.

"Are you ready, Probationer X—?"

"Yes, sir, Inspector."

"Your assignment's under way."

He puts the lights out, but they linger for a moment in the darkness.

He pulls up the window shade, which was down well below the sill.

Opposite, across the square, a sign blazes out, that says "Geety's," and under that, "Drugs."

———

And every night now, where the macabre drugstore cowboy used to stand, there's a ghost-girl waiting for her date. Someone's forgotten girl, waiting for a boy who doesn't come. Eyes always in the semi-distance, haunted, sad, peering, straining, pleading for someone who never comes. Standing in the niche where the toilet waters are, patient, forlorn. Eyes that won't meet any other eyes but some certain pair that they have yet to find.

The crowd passes by like it always passed by and like it always will. Laughing, chatting, pleasure-bound, thick as ants. The current in the lights studding the movie marquee, broken at rhythmic intervals, sends ripples coursing around it. And the same line forms outside it, and the same line melts away. Then the ripples freeze and stop, the lights go out, and it's too late to see the last complete show. A man comes out with a stepladder, climbs up aloft, and changes "Cary Grant" to "Bette Davis," or "Bette Davis" to "Cary Grant." But the show on the outside goes on forever. And your tickets to it are the breath you draw.

They look at her, even more than they used to look at him, for she's a girl and girls draw the eyes more. They look at her with varying meanings and intents, according to their moods, their ages, and their current status of companionship. The girls with other boys look at her comparatively and wonder if they look as good, and measure the discrepancy by the length of time *his* face stays turned that way. The girls without boys look at her with competitive suspicion and wonder if *that's* why they haven't had any luck so far this evening. The boys with other girls look at her, and sometimes wish they hadn't been in such a hurry. But once in a while, once in a great while, one passes by who tightens his arm over his companion's hand and thinks, "*I'm* satisfied; *I* wouldn't change." (He'll make a good husband.) The older women in the crowd tilt their noses in disapproval and think, "In *my* day a girl waited at her house to be called for; didn't come out and meet her beau on a street corner. That's why she's been stood up; no reserve." The older men wish they were the younger men again.

But the younger men *without* girls are the ones who stop and try to do something about it.

The look becomes a smile, the smile becomes a slow-down. The slow-down becomes a full-fledged halt.

She drops her eyes.

Up goes the flap of her envelope-bag. And against the lining, where some such articles have mirrors pasted, hers had instead a likeness of a man's face. A composite, drawn by a competent artist from imagination.

Every little line that has gone into it cost someone's life or caused someone heartbreak.

"He had good eyes, that's about all I can remember; they were hazel colored, but they weren't squinty; they were wide and even honest," said Rusty, Sharon's pal who went out with him one night.

"He had a thin, mean mouth; there was something bitter about it; it was always tightened up," said Bill Morrissey who punched it with his fist one night.

"His nose wasn't very wide; it was even turned up a little; he had a cold one time and was blowing it a lot, that's how I came to notice it," said Jack Munson's landlady.

She drops her eyes, as if coquettishly. And then she raises them again. And then she drops them.

It looks like the coy technique in flirting. But the would-be picker-upper never has a chance to find out if it is or not.

Somebody in the crowd behind him jars him, all but shoulders him along with him. "Keep moving, buddy," a voice slurs close to his ear. "You're blocking traffic." Then before they can disentangle themselves, perhaps the lining of a palm has been glimpsed, soldered with the glinting disk of authority. That's sufficient; the intended dallier continues on his way.

She had made a slight gesture of her hand; pulled open her scarf a little. Eased it a little. That meant: no. If she had made the same slight gesture in reverse, tightened her scarf a little at her throat, that would have meant: yes. There would have been a sudden surge of men from everywhere at once, swift baring of guns, savage struggle, maybe even death. So slight a thing to bring so terrible a consequence.

And then it gets late, there are fewer lights, there is no more crowd; the sidewalk patina tarnishes from gold-plate to lead-dross. Her figure dims to a silhouette in the night gloom.

Far across the square a tiny flame winks for an instant, is gone again. Simply some dilatory casual striking a match to a cigarette. But, as if it were a signal for dismissal, somebody's ghost-sweetheart turns and drifts away into the shadows, as somebody himself once did long ago.

Her feet stand there, so still, so small, so pertly tilted. Planted on the golden-bright sidewalk. And before them in parade, other feet by the dozens, by the score, trudging, shuffling, coursing along. Endlessly, in unbroken succession, almost toe to heel and heel to toe. Anonymous, impersonal, the feet of strangers. They tell you so little, they tell you so much.

Tired, downhearted feet, sloughing along; springy, dancey feet, with a lift and a lilt to them. Anxious feet, in a hurry to get there. Reluctant feet, not caring if they do. The flat, massive feet of men. Achingly-arched feet, with just a toe-hold on the ground. The feet of the town, on the go. A chain-dance of feet, with scarcely a bare patch of sidewalk allowed to show itself between and interrupt their continuity.

Suddenly a crumpled piece of paper falls, cast off by some unde-tected hand above that was not even seen to move. It doesn't fall idly, it comes down at a tangent, strikes the ground just short of her own two motionless feet, lies there close to them. Almost as if aimed toward them.

Something somebody threw away. Or did they? Why right there where she stood? (Unless they threw without looking, and it just hap-pened to land there.) Why not along the rest of the way, both before coming to her and after going past her, where there was no one stand-ing?

It lies there for long moments, just a little crushed ball of paper, no bigger than a walnut.

Her foot moves out a little, touches it speculatively. Then her foot moves back again, to where it was. The whole excursion is only a mat-ter of six inches. No one has seen her do it.

More moments of indecision.

Something about it— Why just there where she stood?

Her hand comes down suddenly, contracts over it, and it's gone.

Behind the sheltering flap of her handbag she opens it. Penciled words strike out. Rough edged, as if done in haste against a brick-pocked wall. A message from death to the already dead.

Dorothy,

I saw you there from off a ways. Last night too, and the night be-fore. I've been watching you three nights. I hated to stand you up, but I'm in trouble. Something tells me not to go to you where you are. I don't know why. I can't talk to you there, too many lights, too many people. They're after me. I'm going to pass by quickly just once and drop this. Hope you pick it up. If you do, start walking away from there slow. Go where it's dark and there are no people around. That's the only way I'll come to you. If I see anyone near you, anyone at all, I can't come.

Johnny.

She swayed a little, though you couldn't have seen it unless you were watching her closely. She moved one hand to the rear and steadied herself against the drugstore glass front. You couldn't see her do that either. Her attitude was, implicitly, that of someone cowering away from something.

Then presently she regained fortitude, her hand left the glass behind her, she straightened up again. She raised her hand, that same one, to her throat and drew her scarf closer over it, as though she felt a chill draught of air. And, prearranged signal or not, that was exactly what she did feel. Closer, closer still, until she was almost holding it taut under her chin. Then her hand let go of it and dropped like a lead weight, and that was the only help she could hope to claim.

Then she turned and started to walk slowly away. Very slowly, driftingly; without looking around her, above all without looking behind her.

For a little while she had the crowd still with her, even had to thread her way through it. Once a man jostled her with his elbow, then apologized mutely with a cursory flick of his hat brim. She showed no awareness of the brief contact, merely tightened her scarf at her throat and continued on her way.

Then the crowd began to thin out, became a scattering, at last an isolated stray or two. As she turned off the square, pursued her unhurried way along one of its feeder thoroughfares, the lights too began to fall behind, dim out. Gaps began to appear in the solid wall of building fronts that lined her way. Black hollows that weren't good to pass.

The street lights stopped, and then the streets themselves stopped, became just countrified roads without sidewalks. And then the houses started stopping, and everything was just wide-open space.

And still she trudged on, waiting to be overtaken. Freezingly expectant of the sudden tread behind her, the arresting hand on her shoulder that never came. Screaming all the while, in deadly silence, inside her.

More and more shadows, more and more trees. More and more of night.

She kept going forward. She wouldn't turn her head. Afraid, maybe, of what she would see if she did.

The ground began to tilt upward, and she realized with a shudder she had taken the road that led upward to the cemetery.

Over to the side, to the right, there was a grassy meadow. She stopped, turned and struck out into that. The field was white in the moonlight. You could see all around you, it was so open. It was like being in the middle of a big open lake of grass, your own height the only thing to oppose the sweep of the eye.

The grass grew higher as she advanced; she had to pick her way. Calf-high, and creeping at last almost to the knees. She still didn't look back. She wouldn't. Maybe by this time she couldn't any more. Fear paralyzes.

She was almost in the exact middle of it now. She stopped. She stood there upright in the middle of it, like a marker.

She turned with quiet deliberation to face the way she had just come.

There was something black coming toward her across the expanse. Small and black. It had broken away from the surrounding black periphery, was striking out on its own. Separate, detached, moving unerringly toward her. Wading through the moon-frosted grass, as she had.

The impulse to flee ricocheted through her; she jolted as she curbed it.

"My God!" she shuddered aloud.

No help could reach her out here in time.

Did he know she was only a replica, the living scarecrow of his lost love? Had he guessed, back there, and was that why he'd refused to approach for three nights? Had the baited become the baiter? The ambuscade was back there, not out here. He had drawn her bodily out of it, taken her away right under their noses and set her down now to wait where there was no trap. Where he was the trapper, and not they.

She had done something wrong, she had made some error in tactic, but what it was she still didn't know, she couldn't have said. She couldn't have done other than she had done, without throwing away all their weeks and months of careful, not-to-be-repeated preparations. Or maybe it wasn't that she had done anything wrong; maybe it was just that his own instinct was so unerringly right, that it had guided him through to immunity. Instinct, in the deranged, can be supremely accurate; it has no reason or logic to contend with.

The oncoming black something was growing steadily larger. Now it had a head, shoulders, arms that swayed to its walk. The moon found where its face belonged, and gave it a face. Small yet, yards away. The moon gave it tiny pin-prick eyes, a tiny nose, a tiny mouth.

A man.

No, the death that walked upright like a man. The death that Sharon and Madeline Drew had mistaken for a man.

It was like looking at some horror in miniature, all the greater for not being life-sized. The moon added details she didn't want to know; the moon left nothing incomplete. It gave him a tiny slanting shadow from his hat brim, it gave him a V of paleness from his shirt front.

He was within the last few yards of her now. He was full-sized, had attained her own proportions. They were within speaking distance. He didn't speak, just kept coming on closer, toiling through the tall grass.

She didn't speak either. Maybe to speak was to betray herself, destroy herself. Was the illusion still intact? Was it already shattered? Or would the first sound of her voice, the wrong voice, only shatter it then?

She could see the expression on his face now. A sort of joy, and a sort of pain, both blended together at once. But nothing there of menace or of abnormality. And that was the ultimate horror; the façade had remained unimpaired through it all, still was now, at this very moment. You had to guess, you couldn't know. It looked a little younger, more boyish, than it otherwise would have by now, perhaps; that was the only indication.

It was hard to meet his eyes. She steeled herself not to evade them.

"Dorothy," he said quietly.

"Johnny," she whispered.

Something broke in his throat. It sounded as if he were crying deep down inside somewhere. Not up where his face was, but deep down in his being. "A fellow's girl—always waits for him. And my girl—waited for me."

His arms went hungrily around her, and she froze. The very flow of her blood seemed to stop.

His voice was close to her ear now, warm, and low, and glad. There was nothing about it—just the voice of a young man.

"I've got that much, anyway. My girl—she waited for me."

He kept saying it over and over, lower and lower, slower and slower.

"She waited for me.

"She waited—for me.

"She—waited."

His head went down suddenly on her shoulder, as if he were awfully tired, couldn't hold it up straight any more.

"She waited for me," he sighed. "Thanks, God; she waited for me."

Over his shoulder, horrified, she could see rippling invisible snakes of the field coursing toward them through the grass here and there. Just the ripples she could see, and not what caused them. They'd stop short, go on again when they dared. Stop, go on again.

Coming toward them, like spokes of a wheel drawing in toward its hub.

He just stood there, mute, inert, his arms about her, his head down. At rest, at peace.

A strange thought coursed through her police-probationer's mind. "How cruel this is. Why does it have to be so cruel? Why couldn't it have been some other way?"

She could feel his heart beating against her. Like a wild bird beating its wings, that has come to rest for only a moment, but threatens to take flight again instantly at the first alarm.

He started to bring his lips around, trying to find hers with them.

The grass whispered a little here and there, as though fingers of a breeze were touching it in certain places, leaving it alone in others. Something rustled, like taffeta being trailed over the ground. Then something snapped smartly. A stick maybe. Then there was silence. All over the meadow silence. Too much silence. Not enough harmless, natural sound.

Instinct.

His arms opened, braced themselves against her sides, holding her at the waist.

Suddenly he gave his body a whirling, spiral twist. She went down, one way, into the grass. He darted off, the other way, bent low, running fleetly, a dark something streaking this way and that. A human-sized rabbit.

Men leaped up everywhere, where there hadn't been any a moment before. They were like dark raisins in the white crust of a pudding, suddenly popping to the top.

Fireflies began to flit here and there all over the meadow, in crazy erratic pattern. Or lack of pattern. Each one seeming to call up its opposite number, back and forth, forth and back. Fireflies hooked up to thunderclaps. Each wink sparking a heavy thud.

Suddenly the rabbit stopped, sank from sight right where it had stopped. A sort of hole remained in the top of the grass where it had gone down. A little dimple.

The thudding fireflies stopped and little wisps of smoke trailed off, as though they had burned themselves out.

There was a silence now of cautiously bent men, creeping in closer toward that hole, closer, but very carefully, very craftily.

Suddenly a moaning cry rent it. "Dorothy!"

The men kept circling, circling closer all the time.

"Dorothy!" rose again, in faint, unutterable loneliness, up toward the objective stars. A love cry, a death cry.

They found him alone there in the grass, head twisted around to look helplessly up at them. Like the rabbit does the hunters.

His eyes were dimming crescents, straining upward into the starred night sky, as if trying to make out, to visualize, some phantom face that no one else could see. And what is love anyway but the unattainable, the reaching out toward an illusion?

He died with her name on his lips.

"Dorothy, hurry up," he whispered. "All the time we've wasted—there's so little of it left now—"

The men stood around him in a circle, looking down.

"He's dead," someone said softly.

Cameron nodded. He raised his hand to the brim of his hat for a moment. He didn't actually take it off, he just gave it a little perk of finality.

"They're together now—I guess. They've kept their date at last."

READING GROUP GUIDE

1. Critics in Woolrich's day considered him the "king of the thriller." Would you agree?

2. *Rendezvous in Black* was a radical departure from the detective stories popular in Woolrich's day. What sets it apart?

3. In the essay "Cornell Woolrich: Psychologist, Poet, Painter, Moralist," Francis Lacassin states that the reader identifies with the main characters through Woolrich's elements of "the noble or pathetic." Is Johnny pathetic or noble? Is he in fact the hero or the victim?

4. Woolrich described his writing as a "form of subconscious self-expression." Some critics have interpreted this statement as Woolrich using his own fanciful crimes as therapy for his personal problems and have gone so far as to suggest that Woolrich's readers view the story in the same light. Is this nontraditional detective story cathartic in any way? If so, how?

5. Does this novel have a hero? If yes, what characterizes him/her as such?

6. Does Woolrich draw any of Johnny's enemies as sympathetic characters? Are Johnny's victims sympathetic characters?

7. In the chapter titled "The First Rendezvous" it is quite obvious what Johnny is setting out to do. It is also fairly obvious that Detective Cameron will triumph in the end. Did Woolrich keep the pace and suspense from beginning to end?

8. Johnny Marr's revenge plots prove ingenious throughout the book, yet his capture could be viewed as quick and anticlimactic. Was Woolrich simply trying to end his book in the favored bad-guy-loses scenario or could Johnny's downfall be seen as more emotional and believable than most crime-story endings?

About the Author

CORNELL WOOLRICH was born in 1903 in New York City. At the age of three, his father, a civil engineer, moved Woolrich's family to Mexico. After living in Mexico and South America for a number of years, Woolrich's parents divorced and he returned to New York with his mother.

In 1921 he entered Columbia University to study journalism, but dropped out after three years to become a full-time fiction writer. His second novel, *Children of the Ritz*, written in 1927, won him a $10,000 prize in the First National Pictures contest and was later filmed in 1929.

After a short time in Hollywood working as a screenwriter, Woolrich returned to New York and took up residence in Harlem. In 1934 he turned his talents to pulp fiction, writing stories for such magazines as *Black Mask* and *Dime Detective*, and earning acclaim as one of the first noir fiction writers. In the late '30s he turned his attention to mysteries and, over the course of two decades, wrote such well-known novels as *The Bride Wore Black*, *Night Has a Thousand Eyes*, and *I Married a Dead Man*. He died in 1968 of a stroke.

A Note on the Type

The principal text of this Modern Library edition
was set in a digitized version of Janson, a typeface that
dates from about 1690 and was cut by Nicholas Kis,
a Hungarian working in Amsterdam. The original matrices have
survived and are held by the Stempel foundry in Germany.
Hermann Zapf redesigned some of the weights and sizes for
Stempel, basing his revisions on the original design.

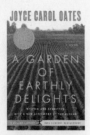